Under a Friendship Moon

D1713975

UNDER A FRIENDSHIP MOON

John M Bullock

To Bill

A fellow Animal lover ...

Best Regards,

John Bullock

iUniverse, Inc.

New York Lincoln Shanghai

Under a Friendship Moon

Copyright © 2005, 2006 by John M. Bullock

iUniverse books may be ordered through booksellers or by contacting:

iUniverse
2021 Pine Lake Road, Suite 100
Lincoln, NE 68512
www.iuniverse.com
1-800-Authors (1-800-288-4677)

Cover photograph copyright by William Bernbeck

ISBN-13: 978-0-595-34619-6 (pbk)
ISBN-13: 978-0-595-83053-4 (cloth)
ISBN-13: 978-0-595-79365-5 (ebk)
ISBN-10: 0-595-34619-7 (pbk)
ISBN-10: 0-595-83053-6 (cloth)
ISBN-10: 0-595-79365-7 (ebk)

Printed in the United States of America

"Do not go where the path may lead, go instead where there is no path and leave a trail." The words of Ralph Waldo Emerson told of the way my friend, Jim Francis, lived his life. He departed too soon but certainly left a profound influence behind. For the many lives he touched, the trail he blazed is paved with the depth of his caring and lighted by the sincerity of his love. Thanks for all you have shown us, Jim. I dedicate this book in remembrance of you.

Acknowledgments

I could not have written this book without the encouragement and assistance of many people to whom I am greatly indebted. My friends in the Hilton Writers Guild have been a constant source of inspiration and support. Their diverse talents and unique insights have helped shape my work and I thank them for it.

My long time friend, John Pockrus, has done invaluable research for this project. Without him, there would be no motorcycle in my story. He certainly went far beyond anything I could have expected in supplying details and insights about the Indian motorcycle.

Friends and former colleagues, Grace Bellave and Jane Schneider, are the best proofreaders a writer could hope for. Without them, my deficiencies in punctuation, spelling and continuity would have been exposed for all to see.

My writer friend, Bill Bernbeck, captured the true taste of autumn's splendor in his poem, *Allegany Green*. Thanks, for letting me share it, Bill. Any further use of this poem requires permission of the author.

Jonathan Keck has been a close friend and respected colleague for close to forty years. He knows the people and the places I have written about. His distinguished career teaching English made him the perfect choice to help edit this book. "Thanks!" old friend.

Friendship, New York is nestled in the foothills of the Alleghenies. You will find it on a map in the southern part of Allegany County. The residents of this rural county are warm, friendly individuals with a patriotic spirit and a love for God that made this the perfect setting for my book. A college friend, Marti Burdick, originally from Friendship, supplied place names and helped add local flavor and authenticity to the story.

This book was originally meant to be a short story. Soon after starting it, I knew it would be much more. It was inspired by my children: Cristin, Ryan and Sean. And it is for them that I wrote it.

And most of all, my gratitude and love goes out to my wife, Marcia, for the understanding, patience and guidance she has shown me during this long journey.

Any merit within the pages of this book is due largely to the caring friends and family I have mentioned above. My sincerest "Thanks" to you!

CHAPTER 1

▼

Twinkling lights from a lonely Christmas tree, hidden in the corner of the bar, failed to lift a single spirit. A brightly-lit jukebox played softly. The voice of an angel swept over sad faces: "You tell me to find someone else to love." That Patsy Cline sure could croon a tune. Her voice was smoother than 50-year-old brandy. Each word she sang legitimized their melancholy more, as she admitted "I Fall to Pieces," but then again, the patrons of the *Black Horse Inn* weren't looking for holiday cheer, unless it came from a bottle.

The Christmas tree stood guard, next to a gray fieldstone fireplace, which harbored the remnants of a once cheery fire. Embers and occasional tongues of flame cast out little heat but enough smoke to sting the eyes of Jack Flanagan, who was hunkered up to the bar in his usual seat. The acrid taste in his mouth possessed hints of Winstons, the beef jerky he'd had for dinner and smoke from the fireplace. He swirled whiskey round his glass several times, staring blankly through the thin film it left slithering down the side. He could see the lights on the Christmas tree reproduce themselves in a cascade of brilliance. *Must be the glass breaking up the light*, Jack thought to himself. But perhaps the tears in his eyes had something to do with it, even though he'd never admit they were tears. Christmas was a great season to wallow in regrets. Jack took a long draw of his drink and held it in his mouth. He closed his eyes but could still see the twinkling lights.

Several strands of tinsel wove their way through his gray hair. Those strands had hung from a gaudy Christmas wreath earlier that evening but Jack's six foot two inch frame hadn't stooped low enough to miss their static grasp. The wreath would probably still be adorning the front archway of the tavern come spring.

"How…how…how are th…th…things?" The bartender struggled with each word. Jack felt like filling in the gaps but that might hurt some feelings. Kenny had stuttered for twenty-some years now, ever since a lightning bolt decided it liked the looks of him, dropped in for a quick visit and lifted a few cerebral connections on the way out.

Jack forced a smile in reply. His eyes were swollen and road-mapped in red. Rough white stubble covered his square jaw and his ruddy complexion might have betrayed a little secret—he liked to drink. Kenny knew the smile was a lie but, like any good bartender, he knew when to agree with the customers.

"Looks like a stor…stor…stor…some bad weather com…com…comin' in."

As if upon cue, the tavern door swung open. A gust of the cold north wind swept in a stranger. A floor-length leather coat hid her boots, making it difficult to tell if the stranger was walking or being blown in by the wind. Her face was animated and she vigorously rubbed her hands to bring back some warmth.

"Damn, it's cold out there! Got something to warm a frigid soul?" the stranger asked to anyone who would listen.

Her question turned a few heads but failed to keep their attention for long. Their true loves beckoned from the bottom of their glasses.

Jack watched her cautiously, not wishing to let the woman know he would pay her the slightest bit of attention. She had a rather ample head of blonde hair that the wind had teased into a beehive of activity. As she passed by a bright Schlitz sign, silver roots exposed her age. Sensing her disheveled appearance, the woman spread her fingers like a mammoth comb and with one swoop of her hand, the hairdo was re-styled, this time with a moderate amount of subtlety. Her rosy cheeks were plump and her eye shadow was a bit heavy.

A barstool next to Jack sat empty and inviting. The heels of the woman's boots pounded against the hardwood floor in excited rhythm that finally slowed as she neared the barstool. As it became apparent the stranger was going to sit next to him, Jack quickly turned his head and stared at the colorful collection of liquor bottles in front of him. From the mirror behind the bottles his sad reflection stared back at him. *"Merry Christmas"* was written across the mirror with spray-on snow. The *"mas"* took an abrupt downward turn as it approached the edge to the mirror.

"Is anyone sitting here?" she asked Jack, nodding at the empty barstool beside him.

When Jack drank, he preferred to be alone. It made the act of feeling sorrowful easier to focus on and, since his ex-wife had left, self-pity had been a near constant companion. "Be my guest," he said, struggling to be pleasant and at the same time trying to convey his wish for solitude.

She pulled off a pair of rag-wool gloves, slapped them down on the bar and rested her hand on Jack's shoulder for some temporary leverage as she climbed onto the barstool. Jack could feel the coolness she had brought in with her. The sweet aroma of leather swirled into Jack's nostrils and he quietly breathed in deeply, holding the scent there secretly, not knowing why.

Jack watched her in the safety of the mirror. She wiggled to free herself from the coat but slowed as the sleeves wedged her arms together behind her back. It took a loud sigh to trigger Jack's less than polished sense of gentlemanliness. He leaned toward her and with both hands eased the coat off. For a split second, Jack turned his eyes from the task at hand to the front of the woman's black mohair sweater that stretched enticingly over her well-rounded breasts.

"You're truly a gentleman. Thanks! My name's Kate…Kate Fletcher. Can I buy you a drink?"

"No thanks. Just filled up and I better slow down after this one," Jack said curtly.

"My family lives out near the dairy. At least Mom does. Dad passed away a few years back," she said.

"Fletcher…yeah, I know that farm. My folks used to buy cottage cheese there," Jack said. "Seems like I remember your name too. You must have been a few years behind me in school," he added.

"Then you're a townie?" she asked.

"Yeah. Been here in Friendship most all my life. My name's Jack Flanagan."

"Oh yeah…I think I remember you. You were a senior when I was in tenth grade. Didn't you date that pretty redhead?"

Jack grinned and nodded his head. The sore subject of his ex-wife was not something he cared to talk about.

"I need a little anti-freeze tonight," she said to Jack then motioned to the bartender. "Creme sherry, please." She took a small black wallet from her purse, pulled out a few dollar bills, placed them on the bar and set the wallet next to them.

"My ex used to drink that stuff…too sweet for me though," Jack said.

The small talk soon faded and the two sat quietly, taking turns stealing glances at one another in the mirror. It was only there that they seemed close. Her face was pretty under the makeup but a vague sadness had stolen her eyes. It took little imagination to see that she had once possessed the looks that would turn young men's heads. Half an hour ago Jack longed for solitude. Now he cursed his silence.

In the lonely quiet Kate began looking around the bar for friendly faces and asked the bartender his opinion on the winter weather. Jack never sensed the woman was making flirtatious overtures toward the other patrons but an emotion he'd suppressed for so long now, was working its way into his well-guarded consciousness. Jealousy was a weakness, worthy of emotional flogging and Jack started mentally lashing at himself. *Look where this got you with your marriage. Just how weak are you? A real man would…*

Jack forced himself to speak—a skill that had atrophied during the apathetic times since his divorce. "You have children?" he asked her.

"My daughter, Sarah, lives in Poughkeepsie. Her husband owns a used car dealership and I do the books for their business. I also waitress at a diner on weekends. That's where I live too, but with Mom sick…well, I figured she could use my help."

Jack half-heard what she had said, as his imagination filled with images of what she looked like twenty years ago. Her plump cheeks had a near rashy quality, probably irritated by the cold night wind. Her face was round and a second chin was in the early stages. Turn back the clock and Jack saw a very attractive woman. But those eyes—deep blue, highlighted with slivers of gold—told a story of difficult times, which no quantity of mascara could obscure, but through the hurt Jack saw a pair of eyes that he found enchanting.

"You have very pretty eyes," Jack blurted out—his boldness fortified by five drinks.

Kate dropped her head, leaving Jack to guess if he had embarrassed her or if she was simply playing the game that women were supposed to play. She quickly raised her eyes to meet his and said, "Thank you."

At that moment Jack wondered what he must look like to her. He stole a glance at himself in the mirror behind the bar. His steel blue eyes were reddened from the smoke and drinking. He ran his thumb across his square jaw and could feel the prickly stubble that hadn't seen a razor in a couple days. His once dark hair was mostly silver now and growing over the tops of his ears. With a haircut, a shave and a few days off the bottle Jack thought he might look presentable. Little did he know that his manly appearance was often the topic of conversation at the local hair salon. His broad shoulders and muscular chest charmed many of the beauty parlor patrons. The spoken fantasy of being swept away in his strong arms produced a number of reddened cheeks there.

"What's wrong with your mother?" Jack asked innocently.

Kate's face sunk as if her heart suddenly pumped lead through her veins.

Jack swallowed the lump in his throat but was a little too late to consume the question that hung in the air about him. He prayed it would just go away unanswered.

"She has cancer. It's spread to her bones," Kate answered. "I don't think she has long."

"I'm really sorry," Jack said. And the conversation slowed into an uncomfortable silence.

Kate pulled a tissue from her purse and wiped the corners of both eyes. "She's lived a hard life and is in so much pain now…heaven will be a blessing for her."

"Do you have any brothers or sisters?" Jack asked, anxious to change the subject.

"No, I'm an only child. It seemed like sometimes she was my only parent, too. Dad could be a real bastard at times." Disdain mixed with the sadness on her face.

"My father was a pain in the ass at times, too. But most of the time he took it out on my older brother, Guy. They were always butting their hard heads together," Jack said.

"Are they still living," Kate asked.

"No, my parents and my brother are gone now."

Jack raised the whiskey glass to his lips and took a sip.

Kate glanced at Jack's naked ring finger and asked, "You said something about your ex. Are you on friendly terms with her?"

The sour mash whiskey caught in Jack's throat. He pressed his fist to his lips to make sure none of Lynchburg, Tennessee's finest elixir would escape. Several coughs and a big grin spoke volumes about the marriage from hell.

"Oh…I'd say the word "friendly" would be somewhat of a stretch. Maybe something more in the line of "detestable" would be a better fit," Jack said and the big grin now appeared laced with bits of a sadistic sneer. He raised his glass and mumbled something…and although the veins on the side of his neck were pulsating, Kate didn't think what she had heard was a comment about, "the twitch!"

"How about you…are you married?" Jack asked.

"I was long ago. His name was Michael and…"

"You fo…fo…folks need another cock…cock…cocktail?" Kenny interrupted.

Jack held his hand up and waved it indicating he was done, a gesture the bartender had seldom seen from him. Kenny smiled, raised an eyebrow and nodded his head toward Jack.

Kate said, "Yes, please," then pushed her glass toward him. Kenny carefully poured her another glass of sherry. The final drop spilled on the side of the narrow neck glass and Kenny gracefully swept it off with his index finger. As Kate took the glass and turned to Jack, Kenny glanced in the bar mirror; saw several strands of hair standing on end in his otherwise perfect part; touched them down into place with his sticky finger and walked to the other end of the bar.

Time and Jack Daniel's had erased the memory of his previous question and Jack went on to ask, "Do you come back to Friendship much?"

"Oh, for funerals, weddings and to see Mom around the holidays and her birthday. I've been here now for a couple weeks. The cancer has been extremely painful for her lately and the pain medication doesn't work all that well. One of her close friends is with her tonight. And I needed just a little time off. So here I am," Kate said, lifting her hands as if she was arising from the dead.

Jack felt very sorry for her at that moment. The make-up did a poor job of hiding her pain. There was something about this woman that told Jack the teased hair and the jovial attitude would be gone in the morning…but her beautiful eyes would still be there.

"What do you do for a living?" she asked.

"I've been roughing houses for the last twenty five years…every since high school. Dad worked the oil fields over in Bolivar and, after a few summers of helping him, I decided that kind of work wasn't for me. So I got into an easy line of work." The crooked smile on his face was there to tell that he was joking about how easy his job was, but the effect actually painted a softer side on this rugged man…one that was very appealing.

"Do you like building?" Kate asked.

"Well, it's a good work crew and my boss is Bob Ames. He's a great friend. Do you know him?"

"Is he that stout gentleman with the great laugh?"

Jack chuckled at the kind way Kate had asked the question. He had often called his friend, "lard ass" and never thought of him as a "gentleman".

"Yeah, that would be Bob," Jack said.

For the next hour the two talked comfortably about family, the good old days, the first Catholic president and the tragedy of his assassination. They agreed that Lyndon Johnson was no John Kennedy but time would tell just what kind of president he would be. Jack drank one more drink to Kate's three, not wishing to deaden his already dulled senses. He thought how wrong he had been when she first walked in and had seemed to be loud and a little too pushy. It now was clear that she was a warm, friendly woman with a good sense of humor. Little things

Kate said led Jack to believe that under the tough image she might be trying to hide several deep-seeded insecurities. It felt so good to talk with someone who looked you in the eyes when you were talking and really listened to what you had to say.

"I had a really long day Jack, and I best be dragging my tail home. Would hate to doze off right here at the bar. All the town would be talking…saying I slept around."

"Well, I ahhh…. I guess I'll see you around town," he said.

She quickly stood, gave him a peck on the cheek, smiled warmly and was out the door.

Jack sat stupefied, rationalizing his actions and inactions. He wondered why this stranger had captured his attention as she did. The black wallet held Jack's blank stare for nearly a minute before the significance of it lying there, on the bar in front of him, pried its way between other thoughts. *She's left her wallet.*

As he scrambled through the archway of the *Black Horse Inn* more tinsel strung itself through Jack's hair and seconds later he stood, wallet in hand, looking up and down the deserted street. Snowflakes began to cling to his red plaid coat. A lock of his wet hair fell over one eye and Jack could now see the shininess of several strands of tinsel. He parted his fingers, ran them slowly through his hair, then walked silently home.

CHAPTER 2

▼

His two-story colonial had been one of the prettier homes on Stevens Avenue. Now peeling paint, several boarded windows, tires stacked on the front porch and a snowblower lying on its side in the front lawn all showed indifference toward appearances. Inside, stark walls, frayed carpet, a three-legged couch and a blackened fireplace with last year's logs greeted Jack with a silent, "Merry Christmas and a freakin' Happy New Year!"

Glare from a streetlight outside lit the room enough for Jack to make his way to a hurricane lamp his best friend, Bob Ames, had given the happy couple as a wedding gift. The globe, with its delicate rose pattern, was but a memory. It had been in the wrong place at the wrong time during one of the Flanagan's little marital spats, which had ended in the exchange of affectionately launched projectiles. As Jack switched on the light, the bare lightbulb gave off light about as subtle as that in the men's room at the *Black Horse Inn*.

His old friend, a bottle of Jack Daniels, sat on the end table next to the lamp. "Give me a hand, old buddy. Let's have a little nightcap. Come on...one or two shots won't hurt." The words flowed over the pleasure center of Jack's brain, making his mouth water. He lifted the bottle, admiring the old-fashioned label and the golden liquid inside then spoke to the bottle: "You've been the best friend I've had for many years now and a hell of a lot more faithful than that red-headed bitch. She was more concerned about money than anything else in life. I should have seen it coming. But you know just what I need to feel good. I did meet a new friend tonight and she made me feel good, too."

Jack flopped onto the dilapidated couch and poured a healthy shot of the fine Tennessee whiskey into a sticky shot-glass that hadn't left its place beneath the hurricane lamp in ages. He rubbed his hands up and down his red flannel shirt several times, as if to wash them or perhaps to alert his stomach it was in for a fine time. Something bulged from the shirt pocket. It was Kate's wallet. Jack leaned back on the couch, staring at the wallet as if it might talk to him at any moment. "I've got to get things straightened out," he said out-loud, then sprawled out across the couch, resting the wallet on his chest.

Morning brought too much sunshine through the uncovered windows and a dull headache. Jack had fallen asleep on the couch, not an uncommon thing, but on this particular morning he actually remembered being there the night before. The severity of the headache was much milder than usual. Jack took this as a good omen. "Guess I'll do something worthwhile today," he said.

The couch had not been kind to his aging body. As he struggled to stand, Jack half-expected to hear the creaking of rusty hinges. Gouty arthritis had invaded many of his joints. The condition had slowed this powerhouse of a man. He wrapped his index finger around the shotglass and the remaining free fingers grasped the neck of the Jack Daniels bottle. He massaged his temple with the other hand then shuffled into the kitchen.

He placed the shotglass in the sink and liquor bottle in the cupboard. "There…I've accomplished something."

Jack sat at the kitchen table waiting for water to warm on the stove. The wallet lay on the table in front of him. Impatience had stolen the whistle from the tea-kettle almost every morning. He firmly believed the Maxwell House coffee was indeed "good to the last drop" but there was no sense waiting for water to boil that he'd just have to wait longer for it to cool. However, today the teakettle's cheerful whistle jarred Jack's attention from the wallet he'd been staring at. He watched for a few seconds as the steam billowed from the pot then disappeared into a fine mist. The cupboard above had discolored and begun to crack in several places.

Jack absentmindedly stirred a mug of coffee as he thumbed through several pictures inside the wallet. She looked so happy back then, sitting on Mom's lap. Jack smiled at the photo that appeared to be Kate's senior picture. *Damn she was pretty, despite the pageboy hair-do.* He recognized a barn in the background of one of the photographs.

Jack decided at that moment to drop by Kate's place, just to return the wallet of course. It was the neighborly thing to do and in a town of less than a thousand people, all were considered neighbors. If she asked him in for coffee or some Christmas cheer…well, all the better.

After a steamy shower, Jack actually toyed with the idea of shaving off his bushy mustache. But the urge passed and instead he shaved only the stubble around it. Generous splashes of Old Spice stung for the usual couple seconds but continued to sting in a small spot under his jaw. "Damn it!" A stream of blood meandered from the spot, diluted to Mercurochrome-orange by the aftershave. A dab of toilet paper would work its magic.

He dressed quickly then walked downstairs. A ghost of Christmas past, his ex-mother-in-law, had given Jack a dark suede coat, most likely in an effort to embarrass him, at least that's what he'd always felt. Now it hung in front of him in the hall closet. The coat had been a Christmas gift and had come after Jack had dated her "little girl" for several years. Plans of marriage were in the making. The previous year Jack had given "Mom" a nice dishtowel and the year before that, a lovely box of peanut brittle that he was sure the coat was meant to trivialize. Jack's mother-in-law had always been a good excuse for his failed marriage. Her precious daughter often ran to her, complaining of being ignored or being mistreated or of some other contrived bullshit that always seemed to cast a bad light on him.

Jack spewed out his feelings about his ex-wife: "God, I hate that woman. She could have driven the pope to drink. I bet things would have been different if we had had some kids…but that wasn't in her damn 'plan'!"

Now Jack stood in front of the open coat closet, eyes alternating between the suede coat and his Red Richie hunting jacket. Good taste won out in the end and dapper Jack drove nervously through downtown Friendship, New York in his vintage Chevy pickup.

A biting breeze stung his freshly shaved face, as Jack stood waiting for someone to answer the farmhouse door. For several seconds he hoped no one would come but when he saw the doorknob turn, Jack knew it was too late to run. An unfamiliar face peered out at him—one raised eyebrow begging his business. Then a smile of recognition filled the woman's face standing in front of him.

Kate wore a Syracuse University sweatshirt, loose-fitting blue jeans and heavy wool socks. Her hair was half the size it had been the night before—pulled back in a tight ponytail. The only hint of make-up was a whisper of eye shadow, possibly left over from the previous evening.

"Jack?" she said, sounding surprised. "Come in. I didn't expect to see you. What brings you out?"

Jack lifted the wallet high and held a toothy smile longer than a relaxed man would have done. He looked like that painfully shy ballplayer on television only a couple nights before. Gary Cooper had played some New York Yankee who had died young, now here he was, reincarnated with a wallet rather than a bat in hand.

"You left this behind," he finally offered. "Hope I'm not intruding."

She took Jack by the arm and coaxed him onto the back porch. "I hadn't even missed the wallet. Been in all day. And no, you're not intruding at all. Mom's asleep and I was just about to start a new book. A friend says it's on the risqué side and that I shouldn't leave it lying around…just in case Pastor Ingles drops by. It's called *Peyton Place*. Have you heard of it?"

"Not actually much into reading myself. But I do follow *Dagwood*." He wished his words back then smiled as if he was just kidding.

"Would you like to come in? I just put the teakettle on for some coffee and there's a pumpkin pie in the oven."

"Well, I can't stay long but a cup of coffee sounds great."

The kitchen was warm and cheery. A pale yellow wallpaper border surrounded the room. The print on it was of an Amish family standing happily in a farmyard. Wooden baskets filled with dried flowers, kitchen utensils and a round loaf of bread accented the counters. The stove was black cast-iron. The sweet aroma of apples and cinnamon filled the air.

Jack sat down at the head of the long kitchen table and watched Kate open the oven to test the pie with a toothpick then pour two cups of coffee. She sat both cups on the table then walked to the refrigerator.

"Cream?" she asked, returning to the table with a ceramic creamer shaped like an elephant.

He lifted his cup and replied, "Thanks."

Kate sat next to Jack at the table and curled her feet under herself. She started to talk about her mother's condition, which was not good, when her eyes paused briefly on Jack's chin. He knew instantly what had drawn her attention. *That damn dab of toilet paper!* For a couple of seconds he plotted several less than subtle ways to retrieve it. *To hell with it!* Jack pinched the toilet paper, eased it from his chin, rolled it between his thumb and index finger then dropped it into his shirt pocket.

At first Kate just smiled but a minute later was holding the back of her hand over her mouth to hide the laughter. A stream of blood flowed again, down Jack's chin. He just shook his head, resigned to the fact he had screwed up. In the grand scheme of things, this would only rate a one on the screw-up scale. Jack had had many entries over the last few years, which would have earned eights, nines and even a few perfect tens. Now Jack sat wondering why he hadn't taken a drink before he left his house…just one to take the edge off.

Kate took hold of Jack's arm with both hands and stared into his eyes. Her laughter subsided. "My dad used one of those chalky things with the green cover to stop the bleeding," she said.

"A styptic pencil," Jack replied. "I would have used mine at home but I wanted to make sure you knew I was old enough to shave, so I left the toilet paper there on purpose," he added then laughed and shook his head.

For the next twenty minutes they talked and laughed. "Oh, the pie!" Kate ran to the oven grabbing a towel from the handle of the refrigerator.

Kate had barely pulled the pie from the oven when a clicking drew Jack's attention to the hallway. A large dog was heading toward the kitchen, claws tapping against the hardwood floor with each step. The wagging tail and near smile on its face gave Jack the impression the dog was glad to see him. When she raised her nose and made a beeline to the oven, the object of her affection became crystal clear.

"Looks like you have a sweet-toothed hound."

"I'm afraid we've spoiled old Darla. Pumpkin pie is her favorite and she knows I'll save her a piece. It's a bit overdone but should still be edible."

"She's a pretty girl. Looks good-natured, too. A golden retriever isn't she?"

"Yes and she's named after that cute girl in *The Little Rascals*—you know, Alfalfa's girlfriend. Folks used to say Mom looked just like her, the little girl I mean, when she was young."

Darla finally noticed someone new in the house and greeted Jack with a gentle kiss on the hand—not too slobbery and very lady like. She looked into his eyes, hoping for a good ear scratching. Jack obliged and immediately knew he'd made a friend.

"I'll be just a couple minutes mixing up some whipped cream. Don't worry Darla...you'll get some pie when it cools," Kate said.

She tied an apron around her waist and took a couple of containers from the refrigerator. There was sugar in one and a dark brown twig seemed to be resting in the middle of it.

"What's that?" A puzzled look crossed Jack's face.

"It's just a vanilla bean. I love the flavor and if you let it sit in the sugar for a couple weeks, the sugar takes on the flavor of the bean. I think you'll like it," Kate said. For several minutes she whipped ingredients Jack couldn't see from the table.

Darla waltzed around in several tight circles then plopped down next to Jack's feet. She released a contented sigh.

Jack did not hear the agonizing moan coming from a distant bedroom. "Mom needs me. Be back in a few minutes," Kate said and hurried down the hallway. Kate's ears were nearly always honed in for needy calls from her mother. And the calls had become much more frequent in the last few days. Cancer had whittled her body to half the woman her daughter could remember so vividly. Kate had cried a great deal in recent days but never in front of her mom.

Jack looked down at Darla. She had been watching his every move and the dog's tail began to wag once she knew she had Jack's attention.

"You're a good girl. Can you shake?"

Darla turned on her side and began swiping her paw toward Jack. "What a smart dog," he said, taking her paw. Her dark honey-brown fur was long and wavy. Gray fur had made its way over most of the dog's muzzle but her eyes sparkled like those of a young pup.

Kate walked back into the kitchen. The look on her face was much more serious than it had been a few minutes before. "Mom's resting but damn…she's in a lot of pain."

Jack still held Darla's paw. "I'm sorry," he said. The dog's ears dropped, sensing all was not right.

Tears welled up in Kate's eyes. She quickly wiped them away and forced a weak smile. Jack watched her cut three large wedges of pie and heap mounds of whipped cream on two of them. She set the naked piece in front of the dog. The threesome sat quietly eating the pumpkin pie. The grandfather clock in the hallway ticked away. Darla burped and Jack took Kate's hand in his. His eyes told her that he was sorry and cared for Kate's feelings but he said nothing.

Before leaving Jack nervously asked, "Do you have plans for Christmas Eve? Maybe we could…spend it together."

"That would be nice," Kate said with a soft smile.

CHAPTER 3

▼

The next day was December 22nd. Rain had transformed a winter wonderland into a slushy mess. The neighborhood was busy with laughing children, enjoying their time off from school. The "twack" of an errant snowball hitting the side of his house would occasionally startle Jack.

For much of the morning he paced, stealing peeks of the cupboard where the sour mash whiskey was resting. He never doubted that he could stop drinking if he wanted to; he just never wanted to. The telephone rang and interrupted his battle with the bottle.

"Hello, Jack?" The voice on the other end was filled with sadness.

Not another word was necessary. He knew who it was and why she was calling—Mrs. Fletcher had died.

Kate hadn't cried. She simply told Jack that their Christmas Eve plans might need to be altered and that she would get back to him. Tears rolled down his cheeks and he wanted desperately to get off the phone. Jack's nerves stood on edge and cold sweat beaded on his brow. The craving for a drink cried out to him.

"I'm so sorry…if there's anything I can do," he said.

"Nothing I can think of right now. I'll get back to you soon. Good bye, Jack." The words rang in his ears with an unsettlingly finality.

"Good bye, Kate…I'm sorry," Jack said, his voice weak. The phone clicked on the other end.

"Show some backbone! Don't make things worse for her by whimpering," Jack scolded himself out loud.

Five minutes later Jack was rolling an empty shot glass between his thumb and finger. The cap of the Jack Daniel's bottle lay on the table. His throat was warm with the memory of the shot of whiskey he had just taken. The one drink he had taken was already bringing back some of the manliness the phone call had made him question. One more stiff one would undoubtedly double the effect. *Why hell, I could be a god damned Humphrey Bogart by the bottom of that bottle. She needs time with her family and close friends. She must have some family and a few close friends still around here,* he thought and poured another drink.

When Jack raised his head from the kitchen table it was dark outside. The clock said 2:30. *Who the hell turned it ahead?* The empty bottom of Jack Daniels screeched back the answer.

Jack stumbled to the bathroom, crashing into walls, doors and furniture that inexplicably jumped in front of him. His image in the bathroom mirror appeared to be that of a total stranger. The other guy's movements were being reflected back in slow motion and "he" looked like shit. "Get the hell out of my house!" Jack dropped his head into the rust stained toilet bowl and his stomach began to heave.

Cold tile made for a very uncomfortable bed. When Jack awoke in the morning it was a toss-up which hurt more—his head or his body. The lingering taste of extra sour Tennessee Whiskey mixed with something he had eaten the day before, fermented in Jack's mouth. "If only she could see me now. Wouldn't she be proud? Maybe I'll stop drinking after New Years."

Several cups of strong coffee washed away some of the bad taste and cleared Jack's head slightly. He thought of Kate and what she must be going through. *Later in the day I'll call her.*

Jack walked to the kitchen window that overlooked his backyard. Snow had fallen overnight, answering the prayers of the White-Christmas sentimentalists and ignoring those of the highway department. Cold weather was in the forecast, so it appeared there would almost certainly be snow on Christmas morning. The gray cloud bank that had delivered in the nick of time was breaking up. A stream of sunshine escaped through a break in the clouds and set the fresh snow to glistening.

Blue spruce trees had been planted on the border of the property during the first summer Jack had been married. Seedlings at the time, only about half of the trees had survived years of neglect. The lot was deep, nearly three hundred feet, and at one time had taken hours to care for. Any urge to mow this once beautiful property had left with his wife. Milkweed and thistle now spread their root where roses and gladiolas once bloomed. Through the scattered spruce trees Jack could see a meadow of golden rod, now in its brown stage and partially covered with snow, spreading like a welcoming mat to the rolling hills that lie beyond. Though his head still pounded, a persuasive voice whispered, "Let's go for a walk."

A pack of Winstons and a lighter in one coat pocket, an apple and a jackknife in the other, were all the essential supplies. He decided to walk to the summit and sit awhile. That was the perfect spot to view the little town. It would be very picturesque this time of year, nestled in the valley, covered with fresh fallen snow. Then he'd mosey over the ridge and perhaps find the spruce tree he had hunted under many years ago. The plans were set and he'd call Kate as soon as he returned. *The old noggin will be clearer then anyway.*

Jack crossed the meadow of golden rod—his arms held just above their tops. Near the back edge of the meadow a snort set Jack back on his heels. His hands instinctively slapped against his heart. A pair of nearly white antlers emerged from the golden rod, followed by the majestic head of a huge buck.

An overdose of adrenaline flooded Jack's veins, causing the scene to unfold in slow motion. The sounds of hoofs stomping on the hardened ground and of the deer gulping in air through its mouth smothered Jack's ears. Black eyes, alive with rage, bore down on him. For a moment, Jack thought the deer might charge, but instead it turned, raised its white tail and bounded toward the hill. Even without a soul in sight, a grin of embarrassment invaded Jack's face. *The great white hunter scared shitless by a little old deer. Why twenty years ago I'd a...*

An old dirt road meandered up the hill and would have made for much easier climbing than the shorter route Jack choose, one that took him through brush and occasional thickets. After ten minutes Jack mumbled, "Jeez, I must have been out of town when the last glacier came through," for the hill was much steeper than he'd remembered.

Under a canopy of hardwoods his footfalls echoed in the crunchy snow. Warm beads of sweat ran from his neck to his chest but cooled quickly when Jack stopped to catch his breath. Deer tracks crisscrossed an abandoned road. One set dwarfed the others and appeared fresh. Jack dropped to one knee and slid two fingers into the hoof-print. He could feel wet leaves at the bottom of the track. The imprint had not had time to freeze over. "That must be him."

By mid-afternoon Jack was standing in a clearing, near the summit of the hill. Tiny houses below followed a distant highway, a few sending up smoke signals from chimneys too small to see. A white church steeple peeked above pine trees. The whine of a distant tractor-trailer was the only sound reaching this peaceful place. The homes, the stores, the farms and the schoolhouse blended together to make up the hometown Jack seldom thought about—pieces of a jigsaw puzzle that each held their own small design and their own unique story.

The ridge that connected several of the hills was much easier to travel. It was virtually level and had few fallen trees or thickets to contend with. Jack had walked this ridge many times with his father while hunting deer and wild turkey. There was a secret place his father had taken Jack to decades ago. About fifty yards in front of him, Jack saw the tall oak, which had marked the spot where the two would turn from the ridge and step off seventy-five paces directly toward a distant grove of hemlock.

Jack turned at the oak tree and began to count. "Sixty-seven, sixty-eight," and Jack stopped dead in his tracks. It was still there! Although it had grown considerably, the tall fir tree was unmistakable. It would certainly make a beautiful Christmas tree but thirty-foot ceilings were rare in this neck-of-the-woods.

As he walked round the tree, Jack dragged his fingertips over the snow-covered boughs. The clean scent of pine floated about the tree. Its needles felt soft to the touch. Memories of time spent with his father in this secluded woodland swept into Jack's thoughts, bringing with them a few bittersweet tears. On the downhill side of the tree he stood to survey changes in the landscape. The hemlock grove straight ahead seemed thicker, the few crab apple trees to the north had now spread to form a small orchard, and the woods filled with beech and maple trees to the south appeared as pristine as they had thirty years ago. A white birch tree had fallen near the point where Jack now stood but had been caught before it hit the ground by what looked to be its twin.

Jack turned to face the fir tree. Brushing snow away to get a better look, he held his breath hoping "they" were still there. Two large branches curved toward each other, obstructing a view of the trunk. Jack parted the branches, stooped a bit and stepped closer.

He saw the two large logs that his father had cut and set next to the trunk of the tree. When Jack and his father would tire of standing—waiting for a trophy buck—they'd sit awhile on the logs and whisper hunting plans.

His father had carried a hatchet with him when he hunted and chopped away several branches that blocked their way to the trunk of the tree. This made it easy to get up close to the tree but eliminated their cover. A wily deer would spot a hunter the second he moved. Dad had solved that problem by pulling several pairs of branches together and securing them with bailing twine. This made a cozy little shelter within the boughs of the tree. Although the twine would break every couple years, after reapplying it three or four times the branches eventually grew together. There was enough opening to see clearly outward but anything more than ten yards away would never notice a hunter in the arms of the tree.

Jack sat down on one of the logs and peered out upon this wondrous place. There was a feeling of security within the little cocoon formed by the fir boughs wrapped around him. Snow flakes, nearly as light as the air, bobbed in front of him. Jack stretched his legs out and leaned back against the trunk of the tree. The magic of this place swept over him, relieving much of the tension he had been feeling. A deep breath escaped as Jack closed his eyes and listened. There were chickadees conversing in the distance but all else was quiet. Sleep washed over him—a comforting, peaceful retreat.

A cold wind startled Jack and he groped with thoughts of where he was as darkness enveloped everything. Parting the branches of the fir tree, he hoped the total blackness would at least subside. But stepping out into the open made little difference. Nighttime had fallen quickly and clouds covered any light the moon or stars might have had to offer. The weight of his dilemma didn't sink in until Jack tried to decide which way to turn. He was quite some distance from home and the walk back would be long, even in daylight. Darkness cloaked the trip in impossibility. "Now what?"

He scrambled for answers. *A fire would help*. But the night was so utterly void of light, the task of collecting any dry wood seemed Herculean. Then Jack remembered the fallen birch not far from where he now stood. He slid his lighter from his pocket and flicked it once. The old Zippo never failed. His ex had given it to Jack on his twenty-first birthday. It was the only remnant of their marriage that worked after all those years.

The flame gave off just enough light to cast a few faint, eerie shadows around the birch. He walked to the tree and found that several of the smaller limbs broke off easily from the trunk. Jack dragged them back to the fir tree, flipped the cover of the lighter closed and groped for one of the large logs that had been used for seats. He rolled it from under the tree then stood it up beside the birch limbs. The log's flat surface would make a perfect shelf for the lighter. Needing two hands to break the limbs, Jack flicked on his lighter again, set it atop the log and hurriedly broke the birch limbs into smaller pieces. He scooped up several handfuls of dried needles from underneath the fir tree. After arranging the birch sticks in a tee pee over the needles, he lit them and minutes later had a small but stable fire.

For the next half-hour he used the light from the fire to help him gather what he estimated would be enough firewood to last the night. Jack fed sticks to the fire and soon had it blazing. Experience told him the birch would burn quickly and that he'd need some hardwood to slow the burn. He eased the large log into the fire. It seemed at first the only thing the log would give off was smoke but finally it broke into a steady flame. A few birch sticks and occasional stoking should keep the campfire burning well into the night.

Jack rolled the second log from under the fir tree, stood it on end and used it for a make-shift camp chair. He stretched his legs to meet the fire, lit a cigarette and began to think this wouldn't be such a bad night after all. The blaze split the night sky and a bed of embers prompted white and light-orange flames to roll like ocean waves in slow motion over the base of the fire. Jack stared for what might have been fifteen minutes or perhaps two hours into the mesmerizing flames—his train of thought derailed uncountable times.

When Jack glanced out into the darkness a faint blink caught his attention. *Must be a couple sparks from the fire,* he thought. But in the distance, near the top of the fallen birch, he spotted two orange-yellowish orbs, which didn't fade away. For a split second one of the orbs disappeared.

"What the hell?" and the orb re-appeared next to its partner. "Damn, it's a pair of eyes," he whispered. And they seemed to be peering directly at him.

He held his breath for a few seconds, then exhaled in a chuckle. "Only a harmless owl."

A deep, "Whoo whoooo," started a conversation. Jack cupped his hands over his mouth and made several mournful attempts to talk back to the bird. Finally he finessed a pair of "whos" that, to an untrained pair of human ears, might have passed for an owl. He sat quietly waiting for a response.

"Whoo whoooooo," spread a smile across Jack's face. The new friends talked for some time with occasional lags in the conversation.

As the entertainment for the evening waned, Jack's eyes grew heavy. He fought to stay awake, fearing the effects of the cold once the fire burned out. In an attempt to keep his mind active, Jack began piecing together images of times, places, people and events he held dear. Kate was among those cherished thoughts. Jack faded into a sound sleep thinking of her.

It was not clear in Jack's mind when morning had actually arrived. He knew he was awake but didn't remember waking. His teeth clattered in the midst of uncontrollable shivering. Gray clouds raced across a bleak sky, catching his attention. A bitter wind stung his face as he stared upward.

"I should get up, but what should I do then? Maybe rekindle the fire. Or walk straight home. Ohhh…I'm so damn tired of thinking."

He struggled to rub his hands over his thighs to warm them but gave up in exhaustion after several strokes. The shivering soon subsided and Jack felt a strange calmness.

"I wonder what Mom's doing for Christmas. Oh, she died. Now when was that," he said to himself.

The fingers on one of his gloves moved slowly. Jack wasn't aware that he was moving them, so he watched curiously, intrigued by the glove's strange movement. Time began to float by in a series of semi-conscious black and white photographs. Sounds were muffled and Jack no longer felt the cold. Peaceful numbness gently soothed him.

Something warm and moist caressed Jack's cheek. He could see movement in front of him but only in trails of dark colors sweeping across his field of vision. His arm lifted involuntarily and far-off sounds rolled into his ears. Jack struggled to understand.

"You'll be okay, Jack. I'll get help." The words crept into his consciousness.

He sat up but had doubts if he had done it on his own. A face came into focus, close to his own. Dark brown eyes peered at him and a long tongue darted in and out between long pointed teeth. The sight startled Jack and he tried to lunge back. Something behind him held him upright. Soft words warmed his ears. "Wake up Jack. I'm here." Someone's lips touched his ear.

Arms wrapped around him and held Jack tight. He could now see the eyes bearing down on him were those of a dog...and a familiar one at that. The friendly animal licked Jack's chin then lay down next to his outstretched legs. "Darla?" Jack questioned.

"Yes, Jack. It's Darla," came a voice from behind.

"Who's back there?" he asked.

Jack could feel the body behind him begin to tremble. "It's me...Kate." Sobs interrupted each word. "I was so worried about you!"

"I'm okay. Just a bit cold and not sure if my legs are working like they should," Jack said. His voice was more relaxed than it should have been, after such an ordeal.

"We'll take care of you." She stretched to plant a warm kiss on his cheek. "I'll get the fire going again."

"I'm not exactly sure what's going on here," he said. Tears began to well up in his eyes then streamed down his face as his mind fought to piece together lost details.

Kate still sat behind Jack, her legs wrapping around his bottom and her chest pressed firmly against his back. Kate patted his chest reassuringly. "We'll get you home."

After comforting her friend, Kate set to work and had a blazing fire going within minutes. She then knelt in front of Jack and poured a steaming cup of coffee from a green thermos. The cup shook as she eased it toward his lips.

"You're cold," he said.

"I was so worried about you, Jack. You sure do play hard to get, running away like that." She forced a laugh and shivered.

Jack squeezed his eyes shut, brushing his fingertips and thumb over them, in a desperate attempt to unscramble the events that had brought him here. Hazy white spots floated across the darkness he saw, reminding him of the gentle snow, so serene and harmless. Yet here he sat, a rugged man, crippled by the elements. His upbringing had molded him into a stoic, tough-it-out, never let a woman see you helpless, type of individual. Now a female savior was kneeling in front of him, rubbing warmth back into his unresponsive legs.

"Thanks," was all he could manage.

Darla sat at his side and wagged her tail at the sound of his voice. The long fur of her tail swept the snow, leaving the imprint of an angel's wing. Jack glanced at the design in the snow then turned to see Kate, a look of concern etched on her face.

"We've got to get you home," Kate said. Her eyes reflected concern. She knew a little about hypothermia and was aware it could cause disorientation.

Finally, the warmth of the fire and the vigorous rubbing seemed to restore some of the physical and mental energy that the cold had sapped. Jack struggled to get to his feet but his will was stronger than his legs. With Kate's help he finally managed to stand. He drooped his arm over her shoulder and forced a weak smile. A clever witticism would have softened the seriousness of the situation, but Jack found himself fresh out.

"Guess I screwed up," he said.

"Don't give it a thought. Can't think of anything I'd rather be doing on the day before Christmas than dragging a big lummox out of the woods." Kate brushed a few snowflakes from Jack's eyebrows.

The walk from the woods was slow. At first they stopped to catch a breath every few yards. By the time the journey finally took them downhill, Jacks limbs had warmed and limbered. His embarrassment and her understanding left the two nearly speechless. They stopped in a small clearing in the woods where they could see Jack's house in the distance.

"Never thought I'd be so glad to see that place," Jack said.

Kate stepped in front of him, obstructing his view. He craned his neck to see around her, giving little thought to what she was doing. A few mental cobwebs lingered in his head. It took several seconds for him to realize she needed him. Her hands slid under the bottom of his coat, momentarily resting on his slim hips. *She's gone through a lot and needs you,* he thought. *Better not say something stupid.*

She pulled closer, her hands wrapping around his back, her head resting against his chest. He could feel her body stiffen then relax several times. A muffled whimper escaped her. Sobs soon had Jack feeling more helpless than he had while he lay freezing in the snow. A few awkward pats on her back didn't seem to help and he finally dropped his head to rest against hers. Jack closed his eyes and held her.

Time passed the two by, neither caring what went on around them or in the little hamlet below. Something brushed against Jack's leg and he opened his eyes to see a pair of sad brown eyes peering up at him. Pools of emotion flowed in those eyes. Darla raised a paw and rested it against his leg.

"Do you want some attention old girl?" he asked.

Kate pulled back momentarily, assuming Jack was speaking to her then broke into a weak smile when she realized the question was directed to Darla.

"She misses Mom and hasn't eaten much since yesterday. I miss her, too."

"I'm so sorry," Jack said, concern set deep in his bloodshot eyes.

A beam of sunshine broke through the muddled gray sky and spotlighted his house in the valley below. It seemed illuminated amid the other homes still shadowed by heavy clouds.

"How did you find me?" he asked.

Kate pointed to a set of tracks near where they stood. "You're lucky there weren't a lot of fools out traipsing through the woods yesterday. Otherwise we might not have found you until next spring. Darla was a big help when we walked through the golden rod and your tracks were hard to follow."

"Guess I owe both of you a big thanks," he said.

Kate could see Jack was shivering again and his lips were grayish-blue. "Let's get home," she said.

They walked hand-in-hand down the hill and across the meadow. At the back steps the idea of asking her in crossed his mind but at times his house didn't exactly look like the Waldorf Astoria and Jack was thinking this might be one of those times.

"I'm going to take a hot bath, then get some rest. Okay if I call you this afternoon?" Jack asked.

"Sure, but I'll be in and out. Still have a few things to do for the funeral. It's the day after tomorrow." Her eyes looked sorrowful as she added, "and I need to find a place for Darla."

"What'a you mean?"

"Well, my boss has been holding my waitressing job for nearly a month now and I need to get back to Poughkeepsie or lose it. It keeps the bills paid and I can afford an apartment but no dogs allowed. And my daughter Sarah has three temperamental cats, so she's out of the question. Darla would have a nervous breakdown after a week with them."

Jack swallowed. "When are you leaving?"

"After Mom's funeral. That's if the weather holds."

A gust of wind sent a shiver up Jack's spine. He'd momentarily forgotten his ordeal but cold air hijacked his attention. Swallowing his male pride Jack said, "I better get inside and get warmed up."

"There's a Christmas Eve service at church tonight. Would you like to join me? There won't be any long sermon," Kate promised.

"Do they have lightning insurance? I haven't been in a church in years and someone up there might not take too kindly to the likes of me barging in."

"Baptists usually welcome even the most despicable into the fold." Her face broke into a broad smile. "I'll pick you up about quarter of eight. Is it a date?"

"I'll dust off my Bible. Do they serve wine there?" he asked with a forced grin.

"You heathen," Kate scolded in feigned disgust. Then she turned and was gone before he could find the word, "Thanks."

CHAPTER 4

▼

Jack's bedroom was about as far from the furnace as any room in the house. By the time any air had zigzagged through the ductwork it was tepid at best and the sheet-plastic stapled outside was a poor excuse for storm windows. Jack plodded up the stairs to his chilly sanctuary and stopped in the doorway. On nights he was not passed out on the couch, Jack would actually enjoy the coolness of this bedroom. The stark white walls all but chattered, "igloo." Jack grabbed a wool army blanket and his pillow from the unmade bed and trudged back downstairs.

The living room was noticeably warmer but, like a slap in the face, its dismal seediness struck Jack with a clarity he had not seen before. Uncovered windows exposed filth. The carpet was matted down, caked with brown and gray three-dimensional stains, resembling the coat of a wild sheepdog. Several dead flies lay feet up, probably pickled and dying happy in the syrup of spilled booze that marbled the coffee table top. The couch might have passed for a Pop-Art masterpiece in another decade but with multicolored stains covering this over-stuffed fleabag, it would be a stretch to even called it furniture now. Jack hugged his blanket and pillow, wide-eyed in disbelief. His eyes dropped to a shiny black bottle, lying on its side next to the hurricane lamp. *How did I let things get this bad?* The answer drifted to him in the gray letters, "J-a-c-k" on the label.

Jack built a fire then worked for the next hour, methodically scrubbing, polishing and rearranging just about everything in the room. Lace curtains that had hung in the guest bedroom now softened the sunlight that had been so truthful a short time ago. A large brown afghan covered the back of the couch. The scent of cedar from the afghan lingered near the couch, grabbing Jack's attention. It made him wish he still took the time to do some of the fine woodworking his father had taught him. A steady fire snapped in the fireplace, warming the room more than Jack would usually have liked.

Satisfied with his work, Jack sprawled out on the couch. He stared into the fire, rubbed his feet together for a few minutes then faded into a restful sleep.

The next thing Jack heard was Westminster chimes. For years he'd meant to change the doorbell, which was a little too formal for Friendship, New York. "Now who could that be?" he wondered.

Reality struck in an instant. He scrambled to the door, assessing his predicament with each step. *What time is it?*

The door opened and Kate stood under the yellow porch light. He could see her warm breath as it hit the cold night air. There was no look of alarm on her face as he might have expected once she saw him. Her date was decked out in a grungy blue flannel shirt and a pair of sweatpants that drooped in the seat.

"What time is it?" he questioned.

Kate reached out and touched Jack's arm. "Don't worry. I just dropped off some stuff at the church and noticed your lights weren't on. It's just a little after 7:00. How are you feeling?"

"A lot better than I did this morning. Finally got some warmth into these old bones. Guess I better get cleaned up. Would you like to come in?"

"No, I need to change and get supper for Darla. Shall we meet at the church?" she asked.

"Nah...I'll pick you up at quarter of eight."

Jack watched her walk away. As taillights disappeared into the cold night air he wondered how Kate felt about him.

The Friendship Baptist Church had always seemed a bit rigid to Jack. Members often carried well-worn Bibles—some even on weekdays. He suspected his drinking might not be looked upon with the esteem he often gave it, especially after a couple belts of JD. But this evening the congregation bustled into the pretty little church, full of friendly slaps on the back and cheery smiles. Kate held his arm while they ascended the steps. As Jack reached for the brass door handle, a family with several noisy children hurried up the stairs behind them. Jack stepped aside, holding the door for Kate and the family. She walked into the vestibule, shook hands with the pastor and turned to look for Jack. Through the doorway and around the taller members of the loud family, their eyes locked. *I'm lucky that I met her.*

Inside, a New England raised pulpit, a choir robed in purple and a ceiling-high Christmas tree greeted all. The choir was just finishing the final verse of "Oh Little Town of Bethlehem". Two stout female singers sandwiched a skinny elderly gentleman in the front row of the choir, almost obscuring him from view. A sheepish smile on his face seemed to indicate he didn't mind a bit. Several dozen candles flickered in nooks and crannies throughout the church. Headlights from cars in the parking lot streamed through stained glass windows, casting brief rainbows of evangelical splendor on an otherwise stark wall. Kate and Jack squeezed into a pew near the back of the church. Within minutes, ushers were setting up folding chairs to accommodate the overflow crowd.

Promptly at 8:00, Pastor Lawrence W. Ingles climbed the pulpit and cleared his throat. The congregation immediately quieted in anticipation. The name Ichabod Crane mysteriously popped into Jack's mind just as the rail-thin preacher let out a booming, "Welcome, all ye children of God". When the preacher paused, the echo of his deep base voice seemed caught within the walls of the sanctuary. "Extend a hand to your neighbor. Tell them, Merry Christmas," he said. And the church was instantly buzzing with seasonal greetings, handshakes and smiles. Kate grasped Jack's right hand with both of hers. He could hear the preacher say something about the greatest gift but his attention was elsewhere.

A half-hour into the message Jack began to realize how Baptists stayed awake through some legendarily long sermons. The pews were hard and angled in such a way as to force the occupant into an upright position, which could generally have been referred to as torturous. The preacher's deep voice massaged the congregation with the story of the Christmas miracle and of newfound hope. Kate sat close to Jack, her arms crossed in a relaxed way. Out the corner of his eye, Jack could see her staring contemplatively up toward the raised pulpit. Several times he felt a fingertip brush against his arm. The gesture was hidden from any Puritan eyes by the arm she had artfully folded over that sinful hand. Jack desperately wanted to hold her.

"Let us go forth, spread his word and be abundant in the joy of this season. May the true spirit of Christmas enter your hearts and fill you with the peace his wonderful love can provide. Amen. Now, let us sing hymn number 143…Silent Night."

Creaks from the ancient pews and arthritic joints accompanied the worshippers as they stood at the pipe organ's prompting. A loud "Pop" startled Jack and many around him, as heads snapped about to locate the source of the sound. An instant later the lights in the church all went dim. It took a few seconds for eyes to adjust to the soft candlelight that now bathed the sanctuary and all looked to the preacher for guidance. "Must be a Methodist fusebox. Let's sing verses 1 and 2 only."

"Silent Night…Holy Night…All is calm…". Jack looked around and sensed a serenity he'd never felt. He fought to hold back tears as soft orange candlelight shown on the faces of those around him. They all seemed painted with inner peace. Then he looked at her.

Da Vinci would have struggled to capture this vision. Her face betrayed a subtle sadness but that was understandable. For the first time Jack stared deeply into her eyes and saw kindness pouring out toward him. He slipped his hand around hers and squeezed. "Sleep in heavenly peace," and she smiled.

A haunting quiet escorted the multitude into the still night air. Not a word was exchanged until the two had driven half way to her home. "That was beautiful," he said. All he heard was a sniffle. Not another word was spoken until they stepped into the farmhouse kitchen. Kate snapped on the light, walked to the stove and lit the burner under the teapot.

"I guess I'm not very good company right now," she half whispered, still facing the stove.

Jack stepped toward her, slipping his arms around her waist and resting his face against her soft hair. "The company couldn't be better."

The two stood silent. Only a nearly inaudible sigh of contentment broke the quiet. Jack wasn't sure if the sound had come from Kate or him. The sigh certainly would have captured his feelings at that very moment. Deep, rhythmic ticks from the old grandfather clock in the hallway drew Jack's attention. As he looked up, his eyes met the sad stare of his new four-legged friend. She was peeking around the doorcase, which lead into the hallway. Immediately Darla looked away, as if she knew she was intruding. "Ahh…you poor girl. It's okay," Jack said softly.

Darla understood and walked over to the embracing couple, her backside wiggling from side to side. Kate turned to see her mom's best friend. "You sure know how to work a guy, don't you? Bet you're just looking for a handout…or maybe a good belly rubbin'."

Kate looked up at Jack. "I don't know what I'm going to do with her. Guess I'll have to look for a new apartment in Poughkeepsie…one that allows dogs. But in the meantime…" Kate ended her thought in a shrug.

Over the years Jack had made a habit of speaking before thinking. Given the chance, he could have come up with dozens of good reasons why keeping a dog would be out of the question but, in the true spirit of his old habit, he blurted out, "I'll take her. Whenever you're ready you can have her back but she won't be a problem with me."

"Jack, don't just say that because you feel obligated. You better give it some thought first."

"Don't worry about me. She'll be great company. Besides, I owe her for coming to my rescue."

"Are you sure?" Kate asked.

"Of course. I can use somebody to keep an eye on me."

Jack slapped his knee lightly several times. Darla turned to him and sat down meekly at his feet. "Must be she wants to seal the deal," Jack said grinning, as Darla raised a paw to shake. They both laughed and the dog wagged her tail.

Over the next ten minutes Kate gathered all of Darla's personal belongings: a collar, leash, brush, food and water dishes, a bag of Purina Dog Chow and a small, smelly quilt. Darla sniffed at the bag of dog food and the quilt, then looked inquisitively at Kate. Jack could see tears in Kate's eyes and decided this was not the time to be interfering. Kate knelt to the floor and cradled the dog in her arms for several minutes. She closed her eyes and stroked Darla's soft fur.

"She's a very good dog, Jack. Won't give you any trouble," Kate assured.

"I'm sure she'll be much more agreeable than my last housemate."

Kate thought for a couple seconds then smiled, realizing he was referring to his ex-wife. "This one might be a lot cheaper, too." Kate said with a knowing smile.

"I know you're leaving in a couple days. Would you like me to pick her up in the morning or take her over to my place tonight?"

Kate looked at the things she had gathered for Darla then into her sad eyes. "Let's let her stay here tonight. Then she'll have a chance to get used to your house for an entire day before bedding down. I'm not sure if she'll whine a bit or not," Kate said.

"Not a problem if she does," Jack said.

Jack thought about suggesting both Kate and Darla come over to spend the night. He rationalized it would have made Darla feel more comfortable in the strange surroundings but deep inside something just didn't feel right about that suggestion. Best just say "Goodnight" then leave, he decided.

As Jack stood by the back door, zipping his coat, something in Kate's eyes spoke to him clearly. "I wish you didn't have to go back," he said.

"Oh Jack, I'd love to stay here in Friendship but my daughter's been so sick the last few days and I want to be with her. And my job."

"I know. It's just...well," and he took her hand, stroking it tenderly. "Maybe I can get out to see you in the next month or so. The construction business is just a bit slow this time of year. How's Darla travel?"

"Best navigator this side of the Genesee. She's great company on a trip. Hasn't ever been carsick," Kate assured. "But we'll need to find a motel that allows dogs since my apartment is off limits to them."

Kate raised Jack's hands to her lips. She slowly kissed his hand then stared up directly into his eyes. "A penny for your thoughts," she whispered.

A devilish smile broke on Jack's face and he shook his head. "Ahh, they're too muddled right now," he lied. He dropped both of his hands to her waist. For a moment he wished he'd had a good belt or two of whiskey. His nerves walked a tightrope and a couple of drinks certainly could calm them. Deep inside he knew nothing good could come of his drinking. As he looked into the eyes of this woman he might be falling in love with, he vowed to conquer his "little problem". Then he slid one hand to the small of her back and the other to her neck, stroking her hair with his fingertips.

Like a gentle breeze stilled before a storm, Kate's breath caught in her throat. He leaned down, resting his head against hers and pursed his lips to her earlobe. As he kissed her ear ever so softly, she shuddered. Jack felt her warm breath seep through his shirt, feeling moist against his chest. Slowly, he left a trail of kisses from her ear, down her cheek then to the corner of her lips. Teasingly he kissed round her lips, finally pulling her lower lip between his. Kate threw her arms around Jack's neck and centered her lips firmly on his. She moaned in a flood of passion that had been dormant for longer than Kate cared to remember. A loud "Rooof...rooof," broke the spell.

"She's quite a guard dog," Jack said pulling from Kate. He knelt to Darla's level and was greeted with a slobbery kiss directly on the chin.

"Was it good for you?" Kate questioned laughingly. She patted Jack on the head and commanded, "Down boy!"

Jack wrapped his arm around Kate's hips and pulled her gently to the floor, growling and nipping like a big puppy at play.

"Don't bite the hand that feeds you," she giggled and the two rolled from side to side on the floor. Darla joined the ruckus, yapping and trying to nuzzle between them. The grandfather clock in the hallway began to chime out the hour of midnight. "Merry Christmas," they both said in unison. The memory of this night would lie indelibly etched in that little corner of Jack's brain reserved for very special moments.

CHAPTER 5

▼

Christmas day was crisp, with a cloudless sky as brilliant a blue as Jack had ever seen. He could recall his father telling of such a sky: "It was over the little Greek Isle of Kefalonia. It hurt my eyes to look at the snow-white sand and the cobalt-blue sky. You could tell the tourists in a minute…they'd squint and stare at that beautiful blue, like it was a color they'd never seen before. Of course, I was one of them and guess I'll never see that blue again." He sounded sad when describing it to Jack.

Main Street was empty as Jack drove his new friend to her new home. Darla sat up curiously in the seat of the truck. Her nose worked overtime, taking in a variety of new smells. She glanced upward and for a moment Jack wondered if Darla sensed the brilliance of the extraordinary sky, then he remembered hearing that dogs couldn't see in color. "It sure is pretty, girl." He looked upward, noticing a hawk gliding gracefully across the sky, wings held perfectly still in the calm air. One glance at Darla and he knew she saw it, too. She touched her nose to the windshield and sniffed several times, streaking the glass.

"You're going to like your new home," Jack guaranteed. Darla examined each word with her dripping nose, leaning closer to Jack's mouth with each syllable. "It's bacon I had for breakfast…you probably can smell the eggs, too. Sorry, it's not on your menu old girl."

Darla began to fidget as they turned into Jack's driveway. The neighbor's Springer Spaniel was inspecting a maze of fresh rabbit tracks near some evergreen shrubbery in their front yard. "That's Freckles. She's a good dog, too," Jack assured Darla.

As the old Ford pulled to a stop, Jack took a deep breath. For no good reason he worried about this new arrangement. Darla watched his every move as the man walked around in front of the truck to the passenger side door. With the formality of a chauffeur Jack opened the truck door and she hopped out. New sights fascinated her. Jack let Darla browse around the property, hoping she'd soon be feeling comfortable in her new environment.

Darla's ears perked up and she circled a small area at the foot of a large white spruce tree. Jack could see that some birds, probably partridge, had been scratching for food there. After assuring herself that the birds were gone Darla pranced up to Jack, tail still wagging. He dropped to one knee, expecting a wet kiss. The dog turned and leaned against her new master. Her eyes were fixed on the open meadow just beyond the tree she had been examining. Jack laughed out loud and patted her. "Later girl."

Inside the house, Jack let Darla have the run of things. He busied himself with little odd jobs that had been put off for years. Kate would be leaving for Poughkeepsie the next day, after her mom's funeral. *I wonder if she's thinking of us,* he thought as he nailed up a curtain rod that had sagged for years. On the floor next to the fireplace, he straightened a bright patchwork quilt. A short whistle brought Darla in from the kitchen. Jack pointed at the quilt and spoke firmly to Darla, "Down girl." After a great deal of sniffing and several trips around the edge of it, she stepped gingerly onto the quilt and plopped down in the middle. His smile assured the dog it was all right to be there. "My Aunt Faith made this quilt many years ago. I used to sleep under it on cold winter nights when I was a boy. It's okay for you to use it now girl, since it's being kept in the family." He reached down a stroked Darla's neck until her eyes began to flutter and finally closed.

Jack picked up yesterday's newspaper, sat down in his easy chair and turned to the sports section. The Olean Times Herald over-reported the details of a basketball game between powerhouse Scio and the underdog Richburg Bearcats. "Must have been a slow news day," Jack mumbled. Terms such as, big guns, attack, half-court bomb, man-to-man defense and offensive blitz lead Jack to believe the reporter must have been a military veteran. The most interesting part of the story involved the lack of seniors on the Richburg team. It seemed they had played in a fund-raiser game earlier in the year. To raise money for their senior trip, the class had sponsored a donkey basketball game. All players were mounted on donkeys for the entire contest. Sectional officials had declared that since the money raised benefited the players, they would now be considered professional basketball players and thus were ineligible. The scrappy underclassmen apparently felt they needed to pick up the slack left by the departed seniors and eked out a last second victory over the heavily favored Scio team.

Jack chuckled at the thought of attempting a fast break atop a jackass. "Damn fools." Darla wagged her tail at the sound of his voice then started to get up. Once she saw Jack's head buried in the newspaper, the dog lay back down. The folded quilt was softer than the throw rug she'd been accustomed to and she sighed in contentment.

From his easy chair, Jack looked over the top of the newspaper and gazed at Darla. Her feet twitched as if she were running after an elusive pheasant. A faint whimper escaped the dog's dream and Jack considered waking her but she soon settled. "We're going to make it just fine, you and I."

The phone rang and Darla barely stirred. "How's the new tenant doing?" Jack was glad to hear Kate's voice. "I found a few of her toys. Okay to drop them off?" she asked.

"Sure...come on over," Jack said.

The threesome spent the afternoon together. It felt good to have a woman in the house. Kate laughed and seemed at ease...but Jack knew the thought of her mother's funeral had to be weighing on her mind. Kate watched from the front window as the sun set on this beautiful day. Jack stood behind her, arms wrapped around her waist. He felt a tear fall upon his hand.

.........Nearly a hundred people attended the funeral at the Baptist church the next morning. Friends and distant relatives offered their condolences and prayers. Kate's daughter Sarah, was bedridden with the worst case of the flu she had ever had, so Kate was on her own. Jack was unsure just how visible he should be but when he saw her standing alone in the vestibule he knew where he must be. Kate squeezed his hand as Jack stepped up beside her.

She left that day, shortly after the funeral. Jack kissed her goodbye and searched for the right thing to say. Kate's eyes told him no words were necessary. Jack knew he had met someone very special as he watched her car turn out of sight.

CHAPTER 6

▼

For the next few days Jack and Darla were nearly house-bound. A bone-chilling Arctic cold front had moved in and even on brief walks outside, Darla would raise a paw almost to her chest, give it a little shake, then switch paws. Jack considered getting her protective footwear but the vision of Mrs. Erma Wilson, the town spinster, walking her Scottish Terrier Miffy, all decked out in plaid sweater and booties was enough to change his mind. "This dog's going to have some dignity," he vowed.

The day before New Year's Eve warmed up to the high 20's. "Great hunting weather, Darla. Let's get some birds." Jack retrieved his bolt-action 20 gauge shotgun from its case under his bed. He'd been meaning to build a gun-rack for years and felt ashamed when thinking how disappointed his father would have been, had he lived to see his son storing a gun under a bed.

From a cardboard box, hidden high in a kitchen cupboard, Jack grabbed a handful of shells and a can of Hoppe's Oil. He squeezed a couple drops on the bolt of his gun, then worked it several times to disperse the oil. Darla watched his every move, sensing the excitement in the air. The farm dog had never been hunting. A whiff of the Hoppe's Oil took Jack back to his boyhood. He explained to Darla, "My dad would meticulously clean any gun he touched. The inside of every gun barrel he owned, sparkled with a thin coat of that magic oil. A spot of rust would have driven him mad. Now I'm passing this information on to you…instead of a son of my own." Jack stood staring at the gun. "Let's go," Jack finally said and ruffled the fur on Darla's head.

From Jack's backdoor, there was a secluded meadow that could be reached in fifteen minutes by foot. An old dirt road crossed the backside of the meadow. A truck-ride there would take less than five minutes but Jack wanted his dog to get accustomed to being in the wild with him before they got down to some serious hunting. So the twosome set off walking.

At the edge of the meadow Jack stood for several minutes breathing in the fresh air, admiring the wintry landscape. Then, at a leisurely pace, he snooped his way down the hedgerow that bordered the meadow. Darla was hesitant to get into the brush there and walked close to Jack's side.

"The object here is for you to run into that brush and flush up some birds. They're not here on the path but in that thick stuff. Now, go get 'em!" he said excitedly, snapped his fingers and pointed at the brush. After the little pep talk, Darla made her way into the hedgerow. *See, it's not so bad after all, is it girl?* Darla made her way through narrow pathways in the hedgerow cleared by various wild-life. The dog's tail soon began to wag furiously and she darted back and forth, nose to the ground. In an explosion of sound, a noisy cock pheasant burst from the hedgerow and into hurried flight over the meadow. A single shot rang out but the beautiful bird continued on its way. A distant cackle bid hunter and dog fare-well.

Darla's head turned side to side and her ears cocked—eyes wide with excite-ment. She'd never heard a gunshot up close, but didn't appear to be gun-shy. Nature turned on an instinctive switch and the dog hunted like a pro for the next hour.

Jack was the first to tire. He stood for a moment to catch his breath and pon-dered the shortest way home. Darla seemed interested in a strange scent and she pranced to the forest side of the hedgerow. In a crash of broken sticks and loud hoof beats, Jack saw a frightened deer bound into the woods. Darla was at its heals, barking wildly. "No!" Jack yelled but his command was not heard in the frenzy of the moment or it simply was ignored. He crashed through the narrow thicket in front of him, only to see the flash of the deer's white tail and sin-gle-minded Darla at its heels.

Jack tracked the two for several hours, yelling her name until his throat ached, then came to a spot where the tracks diverged. The deer had most likely distanced itself so far from the dog that she gave up the chase. Hopefully Darla was now heading home. Jack followed her track for the better part of an hour and noticed the dog was traveling in a large circle. He painfully made the decision to veer from the track in the hope of cutting in front of the dog. Otherwise he'd never catch up to her. It was nearly dusk when Jack knew he had to turn home. Each step he prayed he'd see her tired face on the back steps of his porch. As he neared the back corner of his property, Jack cursed his unanswered prayer.

Over a cup of strong black coffee Jack pondered what to do next. His head throbbed. Rubbing his temples he said, "God, I could use a drink." The cupboard which hid the bottles called back, "Come on over and have just one." Jack pounded his fist on the kitchen table and spit several filthy words in reply to the cupboard.

A shiver brought back the reality of the ordeal he'd been through only a week earlier. One thing was clear: he needed to get into some warm dry clothes. As he sat on the edge of his bed, pulling on a pair of long johns, a plan fell into place. He'd put a set of chains on his truck then travel the dirt roads closest to where Darla had disappeared. Between the truck's horn and his loud voice, a keen eared canine would surely hear something. "She'll be okay," he assured himself.

Night had fallen quickly and darkness enveloped the woods. Ruts in the unpaved road bounced the truck at awkward angles. Beams from the headlights cut eerie patterns through the ebony void. "Darla, Darla come!" The surrounding evergreens swallowed the desperate call. Jack only hoped the blaring horn would fall on his dog's frightened ears. This was Kate's dog lost in the forest and Jack agonized just how he would break the bad news if Darla didn't come back. The truck's horn and Jack's raspy voice continued to cry out into the night.

Fruitless hours crept by. Jack's eyes were heavy, not only with fatigue, but also with the wave of despair that had washed over him. He drove dejectedly into his driveway as the black sky in the east slowly had turned to deep purple.

In exhaustion, Jack crossed his arms against the steering wheel and buried his face in them. A hodgepodge of "should haves" nagged at him. Several disturbing dreams wove their way between states of light sleep and semi-consciousness. At one point Jack was aware he was dreaming and tried desperately to have the dream take him to Darla. A blast from the truck's horn startled him into reality. His arm had slipped onto the horn ring and Jack now sat rigid in the seat. "Damn it…I've got to find her," he swore and started the truck up again.

Tires spinning in the slushy snow, the old truck plowed deep into the forest again. The road was now not much more than a path. Jack had no idea where he was going but knew the dog must be found. Through the dirty windshield he could see a fork in the road ahead. "Which way?" he mumbled. Out the corner of his eye a flash of white caught Jack's attention. Three deer pranced from the woods not more than twenty yards away and turned down one of the forks. "That way!" and the decision was made.

Pine boughs brushed the truck's side panels, the road narrowing even more. Around a tight bend, the forest opened into a small clearing. A dilapidated hunting cabin sat in the middle of it. Broken wooden stairs led to a rickety porch,

adorned with three fallen chairs and a rotted wood-box. Golden rod had encircled much of the porch. Jack surveyed every detail but "No Darla". Seeing no
path exiting the clearing, his only option seemed to be going back the same way
he had come in. "Guess I should have taken the other fork."

There was just enough space in front of the hunting camp to make a U-turn.
Mid-morning sunshine broke over the tops of towering evergreens and bathed
the ramshackle cabin in light. As the truck pulled away, Jack took one last glance
in the rearview mirror. A slight movement caught his eye and there, under the
rundown porch, he saw a face peering around an opening in the goldenrod. In an
instant he was out of the truck and squinting in the direction he'd spied the face.
The spot was empty and for a moment he thought it must have been a fox,
spooked by his suddenness.

Near the goldenrod were spots of blood. Anxiety crept up his spine with each
step toward the cabin. Jack dropped to his knees where he thought the face had
appeared. There, cowering beneath the porch, lay the injured dog. "Darla!"

Jack reached for her and she turned on her side, waving one paw at him. "It's
me girl." It was then he saw the blood. Her lower leg was covered with it. Relief
came seeing the blood was all a brownish-red. At least she wasn't bleeding now.
"You'll be okay. Good dog."

At the words, "Good dog," Darla struggled to get up, never letting the bloody
paw touch the ground. Carefully, Jack slid his arm around her and under her
chest. He stood, his other hand steadying her head. As he walked slowly to the
truck, she nuzzled her nose under his arm and shivered. The driver's side door
was still open. Jack eased the dog into the passenger's seat, climbed into the
truck, said, "Thank you, God," and started back home.

In the driveway, Jack sat in his idling truck for several minutes, staring blankly
at Darla. She stretched to give him a single lick on the hand. A weak smile was
returned to her, from a man exhausted by the events of the last 24 hours. "Let's
get inside and see how that paw is."

In the kitchen Jack filled a bucket with warm water and added a couple drops
of dish-washing soap. Darla fussed a bit as he eased her paw into the soapy water
but relaxed at the sound of his soothing voice. "Let's see what you've done."

After several minutes of soaking the dried blood loosened from her fur. Jack
raised and carefully examined the paw. The dewclaw had been ripped from its
pad and left a nasty gash in its place. "A little Mercurochrome, some gauze and
adhesive tape and you'll be good as new," he said.

The dog watched every move Jack made as he applied the bandage. When he had finished, she limped about the kitchen, testing the patch job. "Guess you'll live old girl."

Darla's coat was still wet. She shivered every few seconds, sporting the "wet rat" look. "Let's get you warmed up," Jack said.

Since Christmas, Jack had split four face cords of hardwood. It had been seasoned for several years. He retrieved an armful of the logs from the woodpile behind his house. Fifteen minutes later, a roaring blaze filled the fireplace. "Come over here girl," Jack said, pointing at Darla's quilt next to the hearth.

The dog limped to the warm spot. She skipped her ritualistic circling and plopped immediately onto the quilt. At the sight of her resting comfortably, Jack finally sighed in relief.

"You sure gave me a scare," he whispered, his own eyes struggling to stay open. "Mind if I join you?"

He grabbed a pillow from the couch and lay down on the floor beside Darla. With eyes closed, she grunted her approval for the behind-the-ear scratching she was receiving. Jack soon began to drift off. His fingers slowed to a snail's pace. Darla, sensing Jack's lack of enthusiasm, turned to her side and lifted the injured paw, obviously wanting her belly rubbed. Instead, Jack drooped his arm over her and coaxed, "Go to sleep, girl". Soon, they were both asleep.

That evening Jack summoned the nerve to call Kate but not before he had mulled over many times just what he'd say concerning the ordeal with Darla. Once she was actually there on the other end of the line he talked about everything else but the episode. Just as Kate was about to say "good bye", Jack casually mentioned, "Oh, Darla chased after a deer today. She's right here now looking guilty after the scolding she got for running out of sight…broke a toenail, too." Tidbits of the dog's romp surfaced every time Jack and Kate spoke but it was months before the whole story got out.

………Two major blizzards in January brought an abundance of snow with them. In a letter to Kate, Jack joked that it only snowed twice here during that month, once for 16 straight days and again for 15. Like clockwork, letters from Kate would arrive each Tuesday. Jack would wait until things had quieted around the house before settling into his easy chair to read each letter twice. The one postmarked January 22nd was read three times.

It said:

Hello Jack and Happy Birthday Darla,

Started to write "Hi" instead of "Hello" and thought it would appear I had terrorist intentions. (Get it. "Hijack") Ha...Ha! Anyway, as I'm writing this letter today, it's Darla's birthday. She's a lucky 7 so the year should go smoothly for her. (No more escapades in the woods.) Give her a special treat from me and maybe a wet kiss!

It's bright and sunny here today but unusually cold. Right around zero degrees, I've heard. Wish a certain someone were here to keep me warm. I have the morning off but need to go into work later today. Here I sit in a pair of long johns my daughter gave me for Christmas. Must look a sight!!

Jack grinned at the image her description had conjured.

Lately I've been very homesick for Friendship. I know it's kind of quiet there but that's okay. At least there, when I go to the store or out for a walk, I know people. Some days, here in Poughkeepsie, I'll go through the entire day and not recognize a soul, except the folks I work with of course and they are nice, but I miss quiet, peaceful evenings just spending time with someone I care about. Well, hope I haven't bored you with all this sentimental rambling.

My daughter and her husband are having me over for pot-roast tomorrow. (One of my favorites.) Both of them are doing well but they seem to be constantly busy. I'm taking over my world famous apple pie. Trying one of those fancy lattice crusts for the first time. I saw one in Good Housekeeping that looked scrumptious.

I want you to make sure you two ne'er-do-wells are behaving. Next time I'm home I don't want to hear any rumors you've been painting the town.

Be sure to let the birthday cake you bake Darla cool before feeding it to her.

XOXOXO,
Kate

Jack rested his head on the back of the easy chair and silently repeated the part that tugged at his heart: "just spending time with someone I care about." A flood of feelings and phrases bounced around in his brain. He knew he had to get them on paper for her. Tomorrow they would be lost.

At the kitchen table Jack tapped the eraser of his pencil erratically. He wondered if the stationery that would capture his masterpiece was too feminine. The ex had stockpiled it and inexplicably failed to include it as part of her divorce agreement. At least the aster laden border was blue. Next to the paper lay the jackknife that had sharpened the pencil to a pyramidal point.

Kate,

How are you? We had a big party here. Darla and I still have our hats on.

Jack waited for the next words to pop out but about the only thing popping were the wood splints from the pencil as he gnawed at it impatiently. "Damn, I know what I want to say but…"

Not much news down here in God's country. One of the Burdick's Holstein's had a two-headed calf. I heard they were trying to sell it to Cornell or Ripleys. Darla and I may go over to see it in the morning.

I'm cooking a pot of chili for dinner tomorrow. Won't make it too hot since Darla may not like it that way. Wish you were here to give me a hand in the kitchen. I like the way you look in that yellow apron. In fact there's nothing you don't look pretty in. Didn't mean to imply you look pretty in nothing. You probably do. Guess I'll skip that subject.

Well, I miss you and hope you can get down here soon!

Love,
Jack

Rereading the letter he'd just written didn't make it sound any better but since it had taken over an hour to compose, Jack decided it was good enough. Sitting in his easy chair later that night, all the missing words and feelings came to him but the energy to start writing again didn't. He'd mail the letter in the morning, on his way to see the two-headed calf. Darla moseyed over to the chair where Jack was sitting. She did her best to position that little spot on her back—the one she couldn't reach—right next to Jack's hand. "Have I been ignoring you?" he asked, scratching his fingers lightly against "the spot". Darla arched and grunted her approval.

CHAPTER 7

▼

The winter months had always seemed extra long to Jack. His construction job was put on hold until the ground thawed, usually sometime in March. For many years he'd plowed driveways during those months but the lift on his truck had given out while plowing the high school parking lot last year. Hangovers and plowing driveways at 4:00 in the morning had never gone well together anyway. Now Jack struggled daily with the urges that had taken him on wonderful and terrible roller coaster rides at various stages of inebriation.

The companionship Jack shared with Darla tempered the urges and his occasional mood swings. At another time, they might have triggered week-long drinking binges. The dog had certainly brought some stability back into his life. But the voices still spoke in a tongue Jack understood far too well: "A beer once in awhile at the Black Horse—what could be more harmless? Afterwards, at home, the slight buzz would feel so good, and for sure, a shot of some hard stuff would hit the spot." Jack had said "NO" for nearly seven weeks. The voice within would say, "You should be proud of yourself," but a deeper, guttural voice—one steeped in indifference—always offered its opinion. "Screw, you're by yourself...who gives a shit. It wouldn't hurt another soul."

Darla and Jack became very close during those lonely winter months. They learned each other's little idiosyncrasies and at times Jack wondered if the dog could read his mind. More than once he'd found Darla standing next to the front door, leash in mouth, ready for the walk he'd just contemplated.

The walks were a special time for both. Darla would sit, not really patiently, as Jack put on his coat, hat, boots and gloves. Her front paws would alternately lift from the wooden floor, like a parade pony strutting proudly. Her nails would tap vigorously on the hardwood as if hail were slapping against the windows, trying to get in.

Nighttime was the best for walks. For the first few minutes Darla would pull just a bit, in unbridled excitement. Then she'd settle into an easy gait, glancing up at Jack every few seconds just to make sure she was doing everything right. Upon seeing the snow covered cannons in Island Park for the first time, Darla growled timidly. Jack let her examine the World War I relics closely. She sniffed and pawed and finally lifted her head bravely. The next time they passed the cannons the dog barely gave them a look.

It was on those night walks that Jack could finally feel at peace with himself. His thoughts were of the cold night air, the glistening blanket of snow and his walking companion. The shortness of breath he had felt during the first few walks had later turned to exhilaration. He'd often think of Kate and silently prayed he could put his life in order before they'd meet again. The clarity with which he could comprehend his life's problems and the clear choices, which might resolve them, surprised Jack. Something, in the confines of his house, where his demons shared residence, clouded the personal blueprint he'd plan on his walks.

Valentines Day had never meant much to Jack. The card he had purchased at the drugstore, way back in January, said little and was mailed only two days before the actual holiday. He had carefully printed a few lines of poetic verse on it and just before sealing the envelope, wished it had been written in pencil. *Poetry is not in a real man's style.* "Ah...what the hell. I'll dribble some tobacco juice on it and save my reputation." Instead, he jokingly crossed out the 'Made in Japan' on the back of the card and neatly printed 'Hallmark'. "There, she won't think I'm too serious."

On the morning of February 14th, Jack walked with Darla to the Post Office. Behind the counter, a jovial Post Master greeted his first customers. "Good morning! You takin' the little lady out for a special Valentine's dinner tonight," he said grinning and nodding toward Darla.

Jack had never warmed up to the pudgy little man with the milky white hands. "Nah...she's got a date with the Padden's Saint Bernard." Mr. Owens possessed a flair for the dramatic, using every part of his body to retell the simplest of stories. Jack bet, before their conversation had finished, he'd see Mr. Owens salute him, cock his head, wink his eye and say "Yes siree!" all in one compact gesture—one that Jack had seen a thousand and one times.

"Just one sweet letter for you today, Mr. Flanagan. Appears to be from that Fletcher girl. Now I didn't know..."

Jack interrupted the most polished of town gossips. "Darla here's gotta pee," and he snatched the letter from under Owens's nose. The last thing he wanted was the town buzzing about something even he wasn't exactly sure of.

Mr. Owens closed his eyes and puffed out his chest, savoring the subtle fragrance he'd stolen from the envelope. "Ou wee! That's some expensive perfume," and the little man grinned up at his customer, showing off a pair of loose fitting dentures, which clacked between every other word. "Now the way I figure it, tell me if I'm wrong, is that…" and Jack turned toward the door.

With his mouth contorted somewhere between a sneer and a smile, Jack said, "Have a nice day, Mr. Owens."

"Yes Siree!" he replied, saluting Jack. And the glass windowpane rattled a good bye.

Jack tugged at Darla's collar several times on the walk home. She looked up each time, wondering why they were in such a hurry. Finally, she resigned herself to the fact that they were taking the Express home. The wonderful scents the Padden's Saint Bernard left for her at the base of their sycamore tree would have to wait for another day.

Back home in his easy chair, Jack held the letter between his hands, his eyes transfixed on her name. He started to raise the letter to his nose but froze for a moment. When Darla's stare turned toward the front window, Jack brought the letter to his face and slowly breathed in the spicy sweet scent. Some past conversation had exposed Jack's fondness for Faberge. Now the perfume aroused a memory of her. He wished time had allowed them to create more.

With the precision of a jeweler, he eased the flap open. His mother had told the story of using cards for his father several times. Apparently she never sealed them, so that four or five years down the road she could present the pristine keepsakes another time. But Jack wasn't sure just why he was being so careful. He pulled the card from the envelope and saw a "too cute" bee looking up at him. It sat atop a red heart-shaped flower with the words, "Bee My Valentine" written across the petals. Inside the card, Jack's eyes skipped over the lame attempt at humor printed there. On the other side he found what he was looking for.

The red ink spoke only to him:

Hi Jack,

Sorry, but this is the best they had at Newberry's. It's the thought that counts though, isn't it! This holiday never really meant that much to me, at least until now. Wish I could be there with you to celebrate. You'd get a big piece of my world famous choco-late-cherry cake and of course an extra big kiss. Give Darla a hug (or a kiss if you pre-fer) from me. It's lonely here on Valentine's Day.

Love,
Kate

Jack read the short note carefully, not wanting to miss something with a hidden meaning. The words "kiss" and "lonely" swirled together in his mind with the scent of Faberge. He looked at the card, still open in his hands but focused beyond it. "It's lonely here, too." Darla laid her head on his knee and sighed. "Guess you miss her, too." The cold February wind howled mournfully outside.

That afternoon Darla watched as her master paced from one room to another. He puttered at nothing, glancing occasionally at the phone. By 4:30 it was nearly dark, an ominous cloudbank cloaking the last remnants of sunshine. Jack impulsively snatched up the telephone receiver and dialed a number he knew by heart—eight rings and no answer. He now concentrated his pacing to the kitchen and consciously kept his eyes from looking up where Jack Daniels called from behind a cupboard door.

A large fabric turkey sat on the floor next to the back door. His ex had spent weeks putting the thing together from scraps of brown corduroy, red flannel and cotton stuffing that now struggled to escape the poorly sewn seams. With a vicious kick, Jack sent the bird flying across the kitchen, where it landed perfectly upright on the stovetop. "Burn, you bastard!" Darla retreated to the living room, tail between her legs.

Jack stomped to the cupboard, threw open the door and snatched a bottle by the neck. He sneered for a moment at the black and gray label. "Old No. 7 Brand...wonder what number 6 tasted like?" and he wrenched the screw cap from the bottom. A casual flip of the wrist sent the cap zigzagging across the linoleum. "We won't be needing your services again." Wickedness infected Jack's smile as he raised the bottle to his lips.

Pleasant warmth filled his mouth and slowly made its way down his esophagus. A droplet of the Tennessee Whiskey trickled down the corner of his mouth. The amber nectar cooled the small path it traveled and Jack promptly brushed it from his chin with the back of his hand. An empty chair next to the kitchen table invited Jack over. He set the bottle firmly on the table and plopped down on the chair. With a shaky fingertip he traced the word 'Jack' on the label then continued his caress to the neck of the bottle. In tender foreplay, he stroked the bottle, then brought it to his lips again.

Jack enjoyed making love very slowly. Meticulously he poured the second drink into his mouth, savoring the rich, biting taste for the better part of a minute. "Oh yes, this is going to be a really good night," he whispered then saluted himself. "Yes sirree! And screw you, Owens, you pathetic little shit."

After the third drink, Jack started a one-sided conversation that meandered from happy, to angry, to melancholy, to vulgar, to dismal and back again...over and over and over. Each subsequent drink stirred the various feelings in his emotional melting pot, and by midnight Jack wasn't sure just what he was saying or how he was feeling. The kitchen spun incessantly and the drunk's imagination transported him to the back of a tiger, running circles atop a cheap carnival merry-go-round he had known sometime in his youth. "I wanta get off!" Jack screamed and he thought of Dad's shotgun. "It's probably getting rusty under the bed. I better oil it...yeah, and clean the barrel. I'll do that first thing in the morning. I need some damn music in this place," and he searched for the radio. "Let me think..." but that was becoming difficult and seconds later he gave up trying.

"Scotch and soda, mud in your eye. Baby, do I feel high." His baritone voice filled the kitchen with the song and he smiled at his cleverness. In a sober state, singing was not something he'd do voluntarily, but Jack surprised himself with the improvement in his voice after quite a few drinks. He slurred his way through a couple more bars. "Oh me, oh my, do I feel higher than a kite can fly...hmmm, hmmmm," and the lyrics were lost.

Jack was losing his bout with the booze and buried his face in his hands, concentrating on staying conscious. Seconds or minutes or hours later—the grasp of time lost—his head slipped between his palms and slammed to the table. He snapped back upright in violent recoil. Several drops of blood splattered on the white Formica tabletop below. Jack's eyes popped. There was very little pain from the gash he'd opened on his forehead but the blood continued to flow. Like a kindergartner dabbling in crimson finger-paint, the grown man drew a stick cat then a stick dog in the blood. And he thought of Darla.

There she sat patiently in the hallway, her head cocked to the side in confusion, eyes fixed on her master. "Come here girl." The dog lifted one front paw then the other, excited by the attention but she held her spot in the hallway. "You need to go out?" and her ears perked.

Jack pushed back from the table and, only with Herculean effort, stood. Rubbery legs, a spinning room, jumbled thoughts...the ensemble of a drunk fought every step to his dog. Garbled words drooled from his mouth and Darla wagged her tail.

When Jack finally staggered into the hallway, he threw his hands to the walls for support. He dropped one hand to pet the dog, but snatched it back as he teetered. Hand over hand, feet shuffling in a clumsy waltz, Jack made his way to the front door. The doorknob darted from Jack's grasp and he spewed profanity in its direction. With fingers stretched wide, he slapped both hands against the edge of the door and slowly dropped to his knees. His hands dragged their way down to the elusive doorknob. A proud smile crept to his lips as Jack finally touched it. With both hands he wrenched the knob and an icy wind did the rest. "Okay girl!" and Darla bolted outside.

Jack slammed the door behind her. He slumped to the floor and laid his head on the arm he'd bent for a pillow. Seconds later he was unconscious.

Harsh morning light and a frigid draft, sneaking in from under the door, roused Jack early the next morning. A hammer thumped inside his head and the wind howled outside. The cobwebs of the lost night slowly unfurled. "Darla!"

Jumping up on wobbly feet, terror gripped his throbbing head. Jack fumbled with the doorknob, turning and pulling it at the same time. The latch released and he yanked the door wide open. Fingers of Arctic air shot through his clothes as Jack surveyed the front lawn for the dog. Winter wind had swept snow in a smooth carpet as far as he could see—not a track in sight. Jack hung his head in pain and shame. "What have I done?" he cried to himself.

She was there at his feet, cowering in fear as if she'd done something wrong. Icy snow covered much of her matted fur. One eye twitched uncontrollably and she whimpered in pain. Jack dropped to his knees and gently lifted her head. "Oh Darla, I'm sorry."

The dog turned her head from him, totally ignoring his touch and soothing words. She dropped her nose between her front paws and shivered. Darla wanted nothing to do with this animal.

An experienced nurse could not have lifted the dog more carefully. Jack eased his hands around her and summoned all his strength to stand. He turned his back to the wind and lowered his face to Darla's ear. "You'll be okay," he tried to convince himself as much as comfort her. Jack stepped back through the open door and kicked it closed behind him. There he stood as meaningless time crept by, praying for Darla and for an answer. "What do I do next?" his whisper accented with a broken sigh.

It had been nearly an hour since the rescue. A huge stack of seasoned cherry-wood crackled in the fireplace. The living room was toasty warm and the frost ferns on the front window had started to drip. Darla was snuggled under Aunt Faith's patchwork quilt, sprawled out on the couch, her head resting on Jack's bed pillow. Jack sat on the floor next to the couch, waiting for some kind of sign. Darla was awake but had yet to look directly at Jack. Her left eye still twitched occasionally. He could have sworn that he'd seen a slight smile on her face once or twice. A venison steak sat thawing on the kitchen counter.

During the course of the next hour, Jack nodded off to sleep several times, only to be rudely awakened by the annoying neck reflex that snapped his head upright. To avoid a severe case of whiplash, he leaned against the couch and rested his head on a cushion. His mind faded in and out of garbled dreams until rhythmic sounds from behind disturbed his sleep. Darla was panting.

Jack quickly turned only to see the dog's head swing away from his gaze. She stubbornly refused to make eye contact. "Ahhh…come on girl. I'm sorry," but Darla wasn't forgiving. (It would be several days before she warmed up to that mean man.)

Darla walked coyly into the kitchen as Jack fried the venison on the stove. Out of the corner of his eye he could see her tail wag, but the instant he looked toward her, the wagging stopped. He cut the steak into small pieces and dropped it into her bowl. She wolfed the meat down.

Jack dropped his aching body into a chair by the kitchen table. He buried his face in his hands as emotions swelled inside. Guilt oozed into every pore on his body. "Damn it!" he cried slamming his palm against his forehead. Throbbing pain swept through his head. He glanced just in time to see her sad eyes. Darla looked at him for only a second then turned and walked from the room.

"That's my last drink," he heard himself say, a promise he'd made numerous time before. But this time, he'd have another pair of eyes to watch over him…eyes that had seen so much hurt after her master got into that bottle. Tears streamed down his face.

The rest of that day was lost in pacing and agonizing. In an unceremonious display of resolve, Jack emptied every bottle of the poison he thought might destroy him. A gurgle from the spout of the last bottle poured down the kitchen sink seemed to plead for reprieve, but Jack ignored the temptation. The garbage pail under the sink was nearly full of empty bottles.

Jack gave Darla her space for the next day. He watched her closely for any ill effects of the ordeal but saw none. For the second time he downplayed an incident involving Darla while describing it to Kate. In a brief telephone conversation Jack matter-of-factly mentioned the dog stayed out for quite some time a few nights back but was fine. He sighed in relief when that conversation ended rather abruptly. "I'll never stretch the truth to her again," he vowed.

A couple days later Jack was watching the evening news—very comfortable in his easy chair. A young anchorman seemed too confident for Jack's liking. "This Cronkite guy will never make it. He's almost singing the damn news," and Jack dozed off.

Sometime later he awoke, oblivious to what had stirred him then realized his hand was wet. She sat there next to the chair looking directly at the man that had done her wrong. But Jack knew he had been forgiven and scratched her ear with affection.

He patted his lap with both hands. "Come on up, good girl," Jack coaxed. Darla hopped up onto his lap and placed a wet kiss on his chin. "Jeez, you're no lap-dog," Jack added wiggling to get comfortable. Darla made herself right at home, eased down and was soon asleep in Jack's lap. He stared down at her with a soft smile. The dog sighed as Jack stroked her head.

CHAPTER 8

▼

Spring broke early that year. Some warm days in early March softened the ground enough to dig foundations. Jack went back to work roughing houses for his friend, Bob Ames, who owned a small construction company. Masonry and carpentry were both things Jack could handle with ease. He was glad to get back on the job, occupying his mind with something other than finding little projects to do around the house.

For the first few weeks back, Jack's age seemed to be catching up with him. There were aches and pains in places he didn't realize could hurt. But, in their own way they actually felt good. Jack was getting back in shape. Winters had always made him soft and this one had brought on a roll of excess skin that hung over Jack's belt. Bob Ames, his boss and friend, occasionally shot jabs at Jack in a near perfect Porky Pig voice. "That little…little…little farm girl's goin'ta have something to gra…gra…grab onto," he stuttered then heehawed, his own massive belly bouncing in ironic laughter.

Bob would often ask Jack to join him for a few drinks at the *Black Horse Inn*. Sometimes Jack would question how a couple of innocent drinks could do any harm…then a vision of a half-frozen dog would expose the flaw in his thinking. Occasionally, Jack would stop in with Bob and have a couple bottles of RC Cola but the desire for something with more kick, never got the best of him. The two would talk of local politics, sports, the weather, fishing and hunting.

Early one evening in April, the pair was finishing one of their bull sessions at the tavern. Bob was slugging down the last of five Rolling Rocks. He looked to the ceiling as if watching a blockbuster movie from his past. A slight slur had invaded Bob's tongue when he said, "Why, remember that time when we went out for bullheads up at Rockville pond? Damn, we knocked 'em dead. Still can see that yellow monster you caught. We should have tried to save it and sell it to some freak show. Let's go up there again this weekend. My wife will be glad to get me out of the house. What'a you say?"

Jack ran several reasons through his mind why he shouldn't go but none sounded good. "Yeah, let's do that. We'll make a late night of it. I'll pick up some night crawlers Friday and we'll go up there early Saturday evening. All right if I bring Darla? She'll behave."

"Sure," Bob replied. "I'll bring the lantern and a couple camp chairs. Let's stop for a burger or two on the way there. Want me to see if I can get a few polly-wogs?"

"Nah, the crawlers will be fine. I wouldn't want to see you drown in the creek trying to net those little suckers." Jack said.

The beam of a large flashlight scoured much of his side lawn late that cold Friday night. Jack swept the light from side to side, hunting for the skittish oversized worms. After a couple dozen were secured in his bait box and placed on the front porch, Jack walked to the living room, shivering from the damp chill outside. He grabbed a couple logs and worked for a minute to revive the embers that smoldered in the fireplace. From his easy chair he watched as the fire gained new life and he thought of Kate. *She's got tomorrow off. Guess I'll call her in the morning. Bet she'll be real excited 'bout my fishin' trip.*

Saturday morning brought a light drizzle and second thoughts about fishing. Jack went through the motions preparing for the trip but found his heart wasn't into it. "Where are those damn bobbers?" Stepping outside, intent on searching the garage, he found the air was clean. A cool breeze stirred the smells of spring. Jack stood by the garage door for a moment, holding in a breath of the sweet air. He went inside eagerly and found the bobbers stored in an old tackle box. "Hope I got enough crawlers," optimism now seeping from his pores.

Later that morning, after every minute fishing detail had been attended to, Jack called Kate. "Good morning! How are things in the big city?" he asked.

"Hi Jack, things are fine out here, but I just stepped out of the bath. Can I put you down for a second, while I slip into my robe?"

"Sure," he said. "Take your time." In the brief pause, his thoughts wandered to images of landing a huge fish rather than the naked woman on the other end of the telephone line.

"I'm back. What's the good news from Friendship?" Kate asked.

"Well…we're both fine and we have big plans for tonight. Darla and I are going bullhead fishing with Bob Ames."

She chuckled and said, "Don't be taking that innocent dog into any beer joints, you hear? I know what those fishing trips turn into."

The three hundred miles between them made Jack's effort to look innocent a futile waste of time. "I would never…there's no way I would let Bob lead us astray."

"Oh, aren't you the holy one! And I suppose you're not going anyplace near the Birdsall Inn. I know about that place!"

"Why…the women there are mostly nuns from that convent up in Canaseraga. We'll actually be on the other side of the county." Darla watched Jack's every move as he talked into the telephone. "Hey, there's someone here who wants to say something," Jack added.

He held the receiver near Darla and whispered, "Speak."

The dog wagged her tail, then barked excitedly.

"I miss you both," Kate said, but only Darla heard the words.

For the next few minutes, Kate heard all she ever wanted to know about bullhead fishing. She patiently listened to all the angler nuances from baiting hooks to landing a trophy bottom-feeder.

"How have you been?" Jack finally asked.

"I've been keeping busy and doing well. Sarah's been trying to fill in the gaps in my social life," Kate said. Her voice sounded empty.

"Gaps? Yeah, right…I bet you're out on the town most every night! Hey, there's a Sadie Hawkins dance at the Grange next weekend. If you were here, would you invite me?" Jack asked.

"It might be a toss up between you and that sexy Mr. Owens at the Post Office."

Jack could see Owens's pudgy little face and that incessant smile. "Oh, I see the competition is stiff…yes sirree!"

Kate laughed at the reference to Mr. Owens. "Even though it would be a tough decision, I guess I'd pick you."

Jack heard the doorbell ring over the telephone. "Someone's at the door," Kate said. "It's probably Sarah. Can I put you down for a minute?"

"No, that's okay…I'm out of clever things to say anyway." He paused. "Oh, I miss you," Jack added, almost as an afterthought. "I'll write you and tell you how we did."

"Good bye, Jack. Have fun," Kate said.

Bob arrived promptly at 6:00. "Come on in for a cup of coffee. Just put the water on," Jack called from his back door.

"Come on out here. I've got something to show you," Bob called back.

In the back of Bob's light blue truck was an army green johnboat. It had brown camouflage spots painted randomly about it. A couple of wooden oars lay against the side panels. With the excitement of a little boy, Jack asked, "Where'd you get this?"

"My brother-in-law asked me yesterday to store it. Great timing on his part and he said I could use it anytime."

"We'll be able to get in that swampy area on the south side of the pond. Better bring a second burlap bag for all the fish we're going to bring home," Jack said.

Bob helped Jack load his fishing gear from the garage. Darla watched curiously, sensing the excitement in their voices. She yipped once, not wanting to be forgotten. "Come on girl," Bob said pointing to the front seat of the truck. The dog hopped in and they were off. For several minutes she sat, watching everything that passed by, alternately lifting one paw then the other. A quick stop was made at the local greasy spoon for burgers to go. Four of them were smothered with onions and a plain patty rounded off the order. Darla wolfed the plain patty down and burped a few minutes later. By the time they reached Rockville pond, she was sound asleep, resting her head on Jack's lap.

When the engine stopped, Darla awoke quickly. She surveyed the abandoned gravel pit where they had parked. It didn't look that interesting but she'd give it a chance. After placing the gear inside the boat the two men carried the aluminum craft a short distance to the pond's western shore. The pond wasn't more than a quarter mile in diameter. A slow moving creek fed it from the north side. Both men eyed the swampy area to their right and smiled in unison.

Darla had never been in a boat. She was nervous at first, her claws clicking anxiously on the metal bottom but she soon got her sea legs, then sat proudly on the front seat.

The men rowed the boat quietly to the "Spot". Jack adjusted his bobber so it would hold the worm just off the bottom of the pond. Not more than five minutes later it disappeared for a split second, sending concentric ripples in all directions. Bob looked up to see Jack nod his head once toward the bobber and smile. A minute later the bobber sunk three times in quick succession. Then, it moved directly away from the boat and Jack yanked his fishing pole up and back in one graceful motion. The hook was set!

Jack gave the fish some slack, letting it swim from side to side for half a minute then began to slowly coax it in. Bob swept a net under the fish as it surfaced for the first time. It was a fourteen-inch, dark bullhead. "Stay!" Jack barked at Darla, seeing she wanted to play with the fish. He lifted the bullhead carefully, avoiding the sharp side fins and removed the hook. "One down, ninety-nine to go!" Bob just shook his head and smiled.

As dusk crept into nighttime, Bob lit his Coleman lantern. The mantle flickered for a minute, then burst into brilliant light. Darla watched with great interest, cocking her head from side to side at the dull hissing sound the lantern made and at the wet burlap bag that flopped from time to time on the floor of the boat.

"Holy smokes…get the net!" Jack cried out as his pole bent nearly in half. "I think I hooked Moby Dick!!"

Bob scrambled to his feet, net in hand. Jack worked the fish to the side of the boat and Bob scooped it from the inky water. Both men stared wide-eyed at the bullhead dangling in front of them, its head pointing at the bottom of the boat.

"You hooked the damn thing by the tail!" Bob shouted and they began to laugh. Darla yapped in excitement.

Bob took the line in his hand and lifted the fish from the net. Jack grabbed the line just above the fish's tail with one hand and groped for the fish with the other. The bullhead flopped and instantly fell to the bottom of the boat. The hook had slipped through the thin skin of the fish's tail.

"Ahhh!" Jack yelled in pain. When the fish broke free, the line that Bob had been lifting recoiled, and the hook sliced through the meaty part of Jack's hand, between his thumb and index finger. The barb was embedded in the flesh.

Bob examined his friend's hand and both men agreed the hook needed to be pushed through, otherwise the barb would tear up Jack's hand. While Bob pushed the hook through, Jack looked away. He winced in pain and continued to look the other way as Bob popped the barb through the skin, then cut it off with wire cutters he'd retrieved from his tackle box. The barbless hook then easily slid back through Jack's hand.

"I'll get a bandage," Bob said.

"Better get two," Jack suggested, after looking at the two holes in his hand that were dripping blood profusely.

Jack washed the hand in the cool pond water then held it out. Bob carefully applied the bandages and the bleeding soon stopped.

"Jeez, you'd do just about anything to get out of cleaning these fish…wouldn't you?" Bob joked.

"Screw you!" Jack said, then grinned at his friend. "Guess you'd do just about anything to hook the biggest one of the night…wouldn't you?"

It was a little before midnight when the threesome trudged back to the truck, Jack using one hand to lift his end of the small boat. The bullheads still flopped in the burlap bag inside. During the ride home, some disk jockey on WLSV, out of Wellsville, kept wise cracking. He squeezed in an occasional tune between bad jokes.

"Now there's a song," Jack said and sang along with The Platters. "When a lovely flame dies, smoke gets in your eyes", he crooned, in a not-so-serious falsetto. Darla's ears perked and a mournful howl conveyed her approval.

"She might be your only fan," Bob joked.

As the fishermen rounded the bend leading into town, they noticed lights on in the volunteer firehouse and several firemen hanging around outside. "They're up late," Jack said. "Must be a hot poker game going on." An uneasy feeling slithered over him.

"What the hell's goin' on?" Bob asked as they turned onto Jack's street.

Red lights flashed through the still night air. There were uniformed firemen next to a fire truck, not appearing too busy. "Damn, I think they're in your driveway Jack."

"The teakettle! Shit!!" Jack jumped from the moving truck as it slowed near his house. He was running the instant his feet hit the ground. Adrenaline gushed into his brain, setting his heart pounding like a maniacal timpani drum. Scrambled thoughts overrode sanity and he yelled out something incomprehensible.

A fireman shouted back, "it's under control, Jack." He motioned Jack to him, then held both hands up, palms facing Jack. "It's okay…try to calm down," the fireman said in soothing voice. "We've saved most of it." He placed a firm hand on Jack's shoulder. Ernie Bishop had done this a few times before. The weak smile on his face was transparent.

"The kitchen and some of the living room are pretty much gone, but we got it under control before it spread to the upstairs. There's going to be some smoke damage on the second floor but you should be able to save everything there…that's after a good clean up. I'm afraid you are going to need a new kitchen."

Jack dropped his head. By this time, Bob was standing next to him, patting his back gently. Darla sat at his side, ears pulled back, sensing the sadness. "Let's take a look," Bob suggested.

Ernie wisely escorted them to the front entrance. He knew it would be less of a shock to see the living room first, where damage was less severe. Jack stood in the middle of the room, shaking his head silently.

"We think it began in the kitchen," Ernie said.

"I know," Jack confessed. "The burner was left on, under the teapot," his voice choked with emotion. He walked slowly to a corner bookshelf and brushed his fingertips over the special books kept on the top shelf. With his thumb, Jack tried to brush away the black soot that now covered his fingers. He lifted a Bible from the shelf and opened it. Beautiful handwriting wished, "Merry Christmas Laura…Aunt Rena…December 25, 1892". Across the bottom of the page was written, "A sword in the face of temptation, a comfort in the time of need". Jack thought back to the many times he'd seen his mother in her old hickory rocker, totally submersed in the Good Book. It had helped her through some very difficult times. In the back of the Bible was a folded piece of paper. It had yellowed considerably with age but without even opening it, Jack knew it well. She had kept it all these years. Jack took the paper and slipped it into his shirt pocket, then closed the Bible. Carefully, he placed it back on the shelf.

"Well, let's take a look at the bad news," Jack said nodding toward the kitchen.

Ernie led the way, looking back at Jack. "I've got a friend, Norman Pettit, who's a great remodeler," Ernie said. "Why Norman can have this looking better than new," he said. "And he's reasonable too boot."

"Nah, I can do this myself," Jack said. Then he looked down at his bandaged hand. In the excitement he hadn't noticed the throbbing. "Second thought, maybe you better give Norm a call."

As they walked into the kitchen, Jack stopped dead in his tracks, not prepared for what he saw. Emergency lights sat upon several counter tops and a spotlight from the truck outside lit the room, casting an unnatural, surreal air.

The room was charred black from floor to ceiling. The refrigerator was covered with grimy soot. Water from the firemen's hoses had left streaks there that looked like tear tracks. Brown droplets of sludge dripped from the cupboards. Axes had slashed open the walls in several places, exposing electrical wires and filthy insulation on the outer walls. Smoke still seeped from various spots around the room. The ceiling light above the table now dangled like a pendulum from its cord. Edgar Allan Poe could have probably described it well but Jack just shivered. He squeezed his eyes shut, running his thumb and fingertip over them, then pinched the bridge of his nose. "Damn," was all he could say.

"You can't stay here tonight. There's still a chance something could flare back up. And the smoke damage…well, you won't want to breathe that stuff in," Ernie said. "Can you find a place to stay?"

"He's staying with me," Bob said firmly. Jack was glad to have the decision made for him.

Darla stood confused in the doorway to the kitchen. She sniffed the strange air.

"We'll be okay girl," Jack assured her.

"Thank God for Mrs. Graves," Ernie said. "She was out for a walk and noticed smoke coming from the back of your house. If she hadn't called us when she did, we wouldn't be standing here now. I'm afraid you'd have lost everything. There's not much more we can do right now. I'll leave a man here for the rest of the night, just to make sure it doesn't start up again, but I think we've got everything hosed down pretty well. We tried to be careful with the water damage but here in the kitchen…well, we couldn't help it."

"Don't worry about it," Jack said. "It was my fault. Got too excited about fishing."

"Yeah, we called around to find where you guys were. Actually talked to your wife, Bob. She said you were fishing but didn't know where. Guess there are some things a man never talks about." A weak smile broke on Ernie's face and he patted both men on the backs. "We'll see you tomorrow morning, Jack, then we can talk about how you can get this thing repaired."

"Thanks Ernie. I appreciate what you've done. I ahh…" And Jack simply shook his head.

"Let me grab a few things upstairs, Bob. I can walk over to your place. Besides, I want to be alone here for awhile. I won't be long," Jack said.

"Take your time. I'll head over home and get some ice on the fish. Cleaning them can wait."

Upstairs Jack sat on the edge of his bed, staring beyond the wall in front of him. Darla rested her chin on his knee. "Oh, Darla…you're such a good dog." He reached down to pat her head and heard the paper crinkle in his pocket.

He pulled the folded paper from his shirt pocket, then gazed at the words he'd written so long ago…must have been thirty years or so. He read the short poem.

Ode to a Traveler

Dusty shoes remembering better times
A lifetime stashed in a bandanna
Heart's hope half full, half empty
Bloodshot eyes stare into yesterday

Baltimore and Ohio's shallow promises
Her whistle sings a Siren's song
Misery despising company
Soothing rhythm of the rails

A photograph of someone he once knew
Raven hair caressing her yellow apron
Mourning doves crying
Cheerful sparrows herald tomorrow's sunrise

Old banjos twang symphonies
Serenading New England's past princes
Harmonicas laugh then mourn
Promiseland lost Promiseland found

Dreams wrapped in normalcy
Faint scents of dusting powder and perfume
How quickly they fade away
Prayers to the Father, come back soon

Emerald pines…scarlet sumac
Amber waves…golden silk
Purple mountains…milky snow
Rainbow sunsets…crystal seas

Jack's older brother had left town and love ones during the depression, looking for some way to support them. Jack had longed to go with him but knew someone needed to stay behind with the family, and even Jack had agreed that he was too young for such an undertaking. Their home had seemed so empty once Guy had left. He intended to cross the country to find work. Jack scrawled the words he now held in his hand a few weeks after Guy set out on his journey. He wanted to pay some kind of tribute to his brother. Now the words sounded so foreign, like someone else had composed them.

"When did I lose that side of me?" he pondered. Jack had been a mess at Guy's funeral. There were many things left unsaid. How did time slip so subtly into lost opportunity? His charred kitchen could be repaired but it was too late to fill in the missing pieces of his brotherly bond. Carefully, Jack refolded the poem and placed it in a drawer of his bedside stand.

Darla had sensed something was wrong and had curled up at Jack's feet, being as inconspicuous as she could. Her chin hugged the floor, not moving an inch but those wet brown eyes watched her master intently.

Jack gathered up a change of clothes and a few toiletries, stuffing them in a pillowcase. His only suitcase was nearly trunk size and the sight of it might have Bob worrying his overnight guest would stay a month. "You're going to like the cats at Bob's place," Jack joked to Darla. The forced grin on his face quickly melted away to a look of gloom.

The teakettle was whistling as Jack walked into Bob's kitchen. He glanced at it, and thought how such an innocent little thing, at times, could be so devastating.

Bob quietly spooned instant coffee into a mug with the words, "World's Best Grandpa" splashed across it. He poured steaming water from the teakettle into the mug and set it on the counter. The smell of fish blended with the aroma of the strong coffee.

"I'm sorry Jack. It didn't help for me to get you all worked up over that boat. I feel sort of responsible," Bob said.

"Damn it, Bob, don't think like that. Why…you didn't even know the teakettle was on the stove. And my insurance will cover just about everything. I'm going to call Kate in the morning and break the news. She won't mind if I stay at her place while the work is being done." Jack said, fighting a yawn.

"Martha has the guest bedroom at the head of the stairs ready for you. It was our daughter's room but since she's moved out, it's yours for as long as you need. You won't mind the pink silk pillow cases, will ya?"

"Heck no! You know I love silk. Wearin' some of it right now in fact," Jack said with a smile.

The bedroom was cluttered with pictures of Elvis, Fabian and Frankie Avalon. A record player sat on top of a dresser, ready to launch a stack of 45s. Jack noticed a Chubby Checker number on top, but passed at the opportunity to twist. Darla circled a shaggy pink throw rug at least a dozen times then gave up, crawling under the bed. Most of the night was spent in restless tossing and turning. Every time Jack dozed off, something would wake him. He heard a distant rooster crow. This would be a long day.

An hour later he heard pots and pans clanging out a wake-up call. Jack slipped into his blue jeans and buttoned his flannel shirt on the way down the stairs. Sniffing as she walked, smelling something good, Darla followed.

Bob's wife, Martha, turned as Jack entered the kitchen, wiping her hands down the front of a faded blue apron, drawstrings tied in the front, easily reaching around her slender body a second time. High cheekbones cradled dark brown eyes and she forced a smile. "Good morning, Jack. I'm so sorry about the fire. If there's anything we can do," and her words tapered off.

Martha and Jack had been good friends since high school. He had once considered asking her for a date, but when his friend, Bob Ames, mentioned that he was considering asking her to a dance…well, things just got too complicated and Jack dropped the idea.

Martha lifted a large mixing bowl and resumed beating eggs. An open carton on the counter held a dozen broken eggshells and a container of cream sat next to it. Bacon snapped in a black cast-iron skillet. Darla's eyes were glued to it. "Hope you don't mind scrambled?" Martha asked. Jack rubbed his stomach in reply. "Bob ran upstairs to get his robe. He's the modest type, you know." She poured the eggs into a second skillet, which was covered with bacon grease.

The house suddenly shook from heavy footfalls lumbering down the stairs. Jack bit his lip to contain a grin as Bob stepped through the kitchen doorway. A bright yellow robe barely made its way around the big man. A thick leather belt held it in place, apparently replacing a not-long-enough drawstring or one that had worn out from the stress Jack's portly friend had put on it. "Morning!" His voiced boomed and he scratched his stomach just above the tight-fitting belt with both hands.

"Damn that smells good. Don't worry Darla, there'll be some left for you," Bob said, setting the dog's tail to wagging. "Have a seat, Jack." Both men sat down at the table and Martha poured each a cup of steaming coffee. Soon after she sat a large bowl of scrambled eggs in the middle of the table, followed by plates heaped with bacon and toast. The three ate in silence, obviously troubled by the situation. Darla made her way around the table, successfully donning her saddest face. She enjoyed everything, but the bacon was certainly her personal favorite. When the bowl and plates were empty, Jack asked politely, "Mind if I use your phone? I didn't check to see if mine was still working and I'd like to give Kate a call to let her know what's happened. I'll pay for the call."

"Why, Jack Flanagan! I wouldn't hear of you paying for a call! Get in there and talk as long as you want," Martha said emphatically, pointing to the living room.

Jack listened to the phone ring seven times and was midway through hanging up when he heard a faint voice on the other end. He pulled the receiver back to his ear. "Hi Kate, it's me."

"Well, let me think, which man could this be," she teased. "Is this Elmer? Nah, he has a much deeper voice. Why, it must be that fine looking Jack Flanagan."

Jack forced a weak chuckle. "I'm at Bob and Martha's, so I better not talk too long. I don't want them to have to take out a loan to pay for my calls."

Kate sensed the tension that Jack attempted to disguise. "What's wrong?" she asked, in a serious tone.

"Don't worry, it's not something I can't get fixed. I'm afraid there's been a little fire over at my place. The kitchen got pretty well charred but the rest of the house is okay. Not a great smell there right now, but I should be able to get it fixed up in a week or so."

"Oh, Jack…I'm so sorry. What happened?"

"It was all my fault. Got excited over that fishin' trip and plum forgot the teakettle on the stove. When we got back firemen were there."

"But you and Darla are all right?" she asked.

"Yeah, we slept at Bob and Martha's and just packed away breakfast enough for thrashers. I'm goin' to see a friend of Ernie Bishop this morning and get started on some remodeling. I'd do it myself, but I ended up on the wrong end of a fishhook last night. Thought I'd have it done in early medieval…stone walls and some torches for lighting." An uneasy laugh exposed his attempt to minimize the situation.

"You need a place to stay. Listen, there's a house key under the doormat on the back steps over at the farm. You and Darla get your tails over there today and no discussion about it."

"Well…" he drawled.

"I said, no discussion. Damn, I wish I could be there with you Jack. I miss you guys."

Those words lifted Jack's spirit. He ached to blurt out feelings that had intensified since Kate had left. The stress of the fire stoked those emotions even more but that inbred, small town stoicism kept them shackled inside.

"Okay, okay…I'll head over there later today. I'm sure Darla will enjoy visiting her old place. Is there anything you need done there?"

"No Jack, I left the furnace set on 50 degrees, so you'll need to crank that up. And light the pilot lights on the stove…oh, and plug the refrigerator in.

Wouldn't want those bullheads to go bad. Feel free to poke around. Maybe you'll find some treasure that will make us rich."

An uncomfortable pause gripped their conversation. On both ends of the telephone line, turmoil clouded what should be said next. "Well…this call's costing Bob a week's wage. I better say good bye. Can I call you from your place?" Jack asked.

Jack could hear Kate swallow three hundred miles away. "Afraid I had the phone disconnected. Guess we'll have to write more often. I'm sorry Jack," she said in a soothing voice.

"That's fine, Kate. The phone at my place might be working. I haven't checked it yet but we'll keep in touch."

"Okay Jack…you keep your chin up. And say 'Hi' to Darla. Bye."

"Bye Kate."

He heard the click on the other end. It punctuated the end of their conversation with heart-sinking finality.

Jack walked back to the kitchen. Consciously he played the role of an unaffected friend, not wishing to involve anyone else in his troubles. He smiled and exclaimed, "Everything's fine in Poughkeepsie!"

Bob gently patted Jack on the back and asked, "Wanta' come over tonight for a bullhead dinner? Martha's making fried potatoes, beet greens and peach cobbler to go with them."

Jack's mouth started watering but he declined the invitation. "I want to get Kate's place in order. She insisted we stay there for a few days. But thanks anyway. Want some help with the dishes, Martha?"

"No thanks. Drying dishes is one of Bob's hidden talents…isn't it dear?"

Bob nodded his head in silence, like one of those new bobble head dolls that were made in Japan. His eyes took on the look of a sad puppy and a sheepish grin crept across his mouth as he trudged toward the sink. Jack smiled as he thought how much his friend looked like that Jonathan Winters character he'd recently seen on the Ed Sullivan show.

"Thanks for everything. Breakfast was great, Martha." And Jack was out the door, Darla at his side.

The cool spring air smelled clean. Jack stood beside his truck, breathing it in, savoring its sweetness. "We'll be fine, Darla." She wagged her tail in agreement.

Much of the day was spent going over details of the remodeling with the carpenter friend of Ernie Bishop. It would most likely take six or seven days to complete the job, as long as the materials were available.

Late that afternoon Jack and Darla drove up to the long driveway at the Fletcher farm. The door on the mailbox had blown open and Jack could see mail inside. He thought for a moment, then decided it would be best if he took the mail inside. He was sure Kate wouldn't mind.

Darla danced on the truck seat as Jack pulled the truck up to the back door. A joyful yip expressed her feelings about the visit. She waited patiently while Jack fumbled for the house key, somewhere under the floppy doormat. "Bet you're glad to be home, aren't you girl? Ladies before gentlemen," he said, making a sweeping gesture with his arm and bowing slightly. The regal Darla stepped lightly up the wooden stairs of her castle. Her humble servant followed.

The air inside was stale but not unpleasant. Scents of musty vegetables and well-seasoned meats still lingered in the kitchen. Jack spotted the refrigerator plug stretched out on the floor. He placed the plug back in its usual receptacle. Instantly the motor whirled and filled the room with its high pitched hum. A box of wooden matches was nestled in the cupboard above the stove. Jack flicked one of them with his thumbnail then lighted the pilots of all four burners and the oven. The kitchen was alive again!

Jack had had the foresight to pick up a few groceries at the local Red & White. Darla sniffed at the bag of Purina Dog Chow Jack had set next to the refrigerator, where he was stuffing hot dogs, milk, Royal Crown cola, cheese, bread, bologna, mustard and ketchup—all the necessities of life. "There, that should hold us for a few days. Let's see how the house looks."

In the hall, the pendulum on the grandfather clock had stopped. The three pinecone shaped weights that powered it were aligned perfectly, nearly touching the dark base of the clock. A light blue moon face smiled at Jack from behind the hands of the clock, seemingly the work of a crazed artist with a dental fixation. "Must have been exactly midnight when that stopped," Jack said to himself.

The subtle hint of rich tobacco permeated the hallway. His Uncle Herb had smoked that brand in his pipe, Jack recalled. He remembered of sitting in a Victorian fashioned sun parlor, his uncle opening a crystal candy jar and offering Jack a pink peppermint candy. That memory now made his mouth water. Uncle Herb secretly let Jack take a puff on his pipe but it tasted nothing like the aroma had suggested. Jack could still hear his uncle saying, "Now don't you be telling your aunt a thing about this. She'd skin me alive! This is just between us men."

A swath of cool air swept down Jack's back sending a shiver through him. He looked down to see if Darla had noticed it. She stood frozen—a front leg lifted in a pose Jack had seen his German Short-Haired Pointer hold many times. "What's the matter, girl?" The question seemed to fall on deaf ears. Her senses were glued to the grandfather clock and not until Jack rubbed her head did she break the point. "Come on Darla, let's go." An uneasy feeling lingered as he stepped into the dining room.

The large table there was covered with a white sheet and eight velvet padded chairs were all leaning forward, their backs resting against the tabletop. A ruby red chandelier, adorned with crystal prisms, hung over the table. One wall of the room was nearly filled with a shiny mahogany china cabinet. It was filled with fancy plates, goblets, cut glass bowls and a variety of knickknacks. The brittle leaves of a philodendron wove their way across the top of the cabinet. Kate must have missed the unlucky plant when she packed the rest away to be taken to their new home in Poughkeepsie. Velvety purple wallpaper looked more suited for an English mansion rather than a country farmhouse. A painting next to the cabinet caught Jack's eye.

He stepped up to examine it closer. It was Kate as a child, probably no older than seven or eight. Her hair was cut in a pageboy style, as blond as summer corn silk. The eyes that had captured Jack's attention at the *Black Horse Inn* months ago were lighter in the picture, but the artist had not failed to notice the golden flecks that gave her eyes such character. The painting stared back at Jack with such intensity that he half-expected to see it move any second but, the young Kate sat serenely, a leather bound book cradled in her arms. "What a beautiful girl," Jack said, loud enough for Darla to hear. She sat calmly looking at the painting.

"Well, let's find our room," Jack said and tapped Darla on the back of the neck. They climbed the creaky stairs that lead to the second floor. At the top, Jack stopped and surveyed four identical doors. Each was finished with a black walnut stain and had brass doorknobs, which had been worn smooth around the outside. Paintings, several of the paint-by-number variety, hung between the doors.

The first room on the left was a sewing room. Reams of materials, in a rainbow of colors filled ivory painted shelves. Two patchwork quilts, blazing in bright reds and deep purples, hung on opposite walls. Several lethargic flies buzzed half-heartedly behind the sheer white curtain that covered the room's lone window. A spool of indigo thread set atop a vintage Singer sewing machine. The machine's foot pedal had worn to silver in contrast to the black cast iron legs that supported it. "Doesn't look like we'll be too comfortable in here. Let's take a look down the hall."

The second room on the left was a bathroom. A large bathtub filled most of the room. It's claw and ball legs were green with corrosion and a rusty stain painted an orange swath from the faucet to the drain. A half dozen dead flies floated in the toilet bowl. Jack flushed them to a watery grave and the bowl refilled with rusty water. A familiar picture of Christ in Gethsemane was the lone adornment on one wall. The Savior was looking heavenward, perhaps searching for paternal answers. His hands folded in reverence—a glorious halo lit the ominous skies in the background with hope. Scattered thoughts of the peaks and valleys that had filled the landscape of Jack's life crossed his mind, intermingling with serious questions of just where religion fit into the grand scheme. The halo that broke into the threatening clouds gripped his attention. In time lost, Jack blinked his eyes and looked round the room. Darla was lying asleep at his feet. "Come on," he coaxed and they left the room.

Entering Kate's bedroom gave Jack an uneasy feeling, as if he were invading something meant to be private. A plain blue bedspread covered the single bed and a brown wool blanket was folded at the foot of it. Two pillows were squeezed together at the head of the bed, embroidered in a simple floral pattern.

An exquisite dresser looked out of place in the country farmhouse. Rich red and gold tones seeped through the matte lacquer finish. A framed photo of Kate as a child, sitting in her mother's lap stood in the middle of the dresser and small matching jewelry boxes bordered it. The mirror above the dresser had black and white pictures of various people surrounding it. An old photo of a handsome young man, dressed in starched Navy whites caught Jack's eye. At the bottom, neatly printed were the words, "Hope to be home soon...Love, Michael". The unknown story behind this seaman was strangely intriguing. Jack wondered if he'd ever hear it.

An old Motorola radio sat on the nightstand beside the bed. Jack's fingers ran over the smooth dark wood that housed the radio. Then he turned one of its ivory buttons. In country twang, a disk jockey announced the big sale at JJ Newberrys. A little jingle concluded the commercial, then Bobby Vinton eased into his tear-jerking hit, "Blue Velvet". "Softer than satin," were the last words Jack heard as he clicked the radio off. "There's not enough time to be sad, is there Darla? Let's get something to eat."

Back in the kitchen Jack stacked bologna and cheese on two slices of bread then topped one of them with mustard. He worked his way around the heel of the loaf. "I'll give the birds a treat later." Looking down at Darla, it dawned on him that she wasn't a real fussy eater. Jack slapped the heel on top of one of the sandwiches and sat down at the table. He ripped the mustardless sandwich in half and handed it to Darla. "You don't mind that crust, do you girl," he said as she licked her lips.

The eventful weekend caught up with Jack. With all the excitement he had rested very little. A steady rain slapped against the windows, making Jack dread the thought of going back to work in the morning. He secretly hoped to get an early morning call from Bob canceling work. On rare occasions, often while his crew was doing a foundation, Bob would decide that working would be fruitless. His typical early morning phone call, complete with weather commentary, would be, "Nice day, if you're a duck. Better take the day off." He'd hang up abruptly without so much as saying "Good bye." Jack overlooked his friend's rudeness...that was just Bob.

"Well, let's go see who Ed has on the show tonight," he suggested to Darla, still busy licking at the taste of bologna on her lips.

Jack went to the living room, turned on the television and flopped onto a crushed velvet couch that appeared to be made for comfort rather than style. Somewhere between the comedian with the mouse and a trapeze artist squeezed into silky leotards, Jack dozed off. He squirmed in restless sleep, dreaming that he was awake or perhaps imagining he was dreaming. A hissing sound grew loud enough to awaken Jack in a panic. The room vibrated in static noise, crackling like a shower of electricity gone wild. Shadows danced in gray and white veils on walls, moving in watery ripples.

Jack sat up straight, attempting to make sense of his surroundings. A flood of disorientation swept over him. "Where the hell am I?" He blinked his eyes rapidly, taking visual snapshots of the collection of unfamiliar objects that encircled him. Mental cobwebs clung in sticky defiance. A dark Indian chief in full headdress stared at the front windows. "The damn test pattern!" Jack finally stammered. And the incessant hiss jumped several decibels, sending sharp pain through his head.

With dizzying effort, he stood, his thoughts consumed by one thing: to turn off the cursed TV. In the middle of his first step, Jack froze in an odd mixture of relief followed by a rush of panic. An eerie quiet cloaked the room and for a moment Jack wondered if he had suddenly gone deaf. Thick blackness enveloped him. Time slipped into an imperceptible dimension, leaving the frightened man paralyzed for several seconds, or perhaps a minute, or maybe an agonizing hour. In syrupy slowness his eyes began to adjust to the darkness. He could see distorted outlines of furniture and his hand, as he raised it in front of his face. Had the power gone out?

Jack groped for a lamp atop an end table. As his fingers gripped its switch, he wasn't sure if he wanted it to light the room or confirm a power outage. A slow turn and a click answered his question. A hundred-watt bulb shone up at him through the top of the lampshade. The room was bathed in a peculiar light, intense to the point it left no shadows. It reminded Jack of the hospital room he had sat in many years before. As his grandmother sighed and gave up her last breath, young Jack looked up from his mother's lap to see if she noticed the curious way the light in the room had changed. And that was a question forever left unanswered.

His eyes fell upon Darla. She lay peacefully asleep, curled up on the floor next to his feet, unaffected by the noise.

"Come on girl. Let's get up to bed."

As he walked past the television, Jack grasped the dial, giving it a turn. It clicked off and the picture tube sent out a contented hum. Then it sat peacefully quiet.

Darla faithfully followed Jack up the stairs to Kate's bedroom. Jack undressed, crawled into her bed and snapped his fingers toward Darla. "Come on up," he coaxed. She hesitated, looking sheepish, then gracefully bounded onto the bed. Jack scratched her behind the ear. She closed her eyes and lowered herself down next to him. Jack forced rationality into the event that had happened downstairs. "It must have been a power surge and I was still half asleep." The logic softened the rough edges and after setting the alarm clock for 5:30, he was soon snoring away.

It took several attempts before Jack located the alarm clock's off-button. He cursed at the sound of rain pelting against the windows. On the job there was nothing worse than working in a muddy hole in the ground, while pelting rain did its best to slap you silly. "Please call," Jack prayed to Bob but the phone sat silent while he dressed, had breakfast, and headed off to work. It was only when he reached the vacant work sight that Jack remembered the phone had been disconnected.

Back at the house, Jack read the Sunday newspaper with day old news. The Buffalo News had always been a step above the Olean Times Herald. With color comics, extensive sports coverage and an interesting article on early spring fishing, Jack occupied the better part of an hour. Like a kid, home on a snow day, he started his day with great anticipation, but by 11:00 was pacing the house, looking for something productive to do. A small wooden bookcase in the living room held a collection of novels. Many of the bindings were slightly frayed, giving the appearance of well-read books. Jack's index finger ran across titles he'd heard of and authors he remembered his high school English teacher, Mrs. Saunders, raving about. His finger stopped on a navy blue volume, trimmed in burnt orange: *Elmer Gantry* by Sinclair Lewis.

With care, he opened the book to the first page and read, "Elmer Gantry was drunk. He was eloquently drunk, lovingly and pugnaciously drunk." Jack glazed at the words, attaching meaning to each. Absent-mindedly he sat down on the edge of an easy chair, pondering his decision to stop drinking. A few cocktails certainly made him more lovable and his tongue would loosen, perhaps not to a state of eloquence but words would, for sure, flow more easily. The word "pugnacious" had been used to describe himself at some point lost in time, but Jack was unsure if that was something to be proud of. By the time he'd read the first chapter, Jack was hooked and held the book against his chest, stunned by the rough honesty this author embraced. Sunshine through the window warmed his feet and he smiled at the change of weather.

"Let's go out for a walk!" The excitement in his voice brought Darla prancing. Minutes later the two were walking down the edge of a meadow that bordered the Fletcher farm. The air was freshened by the rain. An aroma of rich earth and early spring buds intoxicated his senses. A hawk screeched from high above, gliding effortlessly across a large patch of blue sky. Wild leeks peeked up through mossy soil near a gurgling spring. Two woodchucks played tag beneath the rungs of a weathered split rail fence. At the corner of the meadow a large boulder looked nearly dry. Jack sat down in the warm afternoon sun and Darla nuzzled up next to him, claiming the last bit of space on the flat rock. The man drooped his arm over his dog's shoulder and looked beyond the landscape…into days to come. The friends sat silently in peaceful contentment. In a hidden recess of his mind, a minuscule worry festered. Something about the episode with the television just didn't set right. A sloppy kiss on the cheek washed the uneasiness away.

By the time the hikers returned home their appetites had blossomed to ravenous levels. Hearty suppers of Campbells Pork & Beans, hot dogs and dog chow conquered their hunger. Jack couldn't finish the last of the beans. The entire can had been just a little too much for him, but Darla still had some room in her stomach and wolfed them down. She looked up, her eyes still full of want. "No dessert for you, piggy."

The allure of the new found book and the disquieting thoughts of the television were enough to send Jack up to bed earlier than usual. He propped up two pillows and sat in bed for over an hour reading of Elmer's woes. As a young boy, Jack had always gone to extremes, trying to please his mother, vying for affection that came too seldom. Now Lewis's book was revealing a character, not unlike a younger Jack Flanagan. Elmer Gantry had found himself in a predicament, also wanting to shine in his mother's eye but was torn by the fear of making a public spectacle of his religious convictions. "I bet this Lewis guy didn't make many friends in the church community," Jack thought to himself.

For a few seconds the scent was subtle, but not for long. His nose wrenched in unpleasantness. Darla lay innocently on the rug but, at that instant, Jack regretted very much feeding her the beans. He snapped off the bedside lamp. The light instantly disappeared but the smell lingered. Reading had always made him tired and minutes later he was asleep.

Muffled whimpers broke the quiet of the night. Jack stirred, then tried to recapture a dream. Sounds of legs thrashing and more whimpering…she must be dreaming he thought and pulled a pillow over his head. Minutes later he turned impatiently, tossing the pillow to the side. It had slowed his air supply and now Jack was fully awake. With eyes still closed, he attempted in vain to block everything from his senses. The harder he tried, the more amplified each sound became. "No rest for the weary," he grumbled and opened his eyes.

The window must have been left open, for a wisp of fog lingered above the foot of the bed. Jack strained to focus on it but, at that instant, it was gone. The sleepers on his eyelashes must have been playing tricks and with the side of his index finger he wiped them clean. Nothing was there but Darla still whimpered in her sleep. "Wake up girl. You're having a bad dream." She sighed then was quiet. Disgusted, he glanced out the window, noticing moonlight filtering in. From the corner of his eye, Jack could see the fog drift back in and he snapped his attention toward it. *Nothing!* And Darla whimpered mournfully, as if she was being hurt. Jack rolled out of bed, went to the window and placed his hands on top of the window sash. It didn't budge. The window was closed.

Back in bed, Jack experimented with a little game. As he turned his head toward the dresser, the fog reappeared, still hovering over the foot of the bed. The farther away he looked, the more intense the fog seemed to be. Many a night Jack had stood outside, gazing into the heavens, and seen a faint star flicker only to have it disappear when he looked directly at it. When his eyes shifted slightly, the star would reappear. Now Jack was experiencing the same phenomenon, but the peacefulness he had found under the stars was nothing like the uneasiness that currently gripped him.

He snapped his head back toward the foot of the bed. Nothing met his eyes but the closet door, his flannel shirt hanging on its knob. The remnants of some long forgotten horror movie slithered their way into his thoughts. An unfortunate soul locked in some medieval castle, an unseen aberration haunting a silver-screen star, violins screeching in frenzied discord then the mirror of enlightenment. The mirror in which no spirit could hide and Jack snickered at the absurdity of it all. Did some two-bit screenwriter really think the public would fall for some silly magic mirror? Still…and he turned his head slowly.

In the center of the mirror that hung above Kate's dresser something dark stood out amid lighter gray surroundings. It moved ever so slightly and Jack sat up straight in alarm. The darkness in the mirror mimicked his movement, exposing the spirit for what it truly was: Jack's reflection. He repositioned himself until the outline of the footboard came into view and around it Jack saw nothing but darkness. He closed his eyes, not wanting to see more.

During his latter years, Jack's father had developed an eye disease. Now Jack sat in the dark, his heart racing. Could the mysterious cloud he was seeing be the early stage of glaucoma? What he had seen had to be a creation of his vision…didn't it? No good answer came to mind.

Coolness swept over his face, prompting Jack to open his eyes. The room remained unchanged but was now strangely serene. His heart slowed and something told him everything would be fine. As he lowered his head to the pillow, the scent of Kate captured his senses. A clear image of her face, flowed inseparable with her smell through Jack's brain.

Moments later he was in a deep sleep, dreaming dreams that would not be remembered. One minute before the alarm was set to ring, Jack sat up in bed, turned the alarm off, dressed hurriedly for work and was clanging pans around the kitchen when Darla walked into the room. She yawned several times and stretched. The early morning hours were not her cup of tea but since she was up, might as well go outside. Darla scratched lightly on the back door. "Just a minute, girl. Let me get this coffee on."

After doing her dog thing outside with much more sniffing than business, she watched with great interest as Jack cooked breakfast. There was one pancake left when Jack had finished his meal. "I know I'm spoiling you rotten…and not one drop of syrup." She stood over the pancake in her dish and gave one of those prolonged "you better be feeling guilty now" looks. Jack was very stingy with the Aunt Jemima, as he poured it over the pancake. "Don't want to spoil you," he explained. The dog wolfed down the luscious flapjack and licked her lips in appreciation.

"I need to get back to work today. I'm going to leave you in charge. Don't let any burglars in," Jack said. He ruffled Darla's ears and was out the door.

She sniffed her food dish, making sure there was not a drop of sweet stuff she had missed. Outside the truck's engine turned over several times then started. Darla trotted to the kitchen window, nosed the curtain aside and watched as her master drove off. She ran to the living room, hopped up into the easy chair by the front window and peered through sheer curtains at the outline of his truck.

Jack glanced back at the farmhouse. A figure moved behind a curtain in a front window. *It must be Darla*...but an uneasy feeling crept over him.

CHAPTER 9

▼

Across the state, in a rather small apartment, Kate sat covered with blankets on a yellow davenport. Her legs stretched out over a matching ottoman. Kate looked comfortable enough, but under her flannel pajamas a hot-water bottle, a wool rag and Vicks covered her chest. The worst cold she'd had in years kept her from work. Two days in the apartment, with only soap operas and books to keep her company, were enough to bring on the first stages of stir-craziness.

"Wonder how they're doing?" she asked herself in a raspy whisper. Kate's eyes were puffy thanks to contributions from her cold and a restless night. Something had awoken her, then for several hours she felt uneasy. The root of her anxiety never really showed itself but an odd feeling nagged inside. Something was wrong, but Kate was powerless to expose what it was.

A knock on the door broke into her thoughts. It had to be Sarah. Her daughter was the only person she knew, who would pop in unannounced. "Don't get up," she heard from beyond the door and the bolt on the lock receded into its housing. The door swung open and Sarah shuffled in sideways, balancing a casserole dish, a small paper bag, a loud plastic purse and her keys.

"Hi, Mom. Brought you some lunch and cold medicine. I know the tuna noodle casserole won't match yours, but hey…it's the thought that counts. How you feeling?"

"Oh, I'll be fine. It's just a cold and it gives me a chance to get caught up on my reading." Sarah glanced at the copy of *Peyton Place* lying on the coffee table, the bookmark near the end.

"Mom, I can't believe you're reading that! Some of the schools around here have banned it."

"It's not that bad, honey. How'd you get away from work?"

"Just snuck out early. I needed a day off anyway. Jeez, you look awful!" Sarah said.

"Well, thanks. I'd intended to go down to Niesner's today and model dresses. Guess I'll pass on that," Kate said with a pout.

"It's just your eyes look like golf balls. You sure you're okay?"

"Well, I had a tough time sleeping last night. I don't know why."

"You been worrying about that mutt back home? The dog I mean, not Jack."

"Oh, I don't know what is was. It just seemed like something was calling me."

"My psychic mother. Bum, bum, bum, bum." Sarah sang out the four notes in *Twilight Zone* fashion.

"I'm not really worried about them. Usually Jack's as stable as the Rock of Gibraltar. It's just when he drinks...but I don't think he'll ever touch a drop again. For some reason I think there was more going on back there than he's told me. But I guess unless Darla learns how to talk, I'll never know."

"You're really serious over him, aren't you Mom?"

"I don't really know, honey. We haven't know each other that long and you know that no one can replace your dad."

"Mom, that was a long time ago. I'm a big girl now and you need to get on with your life. Damn, you need a man!"

Kate's eyes filled with tears. She did need a man. The one that she truly loved had left her so quickly. And didn't have a chance to say "Good Bye."

"Your dad..." and Kate choked on her words. She buried her face in her chapped hands. Sarah's caring touch on her shoulder was all it took to trigger a flood of tears. "Oh baby, he was a wonderful man." The words squeezed their way in between sobs. "And we were so happy with the news I was pregnant. I wish you could have known him."

"I knew him through your eyes, Mom. There's no need to worry. Nobody's going to replace him," Sarah comforted.

"We had so many plans...then that damned war. It wrecked our lives."

"Mom, I'm really proud of Dad. He sacrificed all he had." Sarah's lips bent in a reminiscing smile. "Remember when the Legion had that ceremony...the one when they gave you that American flag. I thought I'd wet myself when that big man...what was his name?"

"Bob Keyes," Kate said with a weak smile. "They used to call him Turk," and she laughed. "Get it?"

"Yes Mom, I still get it. Oh God, when he sneezed and those buttons came flying off his uniform." Sarah stared back in time and grinned. "And that poor soul that was sitting beside us. She must have been biting her lip so hard it drew blood. Remember how she ran from the room, trying not to laugh?"

Kate threw her arms around her daughter. She closed her eyes, rubbed Sarah's back and tried to mold together an image of Michael. "Killed in Action," the words as pungent as they had been over twenty years ago. She had hidden the letter President Roosevelt sent. Now she silently questioned why. Time had dulled the pain, but never vanquished it. Long ago, Kate had seen a list of the casualties from the attack on the USS Oklahoma. She now wondered how many more widows were crying at that very moment.

Sarah pushed back from her mother, pulled a tissue from her purse and wiped her mother's swollen eyes. "I love to hear the stories you tell, about Daddy and you before the war. Tell me one."

Kate had told endless stories of her courting days to Sarah. She guessed Sarah had heard just about all of them. But there was one that Kate had always felt was just a little too personal to share. "What the hell," she decided.

"Well, just after your dad and I were married, he was working the oil fields over in Bolivar. During the winter, a heavy snow had fallen and your dad had to trudge daily, through waist-deep snow. His pants were always wet and he developed a terrible rash. It didn't go away, and day after day he'd be scratching himself…just making it worse. The skin between his legs was raw. Your dad wasn't actually a shy man but there was no way that he'd go to see a doctor about it.

One day I was in the drugstore, looking for something to help the poor man out. I found this stuff called Sloan's Liniment and the label said it kills pain. There was no doubt your dad had pain so I bought it. At the time, I didn't know it wasn't a good idea to put that stuff on an open sore. Well, I gave him the bottle and he went into the bathroom to give this miracle drug a try. About a minute later I heard blood-curdling screams coming from the bathroom. The door swung open and your dad ran full speed out of the house. I looked through the window and could see him running up the hill in front of our place."

Sarah's jaw dropped and Kate snickered.

"It was at least an hour before he came home. He walked into the house— bowlegged as a broncobuster. 'Remind me to never ask you again, to do any doctoring,' he said. And I fell into his arms and we laughed until we cried."

"How come you never told me that story before, Mom?"

"Well, it's kinda' adult humor, honey. Guess your dad wouldn't have called it humor but we did get some good laughs out of it."

Mother and daughter sat silently, each remembering their own special memories of times they pulled together…a mother without a husband, a little girl without a dad.

"Have you talked with Jack about Dad?"

"Well, he knows I was married and that my husband died in the war, but beyond that, no. I'm not just sure where Jack fits into my life, honey, but I do know I miss him."

"And does he know about Grandpa?"

"No, I don't want to talk about that," Kate said, scowling at her daughter. "That was your grandfather's problem and no one else needs to know."

"Mom…that's just how Grandpa was. I'm sure he loved you."

"I'm not sure that grumpy old bastard loved anybody or anything," Kate said.

"Oh Mom…how can you say that? He was quiet to a fault, but some men are just that way. I bet he had a rough time as a boy. You know, being the oldest of nine kids couldn't have been easy. I'm guessing he was working full time by the time he was ten."

"That's no excuse for a father to ignore his family. An occasional hug would have been nice. I've never told you this but at your dad's funeral there were some problems, and your grandfather was a real ass. I don't suppose it will do any good now, to air dirty laundry."

"I'm all ears. Don't worry, what we say here will never leave this room," Sarah said, her face the picture of honesty. She snuggled up next to her mother on the couch. "Let's hear the dirt."

"Honey, I'm not sure if I'm up to talking about this."

"Mom, it might do you some good to let those feeling out. You can stop any time you wish and I'll understand."

Kate gazed at her daughter. As if a mirror had peeled back time, she saw herself. The deep blue in Sarah's eyes shown like tropical seas at that moment when the last sliver of sun hangs on the horizon and flecks of mischievous sunshine scamper over the water. Before the hurt, Kate's eyes had sparkled, too.

She cleared her throat. In a voice made raspy by the nasty cold, Kate started. "It happened long ago, at Michael's funeral. Our family was seated together at the funeral home, up in the front row, next to the closed casket. The preacher's words were a comfort to us. At that point I thought I could hold up.

Then a naval officer walked silently to the casket and laid a folded American flag next to Michael's picture. I fought to hold it back but burst into tears. Oh God, I sobbed out loud and couldn't stop. Your grandfather was next to me and he grabbed my arm, squeezing it hard to get my attention. I pulled from him and flung myself on the casket. That bastard was rough! He didn't need to treat me like that. He pulled me back to my chair, then reached across my lap, patted my knee then left his hand there, like I was some kind of little kid. Damn him, I know why he left it there…so he could control me…so I couldn't get back to the casket. I squirmed to get loose until he raised his other hand. When I looked into his eyes I saw rage. And his teeth were pink. I can still remember thinking that it was blood, but later I realized it was only from the peppermint candy he constantly chewed to settle his stomach. He held that hand up where I could see it…sending me the message that he'd slap me if I didn't settle down."

Kate snatched a tissue from a near empty box on the coffee table. Equal parts of anger and hurt filled the look on her face. She thought of the stern man old photographs had captured and wondered how her mother had lived so long with someone who was never happy.

"We barely spoke after that day. A polite kiss on the cheek and occasional 'good night, honey' were about the only affection we ever shared. Sometimes I'd catch him staring across the living room at me, but his gaze would quickly shift and I could never really read what was behind those cold gray eyes. I hate to say it, but at times I wished he'd just go away. That would have broken Mom's heart, but in the long run, we might have been better off."

Mother and daughter sat quietly for several minutes. Sarah finally said, "I wish you had told me this sooner Mom. I never knew."

"I think of your dad everyday but only the good memories. And Jack's been very patient. Every time he asks about our family, I drop the subject. He really doesn't know that much about me…thank the Lord."

"How's he doing with Darla? Does she have him trained yet?" Sarah asked.

"Oh, you know it…why that little imp's probably having steak and fries every night for supper. She can get just about anything she wants with those sad puppy eyes."

"I'm going to put the casserole in the oven for you. Then I need to get over to the showroom before Adam actually has to do inventory. God, that's a scary thought," Sarah said.

"Thanks for being such a sweetheart, Sarah. How are those wild cats over at your place?"

"Why, those little angels have made a new friend of the neighbor's hound and play so nice. They know right where his chain ends and strut around just out of his reach. Most of the neighborhood knows when those three are playing. I swear, you could hear that hound dog howling in Herkimer."

Sarah popped the casserole into the oven, kissed her mom on the forehead and was out the door while Kate sat on the yellow couch, daydreaming of Michael, Jack and Darla.

CHAPTER 10

▼

The morning sky was heavy, with dismal purple and gray clouds adding gravity to the dreariness. It was the sort of morning that sleeping-in seemed very tempting, but Jack had to work. Only Darla had that luxury. By late afternoon she had napped in at least half a dozen places and ended up on the living room couch. A lingering smell in the kitchen teased and the dog followed her nose there. As she passed the grandfather clock in the hallway, a high pitched whistle stopped her dead in her tracks. She sniffed around the bottom of the old clock and the hair on the back of her neck immediately stood on end. What started as a low growl ended as a whimper in her throat. With ears lowered and tail between her legs, Darla walked to the kitchen, went to the back door, and looked up at the doorknob. A minute later, Jack's truck pulled up the driveway.

In the kitchen, Jack crouched down, hugged the dog and asked the stupid question, "Do you need to go out?" She scurried to the back door.

Outside, Darla took her sweet time attending to business. When she had finished, the dog pranced toward the field behind the barn, then walked back to Jack. She did this several times. "Sorry girl, I'm too tired for a walk now. Maybe after supper," he said, and they started back toward the farmhouse. Both of them turned their heads skyward, as a screech from high above called down. It was the hawk they'd seen the day before, probably looking for supper. Sunshine had broken through the western clouds.

"Come on girl. Let's get some supper," Jack called. "We'll get back outside later."

After changing into clean clothes, Jack cooked up a hearty conglomeration of sliced potatoes, mixed with ground beef, onions, Worcestershire sauce, Parmesan

cheese, mustard and a heavy dose of black pepper. His mouth watered in anticipation of the delicacy his mother had prepared so often. He hadn't tasted it in
years. On the other side of the kitchen table, he could almost see his father, a fork
lost in the death grip of his downward clinched fist, shoveling down mounds of
the stuff Mom called "shepherd's pie." It took one bite to realize that he'd either
forgotten a key ingredient or that his failing memory had improved the dish's
actual taste considerably. Darla, with a palette somewhat less than refined, had no
trouble finishing what Jack couldn't.

Two restless nights and a hard days work had taken their toll on Jack. He
yawned throughout the meal and was thinking about a good night's sleep, almost
before the evening had begun. His chin was resting on his palm when he felt
Darla lay her head on his lap. The swishes of her tail wagging told Jack just what
she wanted. "You are a demanding woman," he said and patted her head. "But
only a short walk."

The sun had just dropped below the horizon. Cool evening air would have
normally been invigorating, but Jack had worked outside all day and felt more
chilled than invigorated. Darla romped around the lilac bushes—her nose working overtime. Jack shoved his hands deep into his blue-jean pockets and whistled
for Darla as he turned around the back corner of the barn.

Two large wooden doors lay nearly horizontal, adjacent to the back wall of the
barn. Concrete slabs were butted up next to them. Jack thought the doors probably lead to a storm cellar or perhaps a root cellar. There was no lock or chain
securing the doors, so Jack decided to take a peek inside. He pulled on one of the
rusty handles and the door squeaked open. Enough light filtered into the
entranceway to see stone steps leading into the cellar. Darla stood behind Jack,
craning her neck around the back of his legs. "You stay here, fraidy cat," Jack
said.

Using a handrail made of steel pipe, Jack carefully descended the stairs. At the
bottom, he could only see outlines but nothing distinguishable. As his eyes
adjusted to the darkness, a faint rectangular shape appeared above, fringed in gray
light. He moved very slowly toward the shape, shuffling one foot then the other,
praying he didn't walk into some razor-sharp farm tool or fall into an open pit.
As he drew closer to the shape, Jack could see it was the outline of a small door. It
was now directly above his head. Raising his arm and stretching to touch the
door, Jack found it was just out of reach.

"Guess I'll have to find a flashlight and check this out some other time," he
mumbled. As he turned to head out of the cellar, his arm brushed against something. He groped in the darkness, then touched what felt like a two-by-four. Jack

ran his fingertips up the board and found a rung. "A ladder!" It had been secured to the floor and to the frame of the overhead door.

Standing on the first rung and holding onto the top rung with one hand, Jack was able to push the door open with his free hand. Several blades of straw fell onto his face as he peered upward. He climbed up until his arms could rest on the other side of the opening.

The door had opened into the floor of the barn. Bales of hay were stacked high on two walls. Several barn swallows flew nervously about the rafters. Large rakes, scythes, chains and an assortment of small farm tools hung on another wall. Gray light washed everything, creating an eerie mood, like a scene from an old black and white movie. The air was still and the scent of animals still lingered in the barn. In one corner two walls jutted inward, forming a room with the outside walls of the barn. The room was painted dark green and an electrical box was mounted next to the room's lone door. A large steel padlock told that something interesting was behind the green door.

Jack recalled Kate's words when they had talked about him staying at the farm: "Make yourself at home. Feel free to poke around. Maybe you'll find some treasure that will make us rich." He climbed up into the barn and walked toward the room. "There must be a key around here somewhere," and he ran his fingers over the top of the door frame—nothing there. He glanced at the electric box and brushed the top of it with his fingers. A key fell to the floor.

For several seconds Jack stared at the key and wondered if he should be snooping around in someone else's barn. He knew Kate wouldn't mind but an uncomfortable feeling nagged at him. It was her parents that had invested much of their lives on this farm and he was about to invade something that at least one of them wanted to secure from outsiders.

Ten minutes later, Jack was sitting on the couch in the living room. Darla was curled at his feet and he still wondered what was behind the door. Tomorrow, after work, would be a good time to call Kate. He needed to hear those words again, "Go ahead, poke around," and he also wanted to hear her voice. The *Black Horse Inn* had the only pay phone in town. *Remember to take change with me tomorrow, for the call.*

After gazing blankly at the black and white television, Jack decided to shower then retire early. The last two nights had not been particularly restful, and *The Man from U.N.C.L.E.* was just a little too far-fetched for his taste. "Let's go to bed." Darla looked up, yawned and followed Jack up the stairs.

The shower felt wonderful. With the water as hot as he could stand, Jack felt the pressures of the last few days wash down the drain. Steam billowed out from the shower as the hot water hit the cooler air. Darla whined from the other side of the shower curtain. "I'll be out in just a minute girl. It's just steam…and stay out of the toilet!" He heard her paws thump against the door. "Be patient. What's got into you?" Jack stuck his head around the end of the shower curtain and saw the dog lying next to the door. She didn't turn to look at him but crouched like a canine sphinx, guarding the bathroom door.

Jack turned off the shower and snatched a towel from the bar just beyond the curtain. "Damn!" He held a hand towel in front of him and knew immediately that he'd be shivering by the time he dried off with this little rag. Finally, his back still beaded with water, Jack stepped from the shower.

The room was clouded with drippy steam. He reached down to touch Darla. "What's wrong girl?" At first he thought she was shivering under his fingertips but the vibrations on her skin were coming from deep inside. Jack strained to hear a nearly inaudible growl, which seemed to emanate from every pore on the dog's body. A strip of fur from her neck to her tail stood on end, bristling like the scalp of a fierce Mohawk warrior.

The steam masked objects around him, cloaking them in misty gray. Jack opened the bathroom door a crack, to let some fresh air in. Steam poured into the hallway. He saw Darla raise slightly, her head still hugging the floor. She cowered as she crept from the bathroom, looking more like a hyena than a dog. In the hallway Jack watched Darla calm, lower herself to the floor and roll over in submission. A front paw flopped back and forth in a peculiar way, not exactly like the rub-my-belly gesture she often made. "I'll be out in a minute," he said and closed the door…and shivered.

"Have to grab a bathrobe next time I'm home," he mumbled, "and find a bath towel." A few flips of the undersized hand towel over his shoulder failed to catch much water. Raising the little towel to his head, he rubbed his hair vigorously, hoping to be reasonably dry before hopping into bed. "What's got into her?" Jack swiped his face with the wet towel and convinced himself this was as dry as he was going to get. He looked up into the mirror. Shock snapped his hand to his mouth.

The mirror was etched in small slashes, each pointing toward the middle of the mirror. Jack's eyes followed their circular path and his brain feebly attempted to construct a path of logic, which would take him to the source of the markings. His thoughts, as well as his eyes, both ended back where they had started, retrieving no good answers along the way. "What the hell?" Jack fumbled with ways which Darla could have possibly done this but there was no way. He counted twelve slashes laid out in a perfect circle, then slapped the towel against the mirror and rubbed them from his sight. Jack walked naked from the bathroom, snapping his fingers as he passed Darla in the hallway. She followed him into the bedroom and watched her master's hands shake as he groped for underwear in his suitcase.

Jack unfolded the blanket, which lay at the foot of the bed and threw it over the bedspread. He pulled a cocoon of bedcovers around himself. A small electric alarm clock in front of him turned its second hand in silence. Jack squinted at the tiny markings that surrounded its face. There were only numbers at 12, 3, 6 and 9 o'clock. He counted the slashes between the numbers: *10:00 o'clock.* As he shook in the bed, and thought about the slashes on the mirror, the only plausible answer arrived. Someone must have slid their fingertips over the mirror and left a light film of body oils on its surface. The steam would slip from the oily surface and leave the marks. That had to be it. Jack avoided the question, "Why?" He fell asleep satisfied he'd solved the puzzling question. While Jack slept soundly through the night, Darla kept at least one eye open until the alarm went off in the morning.

Although Jack had had a good night's sleep, he spent much of that Wednesday simply going through the motions at work. He daydreamed what he'd be saying to Kate when he called her after work. It took conscious effort to put the strange events of the past few days in the back of his mind. Jack decided it would sound downright crazy if he were to describe what had been going on at the farm. "Just a few weird coincidences, nothing to stir her up about," he tried to convince himself.

During lunch break, Jack half-listened to his work-buddies tell off-color jokes and managed only small talk when Bob asked how things were going. Gobbling down his sack lunch, he thought what a lucky woman Kate was today, not to be close enough to smell him. The peanut butter sandwiches he had made that morning were stuffed full of garlic cloves, a gourmet secret his father had shared with Jack years ago and he knew the odor of pungent garlic would soon be clogging his pores. Darla certainly wouldn't mind. She'd be licking his hands before he got in the door. That afternoon, Jack robotically laid several courses of block on the foundation his crew was working on, then hurried to the *Black Horse Inn.*

It had been several months since he'd last dropped in. The phone was mounted in a small wooden booth with a narrow bench attached for the long-winded. Jack slid his finger into the change pocket of his work jeans and instantly realized the quarters he'd intended to bring were still on the kitchen table. There was no such thing as a short conversation with Kenny, the bartender, but Jack needed to break a five-dollar bill to feed the phone.

"How…how…howdy stranger." Kenny contorted his face with each syllable. A real stranger might think that extracting the words was a painful process but Jack knew Kenny loved to carry on conversations with anyone who would listen. On many occasions Jack had heard the same old stories told ad nauseam, as each new patron would enter the bar. "Thought you got fri…fri…fried," Kenny stuttered then grinned.

"No Kenny, I survived the fire," Jack said with a polite smile. "Nothing got fried but my kitchen. Say, could you break a five for me? I need some change for the phone."

"You ca…ca…callin' that…"

"My dog's having a litter and I need to get an ambulance!" Jack interrupted.

Kenny opened the cash register and counted out the change. He silently reached for his ankle and swatted at some invisible menace. Although Kenny was not fleet of tongue, he was quick-witted. Jack realized he was shoeing away the adversary that had been pulling his leg.

"Wha…wha…what's that sm…sm…smell?" was the last thing Jack heard as he left the barroom.

Inside the phone booth, Jack spread the coins out on a metal tray under the phone and carefully dialed the number he knew by heart. He could hear each ring and worried Kate might be out. After the fourth ring, a deep voice on the other end answered, "Hello." For an instant he thought it was a man. A cough and a clearing of the throat sounded more feminine. "Is that you, Kate?"

"Yes, it's me. Hi, Jack. Sorry, I probably sound a little gruff. I've been fighting off this darn cold for a few days now."

"Hi…wish I could be there to be doctoring you." Jack paused, hoping Kate didn't think he'd implied he wanted to play doctor. "Well, you sound pretty awful. Have you missed work?"

"I just missed yesterday and today. Sarah's been helping out. How are things in the big city?"

"Oh, it's really hopping here. Have you been to a doctor?"

"Nah, Dr. Sarah's been treating me. Says I'll live."

"Darla sends a kiss…she's doing well. And appreciates my cooking. She's about the only female I can say that about. We've been doing some exploring around the place."

"Well, like I said, make yourself at home. Nothing's off limits…except my underwear drawer. You stay outta' there!" Kate started to laugh then broke into a cough.

"Melt some butter and add about a tablespoon of sugar. That's how my mother always cleared my sore throats up," Doctor Jack suggested.

"Well, I'll have to give that a try. Any more advice, doctor?"

"Stay in bed and drink plenty of fluids. Say Kate, there's a room out in the barn…"

"Yeah, that was my dad's workshop. He spent more time out there than inside with us. Did you find anything interesting in there?"

"Well, I didn't feel right snooping around. It was locked and I ahh…"

"There must be a key around there somewhere. Just let yourself in and promise to split the treasure. Probably just his damn tools in there. And you must have found that the padlock on the barn door chain has been cut. When Dad died, Mom couldn't find the key, so we cut the lock with a hacksaw. We meant to replace it but decided just its appearance would be enough to slow down any of those vicious robbers around town."

"Guess I'll take a look as long as you're sure you don't mind. The guy that's remodeling my kitchen should be done early next week. Thanks again for letting me stay at your place. Darla seems in seventh heaven most of the time. I'm sure she misses your mom…and you." Jack wanted to add, "but not half as much as I do," but bit his tongue instead.

The operator cut into the call and informed Jack that $.50 was required to extend the call. After hurried "good byes" he sat in the phone booth contemplating the new direction his life seemed to be taking. There was no doubt things were getting better and damn if he didn't feel comfortable, for the most part, talking with Kate on the phone. Jack swung the phone booth door open and walked back to the barroom.

"What you gri…gri…gri…grinnin' about?" Kenny inquired. He patted his shirt pocket, as if his heart was thumping.

Jack shook his head and replied, "You know Kenny…that's a mighty attractive nose you got there. I'm surprised it hasn't been busted up a few times, you poking it into other people's business so often." Jack raised a fist within inches of Kenny's nose and shook it in feigned disgust. A quiet patron at the other end of the bar peeked out from under the brim of a greasy John Deere cap. The smile on the bartender's face sent his gaze back to the bottom of his beer glass.

"I heard the fireme…me…me…boys are lookin' for some bi…bi…big strong guy to fight the go…go…gorilla at the car…car…carnival."

"Wouldn't want to hurt some overgrown monkey. I heard that beer truck driver from Olean broke a couple ribs on one of those gorillas last summer and that the carnies are in hot water with the ASPCA now."

"Umpah...that's what they ca...ca...call that guy. He de...de...delivers here. Carries three ca...ca...cases at a time. Hasn't got a to...to...tongue."

"Let me have a ginger-ale in a beer glass, Kenny. And keep your damn mouth shut about it!" Jack didn't feel like discussing his teetotalism if some of his buddies dropped in. They didn't—and for the next hour Kenny and Jack shared exaggerations, tall-tales and downright lies. Jack was glad he had stopped in.

Outside the bar, Jack stood in quiet contemplation. Down the street he saw Mrs. Lundy carrying groceries to her old car. He saw Mr. Strickland heading into the post office and Mrs. Willoughby scolding her husband with a shaking finger. Jack knew them all. He felt at home in this little hamlet. It was strange indeed, to be leaving the *Black Horse Inn*, stone-cold sober. Jack felt good about that.

CHAPTER 11

▼

Jack could see Darla's face in the kitchen window as he drove up the driveway. She was at the back door when he opened it, her tail wagging in excitement and her backsides whipping like a salmon swimming upstream. "Oh, you're such a good girl," and he ruffled both sides of her neck. In her excitement, the dog had a slight accident on the floor and lowered her ears back in shame. "Come on Darla. You've had a long day inside." And the companions walked into the backyard.

While Darla romped, Jack moseyed over to the barn. A rusty chain was draped between two black wrought iron handles, securing the barn doors from any hardened criminals Friendship might harbor and curious teenagers looking for a place to make-out. The doors were hung on greasy runners. Rollers attached to the top of the doors would make it easy to slide them to the side, leaving an opening big enough to drive a tractor through.

Anxious chirping from above caught Jack's attention. A pair of song sparrows was fussing around a small nest, which the noisy birds appeared to be remodeling. The nest was precariously perched on the end of one of the door runners. Opening the barn door on that side would terrify the sparrows and most likely dislodge their home. Jack talked to the pair in a soft voice. "Don't worry. I'll be careful," he assured them. The larger of the two sparrows seemed to thank Jack with a beautiful bar from its favorite song, which brought Darla running. She watched jealously as her master talked with the little creatures.

Jack lifted the rusty chain and could see where the brass padlock had been cut. He removed the lock from the chain, then the chain from the door handles. Slowly he slid the barn door, the one opposite the sparrow's nest, open. As he walked toward the workshop, the floor beneath Jack's heavy boots echoed like a deep base drum. For several seconds his mind flashed snapshots of what might be behind the locked door.

The key was right where he had left it. In his excitement, Jack fumbled with it for a moment then slid it into the lock. With a slow turn of the key and a click of the lock, Jack's imagination tap-danced in excitement. *If the door was locked, there must be something important inside.* Like overdone sound effects from a dungeon scene in a vintage horror movie, the rusty hinges screeched out their displeasure at being disturbed. The green door opened into darkness. Jack patted his hand up and down the wall inside, groping for a light switch.

There it was…a wall plate with two switches, both in the down position. Jack flipped the one nearest him. Nothing happened. His fingers pinched the second switch. Two bare light bulbs sprang to life as he lifted the switch. Stark light overexposed everything in front of him. His eyes fell upon the dusty object in the middle of the room.

A motorcycle—one covered with dust sat in front of him. The handlebars curled upward and faced Jack like a majestic bull, sizing up a nervous matador. Several wrenches and ratchets lay on the floor next to a flat back tire. A black helmet rested on a stool in the corner of the room and a price tag dangled from its strap. Behind the motorcycle, four tree trunks—gray bark peeling from each— served as legs under a slab of hardwood. This makeshift workbench was cluttered with greasy tools and small cans of lacquer and paint.

A calendar hung on the wall behind the bench. All the 29 days of February 1956 had been X'd out. Above the numbers a buxom beauty, clad only in red long johns, warmed her exposed behind with heat being thrown from a pot belly stove, which seemed to smile in smug delight.

Jack stared at the calendar longer than he would have, had the scenery been of woodland animals, mountain streams or majestic frigates. Nervously, he shifted his eyes, hoping no one was watching. *What a beauty!* he thought. *Yes, the cycle was certainly a classic.* In a John Wayne-like strut, Jack approached her, ran his index finger over her seat and gazed at the rich brown leather that had been hidden under the dust.

Neurons began to fire like pistons from a two-cylinder engine, igniting memories that had lain idle for years. His brother, Guy had been a hellion—the kind of kid parents could spend many restless nights worrying about. When a motorcycle showed up in the driveway one Saturday afternoon, his older brother and his set-in-his-ways father had a heart-to-heart discussion, which revolved around the type of boy that would own a motorcycle and how it reflected on his family. The two stood toe-to-toe in the driveway—each convinced only he was being reasonable. Jack had watched from a kitchen window, his mother looking over his shoulder as the melodrama unfolded.

Finger pointing and shouting soon spiraled downward to clinched fists and shoving. At the conclusion of their discussion, the motorcycle lay flat on the driveway and daggers of despise filled the non-blinking glares of two stubborn men. Jack's father blinked first and stormed into the house, cursing his ungrateful son. A revving engine landed a final slap to his father's face and a nearby water-pitcher served as a whipping boy for an insolent son. Yellow ceramic shards exploded against the kitchen wall. Then deafening silence cloaked the room. Far off, a lonely engine whined. Time nurtured tolerance, but it never healed the emotional wounds inflicted that day.

"I never want to catch you on that damn thing," his father had warned Jack. Taking him at his word, Jack never let that happen. In fact, he was extremely careful when making plans to meet Guy on the outskirts of town. It would always be a time when their father had commitments. Guy would find some out-of-the-way roads, sometimes paved but often not. The two would sail through wooded glens and serene pastures—Jack's senses alive with blurred rainbows of color, with the smells of evergreens, fresh cut hay and his brother's leather jacket, with the mesmerizing vibration of the iron horse that carried them away.

His big brother had promised the motorcycle would be Jack's someday. The depression hit hard, before that someday came. Jack had never seen tears in his father's eyes, until one day unannounced, Guy dropped $50 on the kitchen table. "I sold the motorcycle. It was getting old anyway."

Their father knew well how much the bike had meant to Guy. "Thanks, son," he said and hugged his boy. Jack was disappointed but knew that Guy had somehow grown up that day, and although he missed that wonderful machine, Jack had not climbed on one since. This was not the only sacrifice his big brother had made for their family. The great depression stole more than money from the Flanagans, leaving behind voids that could never be filled. At that moment Jack wondered if some nameless person, who coined the words, "Great Depression" had meant to portray this historical malady in financial or emotional terms.

The distant dream now materialized in the little workshop. From the side of an ebony gas tank, a red-faced Indian Chief insignia held a steadfast stare, as if looking where an open road might carry. Eagle feathers tapered to a point on his regal headdress. From the curbside, a pedestrian might imagine the wind of the highway, blowing the feathers back in helpless surrender to the power of the machine. A chrome-plated gas cap sat high upon the tank. It had started to pit, a telling sign of the lonely years it had sat in the damp barn.

Behind the tank, the leather seat fanned out atop two black spring supports. Under a coat of dust, the light brown leather had darkened slightly in the spots where the tailbones of a rider from long ago had rubbed against it. The dust could not hide the seat's subtle richness, reminding Jack of the stiff leather of a catcher's mitt, slightly softened with mink oil but never used to catch a ball. The seat curved outward, the way a cartoonist might draw a duck's bill. He rubbed his hand over the leather, raising dust in scattered streaks of sunlight. Jack eased himself onto the seat and closed his eyes.

Electricity ran through his veins and tingled in his fingertips as he grasped the handlebars. From left to right and back, his body moved to the memory of riding behind his brother, so many years ago. The passing wind would straighten their hair—mirroring the image of the Indian's headdress on the gas tank. His foot rested on the kick starter. And for a moment, he wondered how it had gotten there, then decided it must have been an ancient reflex.

The skirted, red fender he could see covering the front tire was a tell-tale sign—this was a motorcycle made by the Indian Company, their Scout model and probably produced around 1941. At that moment, Jack knew he was hooked. The motorcycle would soon be monopolizing a great deal of Jack's free time. Darla sat quietly in the doorway. Had she been human, this would have been the time for a twinge of jealously to rear its head, but being a mere dog, the only twinge she felt was one of hunger. "Let's get some supper," Jack suggested. Darla's tail wagged excitedly.

Like the waters of a hidden forest pool on a still summer night, a calm flowed over Jack that evening. Even Darla seemed more relaxed than usual, as she rested her head on Jack's knee and looked up with understanding, into a face that she had learned to rely on. Several long lashes twitched over her eyes, as Darla watched his every move. The couch's soft cushions rolled around Jack's still body, feeling warm against his back. For nearly an hour he sat there, savoring the quiet. Light from the kitchen came tentatively into the otherwise dark living room, not wishing to disturb the peacefulness. Jack rested his hand on Darla's head and she closed her eyes. A sigh of contentment lingered in the air for a moment and was gone. Darla lifted one ear when she heard a whisper intrude upon the stillness. "You're quite a dog," said the familiar voice. Both could smell the faint aroma of peanut butter on the other's breath.

In bed that night, Jack listened to a concerto of country sounds slipping through the open window: Peepers singing out in soothing rhythm, crickets chirping back and forth in search of a far-off mate, a lonely bullfrog croaking from a distant marsh, two hounds howling at a bothersome raccoon, a solitary owl hooting deep within the woods, and a Buick engine purring as it carried strangers down the road in front of the farmhouse. Only a good listener could hear these nighttime voices. At that moment, the man decided he'd start to listen more closely. The dog already heard much more.

Dawn had not yet broke, when Jack lifted his head to listen. His sleep had been deep and he felt exceptionally well rested. The alarm clock ticked loudly, in monotonous regularity. With no conscious effort, his mind started to form a replica of the sound and fired off an imagined tick precisely midway between the clock ticks. The double time cadence chipped away at his restfulness. In the bat of an eye—less than the time between a real and a contrived tick—Jack bolted up in bed. His head snapped toward the alarm clock. The ticking stopped instantly. A needle-like second hand swept over the face of the electric alarm clock in terrifying silence. That innocent little timepiece hadn't produced a single tick in its entire lifetime. Jack listened, but all he heard was his own heartbeat and Darla snoring.

In the shower, Jack placed his hands against the wall in front of him and let hot water stream down his face. The clarity of what must have been a dream had been uncanny. His senses were acutely aware of the smallest details. Echoes of each disturbing tick were etched in gray matter, so deep within his brain that it would take death or a lobotomy to wash them away. Rationality required the sounds to be a dream, Jack not daring to allow the strangeness to have any other roots. Hot droplets of water snapped into his face, driving reality into his pores. Jack shook his head, assessing what had happened with an abating, "Whew".

He wiped steam from the mirror and whipped up a thick lather in his shaving mug. The man in the mirror looked sane enough, although the soapy foam that dripped from his chin gave every appearance of a mad dog, ravaged by a nasty case of the rabies. The notion of temporary insanity making a brief visit, conjuring up some illusions then leaving Jack mentally intact, certainly had its appeal. Not one of the haunting enigmas that plagued Jack's psyche could escape diagnosis and cure via the loony bin express. A nice ride up to the State Hospital in Gowanda, New York with a couple friendly escorts in starched white coats, followed by a relaxing visit, could have him fit as a freaking fiddle in no time. Jack pulled an index finger across his lips. Their redness contrasted to the milky shaving cream like blood on new fallen snow. With his lips pinched together, he curled a grin, exaggerated to the point of fiendish, threw up his arms as if in rapturous praise and sang out a thunderous, "Mam-my Oooooooaaawwwwwww Mam-my!"

His grin dropped to normal proportion and Jack carefully dragged the cold steel razor blade through a receding mound of lather. The feasibility of being controlled by madness was just about as likely as Darla saying, "Good morning". Jack glanced at her in the mirror. She said nothing, but questions of the strange ticking, the twelve slashes on the bathroom mirror, and the strange way Darla had acted around the grandfather clock all shouted to be heard. Real answers hid well.

"I need to get out more," Jack confided to Darla. "Want to go for a ride in the truck after work today?" She wagged her tail in affirmation.

CHAPTER 12

▼

The hours at work ticked away in mundane slowness. Jack's thoughts touched upon the enigma of the farmhouse, progress on his kitchen, the puzzle of where life was leading him, fishing, the dog back home and Kate. Just about any form of mental escapism seemed fair game that day.

"You guys can go home early today. No sense in just looking busy like most of you goldbrickers have been doing for the last hour," Bob brayed out to his work crew. It was mid-afternoon and they had just finished roughing a nice little Cape Cod on the outskirts of town. The work pace had slowed and Bob guessed his crew didn't want to start on a new job so late in the day. In their position, he would have felt the same way. But being boss, he felt obligated to add, "We'll work late tomorrow to make up for lost time. Tell the little misses to keep those gourmet TV dinners in the freezer 'til just about dark." Five minutes later, a cloud of dust hovered over the skeleton of the house. Pickups spun their tires as they hurried home or over to the *Black Horse Inn*. Jack lingered behind.

"How's the remodeling coming along," Bob asked.

"Should be done early next week. That Norman sure can handle a circular saw," Jack replied. "Say, are you and Martha busy tomorrow night? The firemen are having a Ham & Leek dinner. It's my treat, if you can make it."

"Well, I'll have to check out our social calendar. Can't remember if the opera is tomorrow night or Sunday. Aah…to hell with the opera. Yeah, we should be able to make it but I better run it by the boss," Bob said.

"I'm phoneless, so I'll stop by in the afternoon. We can make plans then," Jack said.

Back at the farmhouse, Jack quickly made three sandwiches, two for himself and one for Darla. He tossed the sandwiches and a bottle of RC Cola into a large paper bag, grinned at Darla and said, "Let's go." After the dog had a few minutes to run, the two set out in the truck on a Friday afternoon adventure.

Darla poked her head out the open window, the wind whipping back her cheeks into a flappy smile. Drool flew back against the dirty back panel of the truck. She took in every detail as birds, cows, kids and less fortunate dogs flashed by and were left sorrowfully behind.

A couple miles outside town, about a dozen houses were clumped together at a fork in the road. The county had erected a road sign announcing to travelers unfamiliar with the area that they were entering Nile. Several street signs preserved the humor of a long forgotten town board that had named the three major segments of macadam, (not one more than one hundred yards long) Fifth Avenue, Broadway and Times Square. Jack turned onto Times Square and thirty seconds later glanced back at Nile in his rearview mirror.

West Notch Road ushered the two over gentle hills, painted in a sea of splendid greens. Wind carried the smells of aromatic pines, sweet grasses and rich soil through the open windows. Jack reached over to scratch Darla's side, but her attention was locked on the panorama of countryside unfolding outside the truck. Beavers had dammed a small stream and the waters, from what was now a pond, nearly reached the side of the road. Two fawns drank at the far side of the pond while a nervous doe watched as the truck slowed. Darla yipped in excitement and the three deer bounded gracefully into the cover of a nearby thicket.

As the truck rounded a bend in the road, Jack could see the village of Richburg sprawling across the windshield. Richburg was even smaller than Friendship and sometime, in their early history, the two towns had been part of the same land parcel. A Red & White grocery store, an Esso gas station and the Casa Nova Grill were the only businesses in the microcosm. A baseball field was set in the middle of town and Jack could see a game was being played. "Let's go see what's happening there," Jack said, nodding toward the diamond.

A taunting "Hey, batter batter!" could be heard through the truck window as it pulled to a stop. About thirty spectators sat in folding lawn chairs, all on the first base side of the field. The purple numbers 1 and 90 were sewn on the gray uniforms of two lonely bench warmers who sat hunched over, chins resting in their hands, gazing at lucky teammates who chirped on the baseball diamond in front of them. The pitcher stood to the side of the mound, rubbing the baseball like he was molding a snowball to launch at some unsuspecting victim. He smiled arrogantly at number 1 and number 90. Number 90 slowly ran his middle finger down the side of his nose. The pitcher stepped up onto the mound and squinted at the catcher. He glanced at the bases, finding each occupied with players donning blue and white uniforms.

Jack opened the door of the truck and pulled a dusty army blanket from behind the seat. As he stepped from the truck, the sound of wood hitting leather resonated a split second before groans escaped the crowd. He watched an unfortunate left fielder scramble up a slight incline into a freshly plowed garden plot. The boy's baseball cap flew off his head, landing in a patch of dark soil. At the base of a scarecrow, Jack could barely see the white dot that the boy was groping for. Finally the boy snatched the ball up, turned and heaved it in the general direction of the infield. By this time the final base runner had crossed home plate, and a dejected shortstop watched the baseball roll to a stop at his feet.

"What's the score?" Jack asked a group of young girls, giggling on an outstretched blanket. The three looked questioningly at one another and a pretty blond in a tight sweater answered, "At the end of last inning it was 27 to 3 in favor of Bolivar. They must have around 33 or 34 now. But it's the seventh inning," she said encouragingly.

The puzzled look on Jack's face prompted her to add, "We haven't completed a game yet this season. Every other one has been called due to darkness."

There was plenty of room next to the blanket the girls sat on, so Jack and Darla made themselves comfortable for what promised to be some interesting baseball. After spreading out the army blanket, Jack sat cross-legged on one side of it and Darla sniffed in the direction of the giggling girls, who had been tossing Cheezies at one another. The skinny batter at the plate had watched three balls fly past him, but none came close to the plate. A rugged farmboy crouched behind him and held his index finger up, plain for all to see. The fact that the batter would see another fastball was not what you'd call "the best kept secret in town". The pitcher nodded in agreement with the pitch selection then heaved the ball toward the plate. The path that it took was several feet beyond the reach of the batter and the catcher had to lunge in hot pursuit of the ball. In the excitement of the moment he absent-mindedly caught the misdirected fastball with his bare hand.

Jack winced in sympathetic pain, but the catcher shook his bare hand once and fired the baseball back to the pitcher faster than it had been delivered. He sneered toward the opponents' bench, wanting each to know the ball hadn't sparked so much as one pain receptor. Then he hacked up some phlegm and attempted to spit on home plate, as the batter trotted to first base. The catcher's mask, which the catcher apparently forgot he was wearing, partially blocked the path to the plate. The cross bar on the mask caught the brunt of the spittle and it dangled for some time as a reminder of the catcher's athletic faux pas. Many lips were bit in an attempt to stifle laughter, but no one laughed outloud. To hell with any joy in Mudville tonight!

The base runner, now on first, immediately took to taunting the hapless pitcher. "Pitchers got a rubber arm," he squawked. Next to him, the first baseman rubbed the brim of his cap. The giggling girls began to whisper and the infielders all trotted to the pitchers mound. Jack could see the first baseman take the baseball from the pitcher and rub it up for him, as if it was a genie's lamp and he was conjuring up baseball magic. And late this Friday afternoon it seemed like magic was the only thing that could produce the final out. All the infielders circled round, as the first baseman slapped the ball back into the pitcher's glove. The girls eyed the first baseman as if he was the reincarnation of Lou Gehrig.

From the edge of the outfield grass the second baseman pounded his fist several times in his glove. He stared toward his opponent on first base and called out, "Bawk, bawk, bawk." The baserunner glared back, desperately trying to look mean. Dark peach fuzz glistened on his top lip, apparently dabbed with Vaseline to look continental.

The pitcher stood on the edge of the mound and threw a devilish grin at the skinny baserunner, daring him to take even a slight lead from the safety of the bag. A protruding Adam's apple dropped in the runner's throat then popped back up resembling a bobber being released by a hungry fish. He took a cautious step off the first base bag. On the other side of the diamond, his coach did jumping jacks to get the boy's attention.

A fly fisherman could not have been more dramatic than the miniature version of Lou Gehrig on first base. The boy swung his glove from his knee, in an arc that would have brought tears to the eyes of his Trigonometry teacher, directly to the chest of the unsuspecting baserunner. Thunderous hoots and cheers from the partisan Richburg crowd followed the "thwap" of cowhide meeting chest cavity. The Bearcats leaped in celebration, seemingly oblivious to the fact they were losing by over thirty runs. Jack had witnessed a stellar performance of the old "hidden ball trick".

The final at bat for the overmatched Richburg team was not exactly a nail biter but it was memorable. A batsman hit by a pitch, followed by a stolen base, placed a runner on second. Bolivar's left fielder had been shifting his weight from one leg to the other since the inning began. From over two hundred feet away, Jack could see the grimace on the boy's face. It was obvious the long game had pressed the limits of this poor boy's kidneys. Suddenly, he bolted from the baseball field into a marshy area that bordered it. Seconds later, only the top of his blue baseball cap could be seen through the tall weeds. It tipped back slowly until the brim pointed skyward then froze, as if in a solemn salute to urinary relief.

Jack noticed he was one of very few watching the mini drama unfold, then a crack of the bat brought his attention back to the game. A tall shortstop leaped high, in a vain attempt to snag the line drive just beyond his out-stretched glove. The baseball rolled up the slight incline to the edge of the garden plot in deep left field. Eyes scoured the outfield for a player that had evidently disappeared into thin air. Raucous cheers from loyal Richburg fans ushered the runners round the basepaths and the blue baseball cap sunk into the weeds.

A minute later, the player who wore the purple number 1, watched two balls cut the heart of the plate. His knees shook, as the pitcher delivered the next blazing fast ball. An impatient umpire snapped his right fist down after the pitch, which was clearly outside the strike zone then added the ultimate baseball insult, "You'rrrrrrre Out!" The shoulders of the batter dropped and he walked in slow motion toward dejected teammates, dragging the bat behind. A batting helmet that would have been too big for the ample-headed Babe Ruth rested on his shoulders. The number 1 on the boy's uniform mingled into obscurity.

Young fans patted the backs of valiant players that had fought their way through the first complete game of the season. Parents stretched stiffness from their knee joints and shoulders. On the far side of the field, the Bolivar coach walked from the marsh with his arm over the shoulder of his missing-in-action left fielder. The giggly girls surrounded a handsome player who seemed embarrassed by the female attention.

A slight breeze blew a smeared flyer onto Jack's blanket. It announced WKBW disk jockey, Danny Neaverth, would be hosting a record hop that evening at the school gym. This was probably the biggest celebrity to visit the little burg since the great John L. Sullivan fought bare-knuckled in the town park, back in the late 1800's.

"Looks like big doin's tonight. We better hit the road while we can still get out of town," Jack said to Darla. "Wait 'til you see where we're going to have supper."

A five-minute ride up a steep hill on the outskirts of town brought Jack and Darla to an open gate. Oaks and maples canopied the road. Between the hardwood trees the waxy green foliage of massive rhododendrons fought to be seen. Jack slowed the truck to a crawl, inching his way into an emerald maze. A single lane of cracked pavement escorted them deeper into the woods. From their tree-top perches, three crows heralded the arrival of the strangers. At the end of a gentle curve, the road widened into a circular clearing, no bigger than the infield of the baseball diamond in the valley below. A fieldstone pathway cut into the dense forest on the far side of the clearing. Jack pulled the truck up to the walkway and turned the engine off. He grabbed the blanket and paper bag then stepped into the clearing. Years ago he and his wife had stood in that very spot. Now Darla was at his side.

The fieldstone was partially covered with wet leaves, which muffled their footfalls, as Jack and Darla walked down the pathway. From the clearing, nothing was visible but foliage. Now, only a few steps down the pathway, a great cedar lodge stood before them. Its shingles had weathered black with time and patches of moss squeezed between them. A large, empty porch seemed to yearn for the contented patrons it once held. One length of chain held a cockeyed sign, which once greeted visitors to the "Hill Top Lodge". Plywood panels protected three hidden windows on the backside of the porch. Black spray paint had defaced one of the panels with what had started in a poor three-dimensional attempt and ended in block letters proclaiming "Beetles Forever". The anonymous artist was apparently oblivious to John Lennon's spelling quirks…as well as impatient.

A few feet from the side of the porch, the pathway split into two forks; one led to a large carport and the other into the forest. Jack stood for a moment, in quiet contemplation of the rich history this once regal building held. His imagination guessed it harbored secrets and scandals that would never be shared. He stepped down the pathway into the woods with Darla at his feet.

Cigar-shaped rhododendron leaves blocked sunlight; creating a tunnel of greenery. Golf ball size buds strained against their green casing, ready to burst into glorious pinks, whites and lavenders. At tunnel's end, the pathway opened to a long forgotten concrete pool. Several feet of leaf-filled water sat at the bottom of the pool and massive ceramic frogs looked into the pool from each corner. Small metal pipes protruded from their mouths. During the lodge's heyday, the frogs would have acted as serene fountains. Metal benches, painted with forest green enamel, rested on marble slabs on the long sides of the rectangular pool. Decorative gnomes, which decades ago, would have been placed next to shrubs and small trees by a meticulous landscaper, now peeked from under overhanging boughs. Childhood dreams would have brought vivacity to these once colorful woodland creatures, but now their pale faces looked lifeless and stark.

Romance had once brought Jack and his wife to this spot. It was at a time before vicious arguments and cool indifference had chilled their relationship. Jack had no regrets about coming here again. He had once sat on one of the benches with his young bride but now held onto that memory, out of a sense of nostalgic reverence rather than emotional yearning.

"What's your pleasure: bologna or peanut butter?" Jack asked, looking into the paper bag. Darla was quietly indecisive and followed Jack to the bench. The decision was made for her: peanut butter it would be! If the entertainment at Hill Top ran slow, Jack could always watch Darla try to lick the peanut butter from the roof of her mouth. He pulled a sandwich wrapped in wax paper from the bag; saw that it was peanut butter; unwrapped it and handed it to Darla. "I'll expect some big tips after this kind of service," he said, as her jaws snapped at the sandwich. While Darla made short work of her main entrée, Jack folded the blanket once and spread it over the cold iron seat. He sat down on the bench and stretched his long legs out in front of him.

This peaceful spot was far removed from civilization, sheltered by dense forest growth. The only sounds that slipped through the envelope of quiet were the occasional chirps of song sparrows and a breeze that peacefully touched only the tops of the tallest trees. Jack placed his hands behind his head and locked his fingers together. He stared into the fading blue sky. Tension that had colonized in his muscles and nervous system began to melt away.

In the eastern sky, the first star of the evening blinked on. Jack felt warmth against the top of his legs. Jack looked down to see Darla resting her head on his lap. Her eyes were closed and her tongue slowly caressed the roof of her mouth.

"Sorry girl, but we better head home," he said. Darla lifted her head and yawned.

Jack carried the remaining sandwiches and bottle of pop back to the truck. For several minutes he just sat there, glad he had revisited Hill Top. The tunnel of rhododendrons blocked what was left of the day's sunshine. Jack flipped on the headlights and inched the truck down the forest pathway. At the point where the pathway widened and the rhododendrons thinned, Jack stopped his truck once more. White streetlights and yellow porch lights twinkled through the indigo space between Jack and the valley far below. The hills on the opposite side of the valley seemed to shiver in envy as the evergreens at their crests caught the last vestiges of sunlight.

His appetite had been lost in reverie, induced by nature and old memories. Now a growling stomach had Jack fumbling in the bag for a sandwich. "Bologna never tasted so good," he thought. Darla took the last piece of crust from his fingers then curled up to sleep the rest of the way home. A distant farmhouse called the travelers back. The peculiar events of the past week slipped back into Jack's mind with equal amounts of apprehension and curiosity.

Back in Friendship, Jack decided to take a look at his new kitchen. From the end of his street, he could see lights on inside his house. A pickup truck was parked in his driveway.

"You stay here," Jack commanded Darla and walked to the house. He called out, "Hello," as he opened the back door, not wanting to scare Norm into pounding a nail through his hand. From inside he could hear the tinny sound of a transistor radio playing an Elvis tune.

"Come on in! Got my hands full right now and the doorman's on break!"

Jack was stunned by the transformation he was seeing, in a kitchen he didn't recognize. A pair of legs extended from under one of the counters. "I just have one more screw to tighten. Be with you in a minute," Norm promised.

Polished brass and cut glass housed five decorative candle flame light bulbs, making the ceiling mounded chandelier the focal point of the room. It hung above a square kitchen table, which was supported by thick, forest green table legs. Maple cupboards with soft satin finish were a tasteful improvement over the bright blue ones that had been there before the fire. A subtle leaf pattern swept through brown linoleum that no longer tried to compete with other kitchen fixtures for the coveted "Most Ostentatious Award". A capped pipe stood waiting to feed the new gas range Jack had picked out from a Sears catalog. "Wow, this looks great Norm."

A head appeared from beneath the counter. "Like William Tell said, 'I aim to please!'" Jack chuckled politely. "The wiring will be finished this week-end and we can have you back in here by Monday."

Norm's face was smudged with various building materials. His teeth sparkled like polished ivory as he smiled. It was obvious he worked outside at times, for his skin had weathered to a leathery brown and crows feet had set prematurely in the corners of his dark green eyes. His lean muscled body carried not an ounce of fat and he moved with crispness, as if each joint had been recently bathed in Quaker State oil.

"Damn, you do nice work! Didn't think I'd catch you here but I was driving through town and thought I'd snoop around."

"Well, I wanted to get these counters done. Wasn't doing anything tonight anyway," Norm replied.

Both men surveyed the room, more for a conversation piece rather than a critical inspection. "The table there, was my sister's. I bumped my head a couple times on that new light and needed a reminder of where not to walk. Sis just bought a new kitchen set and gave me this one. It's yours, if you want. No charge."

For a fleeting moment Jack was tempted to use the corny Jimmy Stewart line from some equally corny Christmas movie: "That's my bad ear…I thought you said, 'No charge,'" but instead just said, "Thanks."

Jack was excited by the prospect of getting back into his own home. He thanked Norm again and left feeling good about the way things seemed to be falling into place.

Darla sat close to him for the short ride to the farm. She seemed to sense he was feeling good and wanted to be part of it.

CHAPTER 13

▼

The headlights of his truck illuminated the barn doors, as Jack drove into the Fletcher driveway. Behind the doors the spirit of the Indian motorcycle reached out and tugged at his imagination. "Soon," he said out loud.

Inside the farmhouse Jack split the last of the sandwiches and gave Darla the bigger piece. She wolfed it down then licked her lips. Six months ago a Friday night without plans would have gnawed at him but tonight Jack welcomed his lack of obligations. *Elmer Gantry* and Darla would be all the company Jack wanted that evening. "Come on girl, let's go to bed." Jack picked up the book from the coffee table and climbed the stairs. He wished there was a working telephone in the farmhouse. The sound of Kate's voice would have made this day just about perfect.

The words of Sinclair Lewis bit their way across a landscape of time and place. Jack sat in bed, pillows behind his back, and let himself be carried with the charlatan preacher, Elmer Gantry, into the lives of innocent, unsuspecting women. At times he felt like a voyeur and admired the way hard-drinking Elmer slid through life. Jack kept any similarities with his own life at arm's length.

His eyes became heavy and the gap between reading and falling into a dream was bridged smoothly. One minute the preacher was Elmer Gantry and the next it was Pastor Ingles, from the little Baptist church where Kate and Jack had spent Christmas Eve. The preacher in the dream pulled at Jack's arms but seemed to have no strength. Jack wheeled a sledgehammer and was viciously knocking the backs off from each pew in the Baptist church then carrying them to his pickup truck outside the vestibule. "God bless you," was all the little man would say each time Jack slammed the heavy hammer into the beautiful wood. Something inside of Jack wanted the preacher to be more forceful but the meek man simply watched his church being destroyed and blessed the vandal.

The dream then took Jack to a distant meadow at the edge of the rhododendron forest Jack had visited that evening. From the mouth of a ceramic frog Jack would retrieve a nail, then use it to attach the lumber he'd stolen from the church to the frame of a house. It was to be a house he would build for Kate. Pastor Ingles stood next to the house, his hands folded in silent prayer. As Jack hammered the last of the pew backs into place, the preacher parted his hands and prayed, "The cow jumped under the moon."

Jack awoke in a cold sweat. The dream would have been disquieting by itself but recent happenings within the old farmhouse now made it extremely disturbing. "What did it mean?" The bedside lamp cast a soft halo of light around the bed but left gray shadows lurking in the corners of the bedroom. Atop the bedspread, next to Jack, the book was still open—yellowed pages exposing themselves. He closed the book, clicked off the light, and replayed the dream once from start to finish, hoping he'd remember it in the morning. He did.

At the breakfast table, Jack sopped up the last of the runny egg yolk with the crust of his toast, then handed it to Darla. She gobbled it down, glad to help him clean his plate. The ham and leek supper would be fun that evening but outside, overcast skies drizzled cold rain, promising a boring day. The last of his coffee left a bitter taste behind. The dirty back windows held water droplets until they were heavy enough to slide down the cloudy glass, leaving trails of clarity. Jack stared absentmindedly through the window at the barn. "The motorcycle," he whispered. "I'll work on that today."

In one of the many drawers under the counter tops, Jack had seen a pad of paper. As he pulled each drawer open, he found it held years worth of accumulated kitchen junk. Partially hidden under a turkey baster and a nutcracker, he spotted the blue spiral pad. From an empty coffee can in the cupboard, Jack retrieved a pencil. At the kitchen table he touched the pencil's lead to the tip of his tongue. The pad guarded several culinary secrets: a coconut spice cake, three-bean salad, chocolate drop cookies and Rice Krispy treats. Jack flipped to the back of the pad and found the last page contained only the thin blue lines that would help organized his "To-Do" list. At the top of the page he wrote in block letters, "Motorcycle Restoration".

Clean gas tank, replace fuel lines, check tires, clean engine, tighten spokes, replace gaskets, check valve clearance, clean carburetor and it went on and on. Jack kept the list to just those tasks necessary to get the bike up and running. Its appearance would have to wait. Satisfied he had touched upon any important work that needed his attention, Jack ripped the page from the pad; folded it; placed it in his shirt pocket and tucked the pencil behind his ear. He pulled a flashlight from the cupboard, hurried to the back door and turned to Darla. "You stay here. There's too much you can get into."

For a moment Jack simply stood in front of the motorcycle, admiring the features he'd first seen only a few days ago but that possessed the familiarity of an old friend. The workbench was filled with tools Jack hadn't noticed earlier that week. An adjustable wrench, pliers, screwdrivers, a tappet wrench, a rubber mallet and a spoke wrench were all laid out neatly. Jars of nuts and bolts were lined across the back of the bench. On the floor, motor oil and kerosene were stored in greasy cans.

The gas tank would be easy to clean. He'd watched his older brother, Guy, perform that very task over thirty years ago, but the method found its way back to Jack. It was as if Guy was standing there; looking over his shoulder; silently gesturing what to do next. After removing the tank from the motorcycle's frame, Jack peered inside. The beam of the flashlight reflected off the shiny bottom of the tank, where gasoline had evaporated, leaving behind a varnished surface. Rust clung to the top of the tank. Jack picked up a jar of nuts and bolts from the workbench, poured them into the tank and reattached the gas cap. He then shook the tank vigorously, like an over-dramatic gourd player in a Mexican mariachi band. Minutes later, his arms numb, Jack stopped; removed the gas cap and turned the gas tank over a wastebasket. Several spoonfuls of fine rust fell to the bottom of the basket. From the greasy can labeled Kerosene, Jack poured about a pint of the heavy fluid into the tank and secured the gas cap. Again he shook the tank but this time for less than a minute, then emptied the fluid into an empty coffee can on the bench top. The residual kerosene would clean and coat the tank until fuel could be added. After wiping his hands, Jack pulled the "To-Do" list from his pocket and placed a check mark in front of the words, "Clean Gas Tank".

Jack had seen a pillion seat, meant for a second rider, on a shelf under the workbench and knew immediately that it needed to be part of the motorcycle's ensemble. A daydream of Kate squeezed up close to him accompanied Jack through every step as he mounted the seat on the back fender of the bike. Someday she would thank him for this place to sit. After Jack had mounted the flimsy seat, he wondered if her "thank you" might actually be a "damn you!"

By noon he had checked off four entries from this list. With each check mark he made, a little more tingle of anticipation flowed through his veins. On the back of the workbench he found a yellowed manual where the motorcycle's tire and spark plug sizes had been written inside the front cover, along with several other less important specs. Jack copied the information into the flip pad. He hoped the Western Auto store in Wellsville would carry the parts. Jack turned for one last glimpse at the motorcycle before switching off the light. The calendar girl on the wall seemed to have a gleam of excitement in her mischievous eyes.

That afternoon Jack wrote Kate the details of playing grease monkey; getting the bike ready to ride, and perhaps, taking a trip to Poughkeepsie. He downplayed his planned night out, mentioning it was Bob's idea in the first place and that he was just going along to keep them company. Some tidbits about Darla and how the remodeling was progressing wrapped up the letter.

Jack had left plans for the night out, somewhat up in the air with Bob. The lack of a telephone made confirming their dinner date a little bit inconvenient. After dropping off the letter at the post office Jack swung by the Ames's place. Martha met him at the door. The curlers in her hair were a good sign. Most women wouldn't curl their hair just to sit in and watch *Gunsmoke* on a Saturday night. Bob was sleeping in front of a baseball game on television. Martha confirmed they would meet Jack at the firemen's hall around 7:00.

The parking lot of the firemen's hall was filled with cars. Jack pulled his truck into one of the last spots. He could smell the salty aroma of ham and the harsh smell of the wild leeks from outside. A few heads turned as he walked into the well-lit hall. An arm waved from the back corner. As Jack wove his way through a matrix of long rectangular tables topped with red and white checked table clothes, at least a half dozen friends slapped him on the back or asked politely how he was doing.

Bob and Martha were seated across from each other. Four white candles spaced equally along the length of the table struggled to create atmosphere. Empty chairs sat beside both his friends. Martha had always had a just-one-of-the-boys way about her and Jack would have felt just as comfortable sitting next to her as next to Bob. He hesitated for a split second and as he stepped to the table, decided if there were eyebrows to be raised that evening, they wouldn't be raised on his account. Three other couples sat further down the table. Jack knew them all. He nodded and sat down next to Bob. At first, he felt somewhat out of place, being in the company of all these couples. But small town camaraderie soon had Jack laughing and almost forgetting he was dateless that evening.

Members of the ladies auxiliary soon began serving large bowls of golden crusted scalloped potatoes, followed by platters of steaming ham and finally roaster pans filled with hundreds of the little second cousins of green onions. The men heaped mounds of the wild leeks next to the meat and potatoes on their plates. Some women had a few of the leeks but their pungent, garlicky smell and biting aftertaste failed to stimulate very many female taste buds. Pitchers of beer and milk were placed anywhere the servers could find a few square inches of space on the food-laden tables. The mere thought of how pleasantly the beer could quench a thirst the salty ham had built up, started Jack's mouth watering. He poured a tall glass of milk and forced his mind to go elsewhere.

Conversation around the table was trite but heaped full of homespun honesty. Plain folks talked about their grandchildren, the weather and their hounds. Nothing said required a great deal of analysis until the town's mayor, who sat at the far end of the table, mused about why only the Democratic presidents were referred to by their initials, such as LBJ, JFK and FDR. From the way he spit the letters from his sneering mouth, a stranger could have guessed Mayor Madison might just be a Republican. Mrs. Madison rolled her eyes and burped, in a less-than-ladylike response, either to her husband or to the beer she'd just gulped down.

Martha, an often outspoken Democrat, peered down the table at the mayor and asked, "What was Ike's middle name, anyway?"

Jack sent the hint of a smile across the table to his clever friend as the mayor fumbled, "Well, let me see...". And the conversation at the table meandered down another road.

By nine o'clock the firemen's hall was nearly empty. A few guests still lingered over coffee and chocolate cake. Bob yawned. "Hey, you got a nap today, Bub. You better perk your butt up!", Martha warned. "Let's go over to the alleys and bowl a couple games."

Jack doubted very much that they'd find an open alley. Even in a town as small as Friendship, there was bound to be a few free spirits that ignored the evening ritual of rolling up the streets each night at 9:00. There were only two bowling lanes and occasionally the boys employed as pin setters didn't show up, making the chances of actually bowling a game, especially on Saturday night, a toss up at best.

"Yeah, at least let's see what's happening over there," Jack added. "If they're busy, we can always drive up the notch and do some deer spotting."

There was nothing Martha would like less to do than be stuck in the confines of a pickup truck, sandwiched between two men who had just consumed massive quantities of leeks. If she wanted to see a spotlight reflected off a pair of frightened eyes, she'd turn out the lights in her bathroom and shine a pocket flashlight into her own. "While you two thrill seekers are stalking Bambi, I think I'll drop into the mayor's place and discuss local politics," Martha said. "That sounds more exciting."

The bowling alley was located above the *Black Horse Inn*. At least a dozen cars surrounded the establishment, but most were likely those of patrons of the inn. As the three stepped into the bowling alley it was apparent, at least for the meantime, bowling would be a spectator sport. There was one small round table with four empty mismatched chairs around it and a ketchup bottle and napkin holder on top. The threesome sat down there, and Bob immediately took drink orders. He and Martha would have draft beers and Jack a ginger ale.

While Bob was at the counter, placing their order, a dark-haired woman, seated at the table next to them, slurred a friendly "Hello". Her dark eyes were caked with mascara and there was a noticeable line under her chin where her makeup stopped and light wrinkles were vying for a toehold. She had been pretty at one time but now tried to hide the fact that years of hard living had stolen her youth. Her age defying arsenal included a lacy white cotton top that plunged between ample breasts. Her black brassiere crept out from under the lace, in a not-so-subtle attempt to be seen. Ruby lipstick smudged her teeth as she smiled at Jack. An innocent spinster might well have imagined this lady to be very tired and in need of some sleep. What Jack saw in those droopy eyelids and sullen lips was also related to a bedroom activity but it wasn't sleep.

The woman glanced up at Bob, as he returned to the table with three glasses pressed against his once-clean white shirt. She looked back at Jack—the cogs of her mind seemed to be clanking away—probably trying to assess which of these potential studs was attached to that woman.

"We're next in line," Bob said, sliding drinks across the table and wiping his wet hands down the front of his shirt. "Shouldn't be too long."

The woman at the next table, silently disagreed with the last few words then dropped her gaze to the half-empty sloe gin fizz that sat fizzless in front of her.

A bowling ball sent a crack echoing through the establishment. Ten pins scattered then some spun on their sides. A lanky boy stood at the end of the alley, waiting for the pins to settle. His hair appeared to have been cut with the aid of a bowl and cherry-red pimples pocked his cheeks. In seconds his nimble hands snatched up the fallen pins and sat them motionless atop barely visible spots that marked their homes. An elderly gentleman walked penguin-like back to the score table, where his silver-haired wife clapped her hands in glee. He patted her back, then she stepped onto the alley and lifted a ten-pound bowling ball with both hands.

The woman at the next table slowly lit a cigarette and rolled her lips around it. She sensuously stroked the filter between her middle and index fingers then closed her eyes and exhaled through pursed lips. When she opened her eyes and caught him staring at her, Jack nervously looked down at his ginger ale. Six months ago he would have held the gaze.

The elderly couple finished their game and walked from the alley to the door, arm-in-arm. From behind a counter, a man in a baseball cap called out, "Mr. Miles," then pointed at the old man's feet. Both of the old folks giggled at the sight of the bowling shoes they were still wearing.

It took several frames for Jack to limber his stiff muscles and actually feel like he knew how to bowl. From the first frame, Bob lofted balls halfway down the alley before they'd touch down, then nearly shatter the pins. By the tenth frame Jack was sliding gracefully through his deliveries, Martha was hooking the ball and Bob had cracked two pins, which had to be replaced.

Martha yawned and said, "It's been a long day and I didn't get a nap like some people," glancing at Bob. She smiled and said good night to Jack while Bob gulped down the last of his beer. Jack said he would bowl one more game then call it a night. The woman at the table covered a devilish grin.

By the fifth frame the woman was sitting close to the score table and asked Jack if he'd like a scorekeeper. She pulled her satin skirt above her knees and crossed her long, shapely legs. Her black, high-heeled shoes were scuffed. As one of her legs bobbed atop the other, she pointed the toe of her shoe at Jack. There was no doubt in his mind, where this situation could lead. A primitive urge tugged at better judgment. "Nah, I'm almost done and at this point, it's best if I don't keep score," he said. A bead of sweat rolled down his back. The need for a drink crawled back up his spine. In the last frame, as he held the bowling ball in his hands, his body felt tight and invigorated. With little effort, he knew he could throw the ball the entire length of the alley, shattering every pin to smithereens, impressing the hell-out-of anyone watching. Instead he rolled the ball smoothly down the alley and returned his bowling shoes to the man with the baseball cap. The woman was pulling on her coat as he passed her.

The streets of Friendship were quiet. Jack had parked on a side street where the lamplights on Main Street were but a faint glow. A light fog had started to settle in when he heard, "Hello there. Got a light?" He turned and the woman from the bowling alley held a cigarette out.

"Sorry," was all he said after patting his pants pockets.

"Maybe we could rub two sticks together. Were you ever a Boy Scout?"

"I never could get that to work," he said.

"Well, I bet I could help that," she said. It was not clear if effects of the alcohol or deliberate clumsiness was to blame but the woman wobbled on one of the high heel shoes then stumbled into Jack's arms. She held her hands flat against his chest and mumbled a less than sincere apology, "I'm sorry, honey…these damn heels. Glad there was a strong man around to catch me." As she pushed herself upright, the fingers of her left hand worked their way between the buttons on Jack's shirt. She held them there for several seconds. The woman then picked at invisible lint on the pocket of Jack's shirt, like a lesser primate grooming her mate. "What's your…" and the train of thought she must have had was derailed. "Name?" finally escaped her lips.

The scent of sweet perfume and tobacco filled Jacks head. Like the nervous Whos from Whoville, every logical brain cell inside his thick skull screamed in unison, praying they'd be heard. "Stop!" With much less than Hortonian willpower, Jack placed his hand on the woman's shoulder and asked, "Are you okay?" He could see the outline of her lips in the dim light.

The lonely woman seemed to sober at the sound of a voice spoken with caring. "I'm fine and really sorry. I didn't mean to…" and her words trailed off, not needing to be said, to be understood. Urges, that had welled up inside Jack turned to pity. More than sexual gratification, this sad woman craved a friendly voice.

"My name's Jack. What's yours?"

He could see her dark outline staring up at him and for a moment he expected to hear, "Daphne" or "Bridgette".

"Blanche," she said, sounding more like a question than an answer.

"That's a very pretty name," Jack said, in the most sincere voice he could manage. "Are you driving?"

In his heart, he hoped to hear "No". "Yes," would have caused some concern for the woman's safety and Jack worried that offering her a ride home might make things…complicated. He chided himself for the selfish thought but was relieved when she nodded toward the top of the *Black Horse Inn*. "I have a room up there."

There was shame in the last two words, "up there." She uttered them softly and the pitch of her voice dropped, giving them meaning the mere phrase could not convey. Both remorse and apprehension washed over the simple words. Pity churned inside Jack.

Jack took one of her hands and held it between his own. "I'm glad I met you, Blanche."

Her hand felt frail as she gently squeezed then released the hand of a man she had considered prey only a few moments ago. Salvaging some respect was far more precious than a couple hours of pleasure.

"My dog's probably dancin' a two-step right about now. I better head home and let her out," Jack said.

Darla was a readily available excuse when being candid might be too blunt. Jack knew she wouldn't mind being used if it might spare someone's feelings.

He reached into his pocket for the ring of keys. As they clinked together in the night stillness, she knew he would soon be gone. Without hesitation, Blanche threw her arms around Jack's neck and hugged him tightly. "You're a nice man," she whispered then released him.

For reasons still unclear, Jack knew he had done the only thing he could. It would have been easy to be holding Blanche this very minute, the rest of the world well beyond a closed bedroom door. A restless demon still murmured for him to sweep this woman from her feet and make her explode in stormy passion. But Jack wanted the man he saw in the mirror the next morning to be one that he respected.

"Good night, Blanche."

She walked quietly from him. He watched until she disappeared into the fog. Her footfalls echoed down the quiet street then the rusty hinges of an opening door squeaked. A window rattled as an unseen door closed. Stillness blanketed the little village. Jack walked to his truck and thought of Kate.

CHAPTER 14

▼

Back at the farmhouse, Darla greeted Jack with inquiring sniffs, just to see where her master had been. The scent of ham still lingered on his fingertips. She licked his hand, savoring the fading taste of the salty meat. Missing her motive, Jack leaned over and patted her head. "Ahhh...you missed me," he said.

A crash outside startled both of them. Something near the backdoor was making a racket, like the sounds of pots and pans being dropped on a kitchen floor. "The garbage," Jack muttered. Darla pranced to the door, barking in alarm. The instant he opened the backdoor, Jack watched helplessly as Darla bolted from the porch and into the darkness. He flipped on the porch light, just in time to see the haunches of the dog disappear around the corner of a hedge. Garbage on the sidewalk told the story: "Raccoons."

"Darla, come!" he yelled. "Darla, come!!"

Several minutes of worry passed. Jack prayed she'd ignore her instinct to hunt and instead heed his calls. The bushes near the barn rustled. Jack strained his eyes to see and a moment later Darla appeared from the fog. Her head was held low. The dog knew she had done wrong.

"Enough excitement for tonight, girl. Let's get to bed."

Darla's encounter with the raccoon had spiked her adrenaline level sky high. For nearly half an hour Jack heard her pacing around the bedroom while he tried in vain to get some sleep. "Darla, down!" he said harshly. He heard the thud of her body hit the floor. "Good dog," but two minutes later the clicking of her nails against the hardwood floor rang through the bedroom again. Sometime after midnight, the two both drifted simultaneously into a restless sleep.

Well before morning, a frantic scratching sound woke Jack. A pathetic whimper put an abrupt end to his rest. *It must be Darla having a bad dream*, he thought. "Wake up girl," he called to her. Jack reached down to stroke the fur on the dog's neck. Darla continued to thrash, now more violently. Phlegmy gurgles mixed in with the whimpers. Jack clicked on the bedside lamp and nervously looked down at Darla.

The dog's legs whipped forward then back and for a second Jack thought she must be in a dream, hot on the trail of the garbage-loving raccoon. But there was stiffness in her legs, like an invisible set of braces was paralyzing her joints. The pads on her feet were separated, exposing the webs between them. Jack knew the dog would stretch her paws like this when swimming but not on a bedroom floor. Something was wrong.

Jack sat up in the bed and rubbed his eyes. The loose flaps of skin on the side of Darla's mouth palpitated with each breath she took. White foam oozed from under them with each gasp. Her eyelids were closed tight but Jack could see eyeballs rolling underneath. She coughed weakly and meringue-like froth spewed from between her teeth.

"Darla!" Jack shouted and shook the dog.

Her body was cold; muscles shivered beneath her fur, which now stood on end. Three loud woofs came from deep in her throat, unlike sounds Darla had ever made. Jack sat and watched helplessly, praying his dog would snap out of this fit. His heart leaped as Darla rose awkwardly to her feet. Legs still stiff; she teetered from side to side. "You gave me quite a scare," Jack said, reaching down to pet her. His breath froze in his throat. Darla's eyes were still closed and foam now covered her face. The dog's stiff front leg shot forward and she began to walk toward the bedroom door. He could do nothing but follow.

Her legs arched forward in a gait immortalized by the Frankenstein monster. Jack called out her name loudly, but Darla seemed oblivious to the sound of his voice or anything around her. Without the benefit of sight, she navigated through the doorway and down the hallway to the top of the stairs. Jack followed close behind; worried she might try to descend the stairs. Near the top step, the dog swayed to her right and brushed against the wall. Darla continued walking down the stairs, her back sliding along the wall, supporting her tilted body. "What the hell?" Jack questioned not only what he was witnessing but also his sanity. There was something that escaped reason, here in this old farmhouse. He silently vowed these two guests would not be spending another night there.

At the bottom of the stairs Darla stood upright again and continued to goose-step her way toward the living room. As she approached the grandfather clock, it chimed out peacefully. Darla lifted her ears, and, as if she had heard an inaudible command, lay down directly in front of the clock. She was still for a moment then Jack could see her stomach begin to heave. Darla opened her mouth wide, ready for her churning stomach to give up something foul…something sinister hidden deep inside of her. Her face muscles tightened in anguish. Like an ocean wave gaining strength as it approached a seashore, Darla's stomach heaved a final time, sending a ripple that turned to a swell by the time it reached her ribcage and it appeared that it might send a tidal wave from her throat. Her eyes popped open in panic yet looked void of life, like those of a china doll when gravity would roll its eyes open in their sockets and the doll would then stare blankly into space. Darla's jaws stretched beyond canine limits, into the realm of mammal-devouring snakes. Every muscle in her upper body surged toward Darla's open mouth. Demonic sounds spewed from deep within her throat but the agonizing retch brought up nothing.

The dog's body then slumped to the floor. Jack knelt beside her and anxiously stroked her head. He willed Darla to breathe when a thumping sound from behind startled Jack. His heart leaped at the sight of Darla's tail slapping against the floor. As his head lowered to meet hers, tears wet his cheeks. Darla turned her head to licked Jack's face. A whiff of peppermint blew from her mouth. The cartoon-like face of the man in the moon smiled down at them from its perch on the face of the clock.

Darla showed no ill effects from what Jack diagnosed as sleep walking and dry heaves. He worried about the foaming in her mouth. What if the raccoon Darla had chased that night had bit her? But he knew enough about dogs and rabies to understand it took quite a few days for the first signs of the awful disease to appear.

On her feet, Darla seemed fine, taking time to show her affection for Jack, who sat beside her on the floor. Then cocking her head she gazed at the clock.

"Bet you don't even remember getting here, do ya?" Jack asked in a soothing voice. "Well, since we're up and it doesn't look like you're tired either, we might as well have some breakfast." Darla wagged her tail at the understanding of that word.

Jack looked out the kitchen window. The first hints of morning crept above the eastern hilltops. Fog still hugged the valley. In the distance, he could see the outline of black rolling hills against a lightening background. A child with watercolors, using indigo paint on black paper, might have painted this sky as it caressed the hilltops. Darla curled at his feet while Jack sat with coffee cup in hand, looking to those hills and seeing well beyond them. Out the corner of his eye, he could see the barn roof peeking over the fog at him. *I know you're there. Don't worry, I'll be back to visit.* The motorcycle sat patiently in the dark.

For the next several hours, Jack cleaned up any mess he'd made in the farmhouse; packed his clothes; gathered Darla's bowls and drove uptown to get a Sunday newspaper.

Back at the farmhouse he poured another cup of coffee and tried to think of anything he should do before heading home. The sounds of truck tires hitting the pavement and of gears shifting made their way through the open living room windows. From the hallway Jack could see the stainless steel dairy tanker whiz by. "Those poor guys must work seven days a week." The Friendship Dairy had a fine reputation for excellent cottage cheese, curd and, of course, milk. Tankers carried the raw milk from farms in the area to the diary and were making runs seven days a week. The local dairy cows hadn't learned Sundays were supposed to be a day of rest.

Jack stepped to the living room window and watched the shiny tanker until it rounded a bend in the road. Then he glanced at the newspaper spread across the coffee table. *Sunday Edition.* The word "Sunday", in particular, caught his eye.

In his boyhood, Sundays were solemn yet happy days spent in church with his family. After the service, grandfolks and occasionally aunts and uncles would gather, often at his house, for Sunday dinner. Much of the afternoon would be spent preparing the feast, eating for what seemed like hours, then engaging in lazy conversations about farming, politics, religion and ne'er-do-well relatives. Jack loved to listen. His grandmother would often critique the morning sermon and never fail to mention how much better her brother Floyd, a Presbyterian minister, could have delivered it. But those Sunday morning messages would make Jack think where God fit into his life.

The Christmas Eve service at the Baptist church had left a sweet aftertaste, not only from the memory of how Kate looked that night but also from the way Pastor Ingles gave his message of faith. Jack remembered the expressions on many faces that night. When the pastor had asked the congregation to greet their neighbors, the entire sanctuary came alive with warmth and friendliness. Sincerity filled the eyes of those people, wishing him a "Merry Christmas". Love abounded in that place, at that moment.

Events of the past week troubled Jack. He could have dismissed all of them, if they had occurred in isolation or been spread out over time. But night after night he could count on something very peculiar happening. An innocent cause might have been behind a dog getting sick, fog in the bedroom, strange noises or streaks on a mirror. Together they were the ingredients of a disturbing stay at the

Fletcher farmhouse. The grandfather clock in the hallway began to chime. *There's something very strange about that clock.*

Jack turned his head toward Darla and announced, "Guess I'll go to church this morning." The dog raised one eye from a peaceful nap. "I'll pick you up after the service."

Jack was relieved to find his home empty and the work nearly completed when he stopped in to dress for church. He wasn't in any mood to explain anything to Norm. Jack's only white shirt could have used a couple additional inches of materials around the middle but a wide tie would hide the bulging buttons.

Church was not a place to make a spectacle by such things as arriving fashionably late. Jack pulled into the church parking lot at 10:35 for the 11:00 service and found only three cars there. Inside the organist was jazzing up her own rendition of *Holy, Holy, Holy* and two elderly women were praying in the front pew. Only the silk scarves on their bowed heads showed over the back of the pew.

Jack walked quietly to a pew in the middle of the church and started to slide across to the far side. Just before he reached the end of the pew a sliver found the meaty skin on the bottom of his thigh. It wasn't a sliver of the hair-size variety but rather one a caveman might have used to spear a small rodent. Jack bit down on his lip but not in time to catch all of the loud, "Ouch!" that escaped. The two scarves in the front row turned and, from under them, four beady little eyes peered back at this newcomer. Jack's forced smile had nearly an equal part wince in it. He mouthed a "good morning" to the ladies and they both quickly turned, without so much as a nod.

With the tips of his fingers, Jack gingerly inspected the damage done by the sliver. On the outside of his pants there was at least an inch of timber. He pinched the nasty piece of wood and pulled it from his thigh. There was no humor as the word, "redwood" scrolled across his mind but the sliver, for the most part, was indeed saturated with crimson syrup. Voices at the back of the church heralded the arrival of the "Loud" family that Jack had seen there Christmas Eve. Mr. Loud pointed to a pew near the front of the church and the little Loudets scurried into it. The scarved ladies must have recognized the Loud voices and slid down their pew, away from the cacophonous clan.

Soon, more sedate families with well-behaved children were filling the sanctuary. Jack had seen most of the friendly faces, at one time or another, around town.

"Hey, you lookin' to have your sins washed away?" The question was intended to be asked in a mere whisper but it was loud enough to turn several heads, as

Bob and Martha sidestepped next to Jack. "Were you bad last night?" Bob grinned until the back of Martha's hand landed on his stomach.

Jack cupped his hand next to his mouth and in a true whisper answered his friend. "No, I wasn't bad last night...just thought this was the best place to pray that your wretched soul doesn't burn in hell." Martha stood between the two men and smiled curtly at her husband, her expression telling Bob very clearly that he got what he deserved.

"You okay...you look a little peaked?" Martha asked Jack.

His manliness told him to lie but the warm moisture he could feel on the bottom of his leg told him he wouldn't get away with it. "Just got a little sliver here in my leg." Martha patted him mother-like on the cheek, the preacher greeted his congregation, and the bleeding stopped.

Lawrence Ingles wore a navy-blue suit, a size too big, but presentable. The knot on his dark gray tie looked like it had been tied by a lynch mob. It protruded, but not nearly as much as his bulbous Adam's apple. Together, this protuberant tandem worked like syncopated ping-pong balls each time the good pastor spoke. The preacher's steel-gray eyes hid under bushy eyebrows, until a rush of ecclesiastical fervor would levitate them and expose a fire in his eyes that willed the congregation to listen and understand. His message this morning would be about "Hope", but first he asked the fold to stand and sing all four verses of *The Old Rugged Cross*...just to get their juices flowing.

Jack tried to ease his way up from the pew, feeling a slight tug at his pants when he began to stand. The blood had partially dried and stuck to the seat of the pew. Martha turned to assess his problem and spotted a small pool of blood on the white painted seat behind her friend. She raised her eyes to meet his sheepish grin...and smiled. The smile she held on her face was polite but ached for some room to expand. Martha felt a wave of inexplicable humor welling up inside and raised the back of her hand to hide her growing smile. Jack scowled at her. As if a vicious virus had leaped between them, he started to laugh, quietly at first. From the corner of his eye, Jack could see Martha's upper body heaving. She grabbed his arm at the elbow and squeezed, summoning as much strength as she could muster. Martha surely thought any bit of pain she could inflict on him might refocus Jack's attention. She was wrong! Instead, her touch sent a jolt of raw comical juice straight through him. He snorted in laughter then clamped his teeth down on his bottom lip but the thought of producing more blood only made matters worse. Martha was now shaking and started to bend over. Jack turned his head, and through watery eyes could see the back of her black dress quiver and hear her muffled sobs. Bob stared down at his wife and shook his head in feigned disdain. Heads around them were turning. Martha began to choke and Jack instinctively slapped her back. She struggled to stand upright. Tears were streaming down her face. Jack felt the total loss of control start to overcome him and decided he needed to sit down. He rested his head on the pew in front of him and prayed for his composure to be reborn.

The first words that actually made their way into a conscious part of Jack's brain were, "It's shame and reproach gladly bear," sung with, what seemed like, more gusto by those around him. He was able to stand and lend his voice to the refrain, "I will cling to the old rugged cross, and exchange it some day for a crown". Martha refused to look his way.

Jack sat down in the hard pew and shifted a few times to get comfortable. Baptists believed there were no shortcuts to heaven and the sermons supported this belief. His frail appearance betrayed the preacher's deep, booming voice that could soothe, scare or assure the faithful. He started his message with the question, "What is hope?" Like an anxious child waiting for a "Once upon a time," the congregation sat in anticipation. It would not come in a curt little minuet but rather in a languidly unfolding symphony. For the next hour Pastor Ingles would preach a sermon, which was no less moving than a Rachmaninov concerto.

In a soft, melodic voice he started: "What is hope? Well, a vague notion comes to mind when we usually think of hope. On the surface it seems so very simple, for we think of hope as a feeling, sometimes a vain feeling that something better is just around the corner. We might "hope" that a fortune magically appears on our front doorstep or we might "hope" that the preacher isn't long winded today. (Several heads shook in disagreement and a few people chuckled.) But, to more fully understand hope, we must look much deeper, for it is a gift from God…a priceless gift more precious than our wildest dreams of earthly fortunes.

True hope comes only from God and it is given to all that believe. The gift of hope is wrapped inside another gift. Our children find great delight in opening one brightly wrapped package only to find another. God's greatest gift was his son and once we accept that gift we can also have the second gift. Hope!

Brothers and sisters…close your eyes…watch and listen. Can you see a soul at peace because hope has filled a heart? Can you hear the distant quill gliding over parchment? Emily Dickinson sent us a message. Do you hear it in her words?

> *"Hope" is the thing with feathers—*
> *That perches in the soul—*
> *And sings the tune without the words—*
> *And never stops—at all—*

I can see her in a garden; song sparrows and larks singing all around her; a lady in a white dress, translating their songs to words. "That perches in the soul—." Yes, that's exactly where hope lives. It perches in the soul and nourishes our spirit, if we will but take it and eat.

"Be of good courage, and he shall strengthen your heart, all ye that hope in the Lord." David, the shepherd boy, wrote those words to the Chief Musician in the 31st Psalms and don't they still ring true today?

Our hearts can become heavy when we see our young President taken by an assassin's bullet—or when we hear that the nuclear arms race has produced enough weapons to destroy the Earth many times over—or when we read of the most basic human rights being stripped from so many around the world. But be comforted…because for every story the media sees as newsworthy, there are thousands of untold stories—stories that abound in goodness and in love. You might not read about the volunteer fireman that risks his own life, running into a burning building to save a helpless child—or about a nurse sitting at the bedside of a dying patient, while her own family waits for her at home. You might not see a story on the nightly news about a soldier turning his weapon away from a boy trembling in an enemy uniform—or about a poor child hoarding her pennies, just for the joy of dropping them into the collection plate at Sunday school, knowing she'll be helping the less fortunate.

But as good Christians, isn't it our job, our responsibility to spread the good news—the news about Hope he has given us? Mark tells us to "Go ye into all the world, and preach the gospel to every creature." You may want to shout it from the rooftops or share it in a letter to an old friend. But don't keep it secret…let us pray."

The words of this small town preacher touched many hearts in the congregation that morning. Through double windows hung high at the back of the church, rays of yellow sunshine beamed down on the regal purple carpet that covered the main aisle. The preacher stepped down from the pulpit, raised his arms toward heaven and asked his people to, "Take the word of the Lord with you." From a pew near the front, Mrs. Ingles joined her husband and the two walked like newlyweds, hand-in-hand down the aisle. Tranquillity lingered over the believers as they sat in quiet contemplation, waiting for Pastor Ingles and his wife to reach the vestibule. The sweet notes of *I Come to the Garden Alone* flowed softly from the pipe organ.

Jack bowed his head and rested his hands on the pew in front of him. Thoughts of the pews he had destroyed in his troubling dream crept into his head. Yesterday morning a malignancy had woven its way through the nightmare but healing had occurred in this place today.

The two large doors at the entrance of the church were propped open, letting the warm air of spring baptize the worshippers with their first scent of lilacs that season. Demure, dressed in a plain black dress more suited for an Amish wife, Mrs. Ingles stood next to her husband, grasping his arm with both hands. A Bible rested in the cradle of her arms. She greeted each person who passed, with a nod of the head and a tender, "God bless you." Salt and pepper hair was pulled back in a bun and a touch of rouge was the only makeup that graced her pale face. As he stepped in front of her, Jack detected the faint scent of the same dusting powder his mother had worn.

"Good morning, Mrs. Ingles. We certainly are blessed with this beautiful day, aren't we?" Jack said.

She nodded her head twice and simply replied, "Beautiful".

Lawrence Ingles made sure every person that had taken the time to hear his sermon that morning felt they were welcome to come back for more. He gave firm handshakes to everyone in the Baptist processional and added, "Hope to see you again next week."

Jack shook the preacher's hand and held on longer than any polite Baptist would do, but several seconds shy of the typical Jehovah's Witness handshake. "Great sermon this morning, Pastor Ingles," Jack said in a loud voice then lowered it to add, "It was very meaningful."

"Mr. Flanagan. It's nice to see you again. I was just thinking of you the other day. Heard about the fire. I'm very sorry."

"Well…things are almost back to normal. In fact, I'm moving back in today."

"It was sure nice of Miss Fletcher to open up her home to you. Say, would you like to have dinner with us this evening. Won't be anything too fancy."

Jack instantly decided to decline but contrary words escaped his mouth: "Why…sure, I'd love to." The reasons he had accepted weren't clear in Jack's mind, but he knew there was more he wanted to hear from the country preacher.

"How does 5:00 sound for you?" the preacher asked.

"Great, I'll see you then," Jack said and walked to his truck, glad he had accepted the invitation. The crimson spot on the back of his pants had dried and went unnoticed. Had Jack remembered the earlier bloodletting, he might have back-stepped from the church.

CHAPTER 15

▼

Back at the farmhouse Darla had made herself comfortable amid Jack's bags, which had been placed near the back door, ready for the move. Any other time he would step into the house, the dog would prance around the kitchen floor, her claws clicking on the linoleum in a dance of excitement, but today Darla held her jaw on the floor when Jack stepped into the room. Her eyes drooped like a bloodhound's. Jack knelt beside her and comforted, "Don't worry girl, we'll be back.

Before they left, Jack wanted to take one last look at the motorcycle. Perhaps he'd tinker a bit, so Jack pulled a pair of blue jeans and an old T-shirt from one of the bags and changed from his church clothes. Darla followed him to the barn and sat obediently by the entrance to the workshop. The flick of the light switch revealed the Indian motorcycle sitting motionless but ready to spring. The solitary headlamp gazed up at Jack, like a mechanical Cyclops looking for a liberator. The aromatic smell of kerosene lingered in the workshop.

Jack looked back at Darla, "Just a few minutes with the bike, I promise." He picked up a grease rag and absent-mindedly rubbed his hands with it, deciding what to do next. On the floor, under the workbench, cans of Marvel Mystery Oil sat in a neat row.

"I'll clean the motor."

Jack drained the old oil, removed the exhaust pipes and valve caps then he poured a small amount of the Marvel Oil on the cylinder heads and waited for it to seep into the engine. After replacing the valve caps, Jack filled the crankcase with the rich oil and cranked the motor with the kick starter. He left the ignition off, which forced the fluid through the engine, completing the Mystery Oil enema. He rinsed the carburetor with rubbing alcohol and checked the valve clearance. Once the valve train was lubricated, Jack stood back and smiled in satisfaction. The job brought him one step closer to riding this incredible motorcycle.

Jack looked at his watch and shuddered at the sight of 4:30. The afternoon had literally disappeared and he still needed to get cleaned up for dinner at the parsonage. With his hand on the light switch, Jack stole one last look. She would wait here for his return, as loyal as Darla. However, unlike the low maintenance canine friend, the motorcycle would require much more attention, at least until she was up and running. Darla pranced beside Jack as he hurried to the truck.

Waiting at the front door of the parsonage, the sour smell of cabbage met Jack's nose with a nostalgic slap. Once a month his mother would pull out a tarnished pressure cooker and prepare a meal Jack soon learned to hate. A conglomeration, which included cabbage, potatoes, carrots and ham, would be mixed together into what Mom always called a "boiled dinner." Jack and his brother, Guy, referred to the meal as a "spoiled dinner," but never in the presence of their mother. A quiet prayer was sent heavenward requesting anything but...

"Hello, Jack. Come in, come in! Hope you like a good old boiled dinner," Pastor Ingles said as he opened the parsonage door.

"Oh, I love them," Jack lied. "Mom used to make them all the time." Jack wondered where the sin, "lying to a minister", would fall on the sin scale—probably somewhere between "spitting in a cemetery" and "having lewd thoughts about the Good Witch of the North."

The front room was neatly arranged with a desk, leather couch, an easy chair and several bookshelves. A large picture hanging above the couch immediately caught Jack's eye. At first it appeared rather drab, full of dark colors and a dismal overtone but there was an interesting quality in this picture of *Daniel in the Lion's Den*. The lions had not yet arrived and Daniel stared upward, at a small window near the top of the den. A golden ray of sunshine shone down on Daniel through the window, illuminating his face and a small part of his deep purple robe. The face had been painted in such a way that even a casual observer could see the inner peace within this man. A thin border of metallic gold matting was bordered itself by a wider purple mat board. Dark mahogany with hints of its own rich purples framed the interesting picture.

"It's Daniel," the preacher said.

"Yes, I know...it's beautiful."

"Thank you. We had it stored away for years—seemed too depressing to hang on our walls. Then a friend with a keen eye for color suggested we frame it with the metallic gold and purple mats. We both love it now."

Jack noticed many of the books on the shelves were leather-bound, old, and had titles, which might scare away any casual reader.

"I'm reading Elmer Gantry. Are you familiar with it?" Jack asked.

The preacher's eyes popped like those of a proctologist's patient hearing the snap of a rubber glove. "Why yes, I'm familiar with that work. It rather demonizes our religion, don't you think?"

Honestly, Jack had only viewed the book as an entertaining work of fiction. Gantry, the shyster, the womanizing preacher, seemed at times laughable and at times pathetic but never the stereotype of a real Baptist pastor. "Well, I ah...I saw the movie and it wasn't that great. Thought the book might be different and have some redeeming qualities. I just started it," Jack lied again. One more lie and he might as well jump onboard the express train to Hades.

"Well, I read the novel myself years ago and that Gantry fellow is, for sure, pure evil. It's a sad state our country is in when this type of filth hits our libraries and our theaters."

Salvation came in a weak voice from another room. "Dinner's ready," Mrs. Ingles called.

As the men entered the room, Mrs. Ingles was placing a steaming bowl of food in the center of the table. The kitchen was small but cheery. "That smells wonderful," Jack said then looked over his shoulder to see if a red man with a pitchfork might be attacking him at that moment. The look on Lawrence Ingles' face betrayed the fact that the boiled dinner might not be his favorite cuisine either.

Mrs. Ingles moved mechanically about the kitchen, attending to details with the resolution of a Geisha girl. Jack had a sense that if he spoke to her, it would throw a monkey wrench into the routine, so decided to wait until the threesome could all talk during the meal.

Finally she stopped scurrying and wiped her hands down the front of her apron. "There," she said softly.

Jack waited politely behind his chair at the table for the lady of the house to be seated. Pastor Ingles started to sit, but quickly stood back upright when he noticed Jack still on his feet. For a second, a look of alarm filled her face, thinking she had perhaps overlooked some critical part of the meal. Then Mrs. Ingles' eyes brightened as she realized Jack had obviously been taught proper table manners. With a meek nod of appreciation she sat down and closed her eyes. The two men then seated themselves and Pastor Ingles bowed his head and began to say grace. "Our most gracious heavenly Father. We thank you for the food you have placed before us. Bless it to our bodies and let it provide sustenance so that we might spread thy word and honor thy name." Three "Amens," concluded the prayer.

Jack loaded his plate with potatoes, carrots and ham, leaving not a square inch of space for the cabbage. "Oh, Mr. Flanagan…let me get you a bowl for the cabbage. I see you're out of room."

Mrs. Ingles was up and at the cupboard before Jack could protest. She scooped a mound of cabbage into the bowl that could have choked a horse. Jack smiled politely and said, "Thank you." A delicious looking three-layer chocolate cake sat atop the counter next to the sink. Neither a cabbage-loving hound nor the long distraction Jack had prayed for actually materialized, so he picked at the cabbage between bites of edible food.

Conversation moved at a leisurely pace. They talked of the morning sermon, of their ancestry, of mutual friends, of baseball and of Darla. Mrs. Ingles laughed several times, especially during stories of the impish dog. Layers of uneasiness peeled away, exposing a woman much more profound than most people knew. A cloak of awkward shyness had hidden much of the real Penelope Ingles. A gentle smile turned her face from plain to lovely.

In a seesaw battle between better judgment and possible enlightenment, Jack made up his mind that the disturbing dream he had had several nights before was not worth mentioning. The fact that his mind would have been invaded with thoughts of desecrating a church, even if it was within the framework of a dream, would raise judgmental eyebrows and maybe questions concerning his sanity.

Jack also weighed the possibility of broaching the topic of the strange goings-on around the Fletcher farmhouse. His curiosity outweighed any reservations. Anyway, the preacher already knew Jack had stooped to the depths of literary lewdness by reading the works of that Anti-Christ, Sinclair Lewis. *Might as well take the plunge into total heathenism.*

"I've been seeing a few odd things happening around the Fletcher farm," he admitted. "No ghosts or anything," Jack said smiling, but then winced inwardly at his choice of words. Overstatement of the occurrences would have the Ingles giving him the "carrots growing out of his ears" look.

"Just some strange noises, a few odd markings on the bathroom mirror, and the dog acting quite peculiar last night. I guess there's a logical explanation for everything that's happened there but the combination has left me feeling uneasy."

"Those old farmhouses can have a personality of their own. Perhaps some little critters are getting into the attic. I've heard they can make quite a racket. And those old beams can do a bit of shifting and cause some ruckus," the preacher suggested.

"Well, I thought of that, but what I heard wasn't noise made by any animal. Maybe I was just dreaming." Jack didn't really think this was true but wanted to leave himself a plausible way of stepping away from the circumstances and back into the neat, explainable world of civilized Christians. At that moment he wished he'd never brought up the subject with the Baptist preacher.

"Jack, there are things in this world that no man or woman can explain. I'm often skeptical when I hear stories that seem to lack explanation but then I step back and think of my own faith in God. There are doubters that question many things that I personally accept as the gospel truth. Christianity is all about believing in things that might defy logic, for nothing else in the history of mankind can be likened to the events that are the basis of our faith...but that does not make it any less true. The Old Testament has an abundance of passages that describe events that seem to contradict plausibility, at least by today's standards. So, I'm at a point in my faith that I can't be too judgmental. There are going to be inexplicable things that God allows to happen."

Jack nodded his head in silence. He had been wrong in his first impression of this meek looking man. The Christmas sermon that Paster Ingles gave was moving but could have been dismissed as a seasonal fluke. Spirits ran high on Christmas Eve and any sermon, which might be judged mediocre at another time, could draw tears on that special night. But the message of "Hope" the skinny preacher had delivered that morning was filled with such passion, so much understanding and insight that nary a soul left the sanctuary without being spiritually lifted.

"There have been many times when life has dealt an ugly blow, making a doubter out of me or overwhelming me with fear. But I've found answers, Jack. They're not always obvious, but if you search for them, the Bible holds many keys that unlock the doors of understanding. One of the wisest rulers the Earth has known sent us a gift eons ago. The shepherd boy, who slew the Philistine and later became King of all Israel, wrote beautiful passages, which we call the Psalms. They're not only radiant poetry but also contain messages we might overlook. A brilliant mind disguised a map to understanding in the lovely verses and I think he knew just what he was doing. The "still waters" and the "green pastures" were used to keep our attention for untold millennia but there's so much more hidden within these passages."

Jack sat intrigued by a revelation Pastor Ingles made so obvious. The night of the fire he had held the *Good Book* in his hands—a gift from his mother, which until this moment, held only nostalgic worth. Its worn pages and underlined passages sent back a message from another place. It would not have been clearer if his mother was sitting right beside him. She knew where answers were.

"I don't mean to be telling you where to look, Jack…I just used the Psalms as an example but the Bible can help you."

Mrs. Ingles nodded in quiet agreement. That morning at the church she gave the appearance of being painfully shy, and perhaps a mere extension of her husband's personality, as she clasped his arm and looked more at him than into the eyes of the departing congregation. Now, the same gesture took on an air of contemplation and when she looked into Jack's eyes, he could see she possessed the soul of a woman more concerned with the well-being of others than with her own appearance. Without makeup or lipstick, her face glowed in a naked radiance, like those of the angels painted on the pages of his family Bible.

The engaging conversation had diverted attention from the meal and, in what some might call a modern day miracle, Jack had finished all the cabbage in the bowl. Had the foul stuff been in a little boy's basket two thousand years ago, Jesus might not have had to use his heavenly powers to divide the bread and fishes. The cabbage in one boiled dinner would surely have been enough to provide the multitudes with all they wanted.

Penelope Ingles walked to the counter, picked up the three-layer chocolate cake in one hand, plates, forks and a knife in the other and walked back to the table. "Devil's Food cake, Mr. Flanagan?"

Later that night Jack sat in the easy chair back in his own house, staring at the boxscores in the Sunday newspaper. Don Drysdale and Whitey Ford had both won brilliantly pitched games. Darla nosed around in the kitchen. When he had finished reading the paper, Jack picked up the Bible his mother had given him years ago. He began to read passages she had unlined just for this moment. *There are answers here.*

In bed, Jack thought about the last time he had prayed. That time unremembered, he decided it was time to start again. Jack closed his eyes and began:

"Dear Lord…I know it's been a long time, but I want to say I'm thankful for so much you have given me. Pastor Ingles has showed me a pathway to find peace within myself and he has done it through your Word. Kate has been the answer to a prayer I didn't even make. I'm sorry I've overlooked you all these years, but you being you…I know I'm forgiven. Oh, if there's anything unholy at the Fletcher's farmhouse, please make it go away. Thanks for listening. Amen."

Jack snapped his fingers and patted his hand on the bedspread several times. Darla sprang onto the bed before his hand stopped patting. Jack knew the dog had this old soft-soap wrapped around her little paw. The two slept peacefully throughout the night.

CHAPTER 16

▼

An unusually pleasant spring leaped into summer. By early June most days were hot and dry, which was expected since the *Farmer's Almanac* had forecast it. Many a warm evening found Jack in the Fletcher's barn, puttering on the motorcycle. He changed the plugs, oiled and greased the throttle and the brake cable. He checked clearances, bearings, the magneto point setting and replaced gaskets. A friend on his work crew suggested Jack contact Bob's Indian Service Shop, in Etters, Pennsylvania. They seemed to know everything there was to know about the Indian motorcycle. Jack talked with someone in the shop several times a week and planned a day trip there when the bike was up and running.

During all the weeks of restoration Jack had not once tried to start the motorcycle. He assured himself that the only reason for delay was to make sure the bike was ready but as restoration neared completion, Jack began to find many insignificant details that he felt needed attention. Settings were adjusted second and third times, nuts and bolts were painstakingly cleaned and oiled, more saddle soap was applied to the motorcycle's leather seat and cosmetic trivialities were becoming an unwarranted center of attention. It was not the mechanics of the machine but rather the mechanics of Jack's psyche that were postponing the Indian's maiden voyage.

The beauty clad in red long johns watched from the calendar as Jack worked each night. Her painted smile seemed to grow impatient until Jack stepped up to her late one Friday night and printed, "Start up the Indian tomorrow!" The two exchanged grins of anticipation.

The next morning Jack was up to see the first rays of sunshine pop from behind the distant eastern hilltops. Darla sensed something was different about this particular morning and paced the kitchen as Jack prepared breakfast. He nearly tripped over her while balancing a plate of bacon and eggs and a cup of steaming coffee on his way to the table. "Darla, down!" he snapped and nodded his head toward her small throw rug, near the refrigerator. Her head dropped and her tail curled between her legs as she slunk down on the rug. Jack glanced her way after a few bites of his breakfast. Darla had been looking at him but quickly turned her head and stared at the wall.

"Enough of the games. Come over here," he said—the warmth in his voice perking her ears. Darla trotted over and laid her head on his knee. Jack stroked behind her ears and daydreamed of what the day would bring.

A velvet-voiced radio announcer had just concluded the Farm Report from an old Motorola radio that sat atop the counter when the Shangri-Las broke into their biggest hit. Poor Jimmy…Jack knew he was toast when the girl group screamed for him to, "Look out! Look out! Look out! Look out!" A boy from the wrong side of town and a motorcycle made for a really bad combination and the *Leader of the Pack* was probably pushing up daises in some Hell's Angels' graveyard. Jack gulped down a third cup of coffee, grabbed his keys and was out the door before Darla could play her sad-eyes routine.

In the workshop, Jack talked to the bike like it was a pretty woman. He walked around her several times, wondering if he'd adequately taken care of all the details in preparation for their first date. With the inside of his T-shirt, he wiped a tiny smudge from the mirror. Jack took a shot glass he'd brought with him and added two shots of the Marvel Mystery Oil to the gas tank, which he'd filled the night before. When it entered the combustion chamber and ignited with the fuel, it would vaporize and soak into the carbon buildup in the chamber and valve guides. The carbon would loosen up and eventually blow out through the exhaust. At least the bike was ready, Jack thought. He took a deep breath and pushed her slowly into the driveway.

Jack eased himself into her saddle and patted the gas tank. "Easy girl," he said as he raised his foot to her starter pedal. One of the employees at the motorcycle shop in Pennsylvania had told Jack the starter might kick back like an ornery mule for the first few times. With his hand squeezing the front brake lever, Jack stepped down on the starter and sure enough, she kicked back. Four more tries and nothing. Finally, just as Jack was beginning to worry, the engine turned over. It sputtered and spit. Billows of white smoke welled up from the exhaust pipe. Jack let the engine idle for several minutes, occasionally revving the throttle. The engine slowed. Jack knew she was ready.

With his right foot, Jack engaged the clutch and shifted the 1941 Indian Scout into gear. She lurched forward, startling Jack but by the time they reached the end of the driveway, the motorcycle was gliding smoothly. It had been many years since Jack had been on a motorcycle, making him feel clumsy and unsure of himself. A couple circles around town acquainted Jack with the controls and had the engine purring.

East Notch Road meandered through hills and meadows. A small stream wove in and out of view of the highway and several dairy farms dotted the landscape with herds of Holsteins. Jack eased the motorcycle through sweeping curves in the road as curious cows chewed their cuds, watching this loud machine pass their serene pasture. At the base of a steep hill, he opened her engine up, unsure how she would respond. The motorcycle's 75 cubic inch engine had more than enough "umph."

Jack had intended to wear the helmet he'd found in the workshop, but in the excitement of the moment, it still hung on a hook, waiting for the next ride. The engine puffed its chest, popping buttons and rippling with power. To the summit of the hill, the bike carried its rider without so much as one knock or sputter. Jack's hair shot back like the headdress feathers of the Indian on the gas tank. His face tingled—warm summer air biting gently as it passed. "Whoa," he said, backing off the engine as they crested the hill.

A valley painted in the rich greens of maple, hemlock, pine and grain spread out between the hills in front of them. For a moment Jack considered pulling off the road to gaze down at the beautiful vale but he knew where he wanted to be. Through the little hamlets of Richburg and Bolivar he rode. A couple of old men waved from a park bench and gave him longing smiles.

Jack turned the motorcycle from the main road and headed into forested hills. At times the limbs of majestic maples reached across the back road to touch the limbs of a sibling tree, that had been separated long ago by the macadam reef. Sunlight flickered through the outstretched branches, trying vainly to touch the machine as it slipped by.

Finally, Jack approached an unnamed dirt road and slowed the motorcycle to a crawl. Leaves and puddles covered the rutted road and at one point Jack considered turning back. But in a memory, clouded by time, the journey's end was just around the next bend in the road. In a clearing of grass that had been matted from tire tracks, Jack stopped the motorcycle. He walked the bike a couple feet to a spot where the kickstand could rest on top of a flat rock.

"I'll be back," he said. The bike still needed some cosmetic work but there in the sunshine she stood with a spirit of her own.

The woods had changed a great deal. Saplings had become great trees and thickets filled in once open spaces. A short distance down the road a path cut into the woods. Brambles of blackberries skirted both sides but the path itself was still passable. A minute later Jack stood there as awestruck as he had been the first time he had seen these prehistoric behemoths. His high school science teacher had called them "glacier conglomerates". Trees had grown around this house-size rock, hiding it from a clear view but there it stood, marking the exact spot where an ancient glacier had come to rest.

About a dozen similar rocks marked the hilltop near where Jack stood but none held the memories that this gargantuan boulder did. The base of one section of the rock sloped sharply inward, exposing the earth beneath it. Black coals marked the spots where campfires had warmed unknown adventurers. Jack grinned to think that the tradition of partying under the rock had survived all these decades.

Once or twice each summer the secret would spread, "Party at the Rock tonight." By nightfall, every teenager in the town would know all the important details and a caravan of jalopies would weave their way through the forested back roads—their headlamps cutting the darkness like a chorus line of fireflies. A campfire was always burning by the time Jack arrived. A quiet kid everyone knew as Coal Dust invariably tended it. By evening's end, the toothless boy would have black soot smeared over every inch of his face. Jack guessed Coal Dust actually took pride in scaring an unsuspecting young girl with his maniacal smile in the eerie light of a campfire.

In a light rain, the rock's overhang could shelter a dozen partygoers and the need to stay dry would make things quite cozy. Jack thought of a girl named Nora, who had cuddled with him under a smelly wet blanket there one night. They had kissed and watched shadows dance across the face of the Rock. A blue-jay screeched overhead and the images evaporated. Jack stepped up to the Rock and ran his hand over its bumpy surface. The Rock's long journey to this final resting-place had likely been mundane, but if it could speak it would surely tell some interesting tales of the last hundred years.

In the distance, a rodline sent two high pitched squeaks through the forest then repeated them again and again. Jack had worked these lines when he was fresh out of high school. In those days the oil fields flowed with rich Pennsylvania crude and a boy could make a decent living working long hours there. The rod-lines had to be kept greased at those spots where they rubbed against the log supports under them. At one end a powerhouse, driven by a huge diesel engine, would push then pull the iron rods not more than four or five feet. This supplied the power that raised and lowered the pump jacks on the other end of the rods, lifting black gold from deep within the earth.

Just over a couple of hills, the little town of Cuba had been the first location in North America where any mention of oil had been made. In 1627 a Franciscan Missionary, Joseph DeLa Roch D'Allion, described seeing oil literally seep from the ground. The Seneca Indians inhabited this land at that time and had used the crude oil as a topical medicine. They would harvest it by throwing blankets into a pool of oil then after retrieving the blanket would wring the oil from it and into earthen vessels. Before the Senecas, the Wenro tribe had settled in this area during the early 1600's and derived their name from the Huron word, Wenrohronon, meaning "the people of the place of floating scum." A monument now marked the sight of what the townsfolk called, "The Famous Oil Spring."

The Flanagans and these oil fields had been intertwined for many years. Jack's grandfather was a flamboyant oilman, who often strutted around some of the finer establishments in Wellsville, his hometown, showing off a three-piece suit and gold watch he wore. One oil well that he owned had been very profitable but its success was short-lived. Grandfather Flanagan had died poor, living his final years in the Almshouse in Angelica. Jack's father worked in the oil fields when Jack was young, and later at the Quaker State Oil Refinery in Bolivar. As Jack stood listening to the squeaking rodline, he realized the vein of oil that ran through the Flanagan bloodline would end with him. He looked back at the Rock and wondered if Kate had ever seen this spectacle. Someday he would bring her here and tell her stories.

The motorcycle kicked up some mud on the way out of the woods. An urge to fishtail the bike slipped into Jack's mind but maturity quickly transformed the urge into a bad idea. His brother had done that many times with Jack clinging to his back in nervous excitement but they were just boys. As he neared the paved road, an unexplainable twitch in his wrist gunned the throttle and the motorcycle's back tire spun wildly from side to side. Dirt and gravel shot into the air and the bike's engine growled. Jack slowed the wild machine to a stop at the intersection, looked both ways and seeing no other vehicles, broke into a boyish grin.

All the way back home Jack thought of improvements he'd make on the motorcycle and of trips he'd take over the summer. A weekend ride to Poughkeepsie cemented itself in his plans. The warmth of Kate's body squeezed tightly against his as they rode to some secluded spot in the beautiful Hudson Valley was the last thought Jack had before he saw the lights.

Red, white and blue lights flashed out a warning in the road ahead. A fire truck, police car and ambulance formed a semicircle around something totally obscured from view. Jack slowed the motorcycle to a crawl, straining to catch a glimpse of the cause of all this excitement. A fireman stood in the middle of the road in a shiny yellow slicker, ready to direct traffic around the scene. He looked between the emergency vehicles; his stern face seemed wrought with worry. As Jack inched closer, the fireman snapped his head around, startled by the motorcycle. He motioned Jack to pass but patted one hand through empty air. The gesture of caution was not necessary but Jack still nodded in appreciation as he passed the volunteer. Shards of glass glimmered on the pavement. The smell of gasoline hung in the air and another fireman walked toward Jack with a street broom. Between the ambulance and police car, the bottom side of pickup truck came into view; its front tire still rotated slowly, six feet above the rutted shoulder of the road. On top of the rolled vehicle an open space yawned skyward where a door had been earlier. The hood of the truck rested against the barkless blonde wood of a sugar maple. Cast off in a ditch near the fire truck, a light blue door lay among weeds. A bolt of terror leaped through Jack's head and zigzagged its way down his spinal cord. "Shit," he moaned, staring at the door of Bob's truck.

Jack could see the back of the ambulance was open as he hurried around the fire truck. Dizzying lights danced over the top of the ambulance. The backs of two people were bent over a gurney that rested in the back of the ambulance. One wore a white starched shirt and the other was in flannel. "Bob," Jack choked out, but the flannel shirt didn't move.

The vision of Martha trying vainly to smother uncontrollable laughter in the church flashed across Jack's mind. He placed his hand on his best friend's shoulder. Panic monopolized Bob's eyes as he turned to his friend. He squeezed them closed and tears trickled down his beefy cheeks. "She's alive," he whispered.

Inside the ambulance Jack could see her body wrapped in a snow-white sheet. Crimson poke-a-dots violated the linen's purity and made Jack feel as if he were intruding. He felt like a teenage boy gawking at a rack of girlie magazines—knowing he should look away but slow to respond. A paramedic was leaning over Martha, obscuring her face. The end of the stethoscope that hung from his neck rested on her chest. Jack imagined he heard a heartbeat.

A gunshot rang out then echoed through the valley. Bob stood frozen—immune to the noise—shock dulling every sense. Jack turned to see a policeman holstering a pistol, staring down at a deer that lay lifeless near the blue truck door.

"We're going to Cuba General," Bob said. Each word he spoke seemed to puncture his spirit more deeply than the previous one.

"She's unconscious," he added and the big man brushed tears from his cheek.

Jack embraced him. This friend who often appeared bigger than life now felt diminished—lifeless in Jack's arms. One of the men in the white uniforms slammed the back door of the ambulance. The sound slammed into Jack's ears, like the lid of a casket being closed in a funeral parlor. Over Bob's broad shoulder, Jack could see the ambulance attendant. He was an unshaven man with bedroom slippers on his feet. Most likely he had rushed from what he thought would be a leisurely Saturday at home. The fire whistle often caught volunteers off-guard.

"I'll follow you there," Jack said, stepping back. Bob nodded in silence then climbed into the front seat of the ambulance.

A tidal wave of thoughts flooded Jack's head—all cloudy and incomplete. Red and white lights flashed atop the ambulance, rotating inside the gumball machine. The tears on Bob's cheeks, the tongue hanging from the dead deer's mouth, the pulpy wood on the tree trunk, the smell of hot rubber, Pastor Ingles message of hope, the taste of Tennessee sipping whiskey—they all fought for time and space in Jack's brain.

Jack sat on the motorcycle, gazing at nothing; not knowing how he got to the bike. Gravel kicked up as the ambulance pulled from the shoulder of the road and onto the pavement. Jack's best friend sat motionless behind the ambulance window as they passed.

The Indian motorcycle took over. Its rider was more like a spectator than a man in control. As the little caravan sped out of town, Jack gazed at the ambulance's flashing lights. For untold minutes the Indian motorcycle followed the ambulance, carrying an unthinking rider.

A plump, juicy katydid flapped its wings frantically to avoid the oncoming machine. The bug was drastically outsized but would leave the world of the living in splendor. The "Splat!" left legs, wings, antennae and green juices strewn over the insect's final resting-place.

Jack shuddered in pain and grasped his forehead. His fingertips probed for the bullet's entry point but all they found were bug innards. His eyes welled with tears that trickled to his cheeks. As the wind swept over his face, his skin stung. The tracks of his tears felt cool. Red and white lights shot to the core of his brain, giving his consciousness a boot on the ass in the process. The ambulance hugged the double solid line on a curve in the road. Jack banked the Indian into the curve with such fluidity that he felt like he was riding a chairplane at an amusement park he visited as a boy. He saw the white lines in the road—ski tracks on black powder. The edge of a field of timothy bowed then stood from the side of the road, as the ambulance stirred the air. Jack now saw everything with crystal clarity.

He glanced at his feet as they glided over asphalt five inches below. Lowlands to his left were filled with rich muck and swamp plant life. Their earthy smells wafted across the roadway and mixed with the scent of wild strawberries. Cattails bumped their brown heads against each other and several red-winged blackbirds clung to their tops. At that moment a transcendent spirit flowed between the Indian motorcycle and Jack. He realized it would be impossible to share this feeling, this indescribable sense of knowing his place, with anyone. *Martha will be all right!* There was no way of knowing this but Jack perceived it with certainty.

The ambulance slowed as it approached the outskirts of Cuba, a village not any bigger than Friendship but it had a hospital. With the siren announcing their arrival, the ambulance and the motorcycle pulled into the emergency entrance of Cuba Hospital. Jack parked the bike in the small parking lot and hurried inside to wait.

Bob's eyes were puffy and bloodshot. After he attended to paperwork at the front desk, the two friends sat down in a sterile white waiting room shrouded in silence. Nurses in rubber-soled shoes walked by; their soundless steps conjuring images of angels walking on clouds. Drab organ music filtered into the little alcove. A sleepy lullaby was more annoying than soothing. Tinny speakers hung loosely on stark walls rattled with every low note. An old man, bent over a walker, shuffled by, tapping a crooked finger in time with the music. Jack and Bob both gazed blankly at him then simultaneously they turned their heads to avoid the sight provided by the old man's untied hospital gown. Bob grimaced, then grinned.

"I didn't kiss her good bye," he said. "She was heading over to Susan Shaw's place to make some plans for the church bazaar. I don't know exactly what happened but I guess that deer must have jumped in front of her."

Jack could see a mixture of puzzlement and pain painted on his friend's face. Then Bob's eyes shifted their gaze to Jack's forehead. "What the hell happened to you?" Bob asked.

For an instant the question had no meaning then a faint tingle reminded Jack of the collision. "A kamikaze bug. The damn thing must have weighed a pound. Got my attention right quick." Jack touched his forehead and could feel the dried insect remnants.

Someone behind them cleared his throat and the two turned to see a short man in a white doctor's coat. His dark hair was thinning; cut short and perfectly groomed. He peered through silver rimmed glasses.

Vincent Chompa was no stranger to either man. He had delivered Bob's daughter and been Jack's family physician for years. The neutral look on his dark complected face gave no hint of what he had to say. Doctor Chompa folded his hands, cleared his throat again and in a deep, deliberate voice began: "Martha has sustained a severe, grade 3 concussion. She's also lost a great deal of blood from the laceration on her head. There's a compound fracture of the fibula. These are the major complications and there are various other minor injuries but nothing we've seen here is life threatening."

The breath Bob had been holding shot out in a gust of relief. He dropped his head and started to weep. Doctor Chompa placed his hand on Bob's shoulder and softly said, "She'll be okay. Its going to be awhile before she's back on her feet but we have every reason to believe Martha will make a full recovery. Right now she's conscious but needs rest. Before I give her a sedative you can see her...but only for a few minutes."

Bob smiled through tears. Jack patted him on the back and said, "Is there anything you need done around the house...or anybody you want me to call?"

"I don't think so...Oh yeah, would you mind letting Susan Shaw know what's happened. She's probably worried sick and with the ambulance and all—she's probably thinking the worst."

"I'll call her when I get home," Jack said.

"Thanks Jack...Thanks a lot," Bob placed his hand on Jack's shoulder and offered a weak smile.

"Call me if you think of anything you need done or if you just need to talk. I'll be at home tonight and will see you here tomorrow."

Bob turned and walked toward a pair of swinging doors where Doctor Chompa was waiting. As the doctor and Bob disappeared behind the doors, Jack raised his head skyward. "Thank you," he whispered.

On the ride home Jack felt relieved, knowing that Martha would be all right. The time he had spent among the boulders in the woods had been relaxing, then things had spun wildly out of control. His nerves had worked overtime since the first sight of the flashing ambulance lights. Now the Indian motorcycle carried him home, it's gentle vibration easing the tension.

Darla playfully pranced out when Jack opened the backdoor. She hesitated, giving Jack a puzzled stare when he called for her to come inside after only a couple minutes of romping in the backyard. Then she dropped her head and walked slowly to the door. "Sorry girl. It's been a long day. I'll make it up to you...promise." Jack called Sarah Shaw with the news, picked at leftovers and sunk into his easy chair, intent on reading the final chapter of *Elmer Gantry*. The western sky still held vestiges of purple and indigo when Jack went to bed. Exhausted, he fell into a deep dreamless sleep and did not wake until church bells announced 9:00 the next morning.

CHAPTER 17

▼

When Jack arrived at the hospital late that morning, a steady stream of familiar faces met him. Word of the accident had traveled at the speed of sound around the little town. As Jack walked quietly into room 144, an elderly, nearly bald woman mumbled in her sleep. On the far half of the semi-private room, the inventory of a small gift shop cluttered every shelf and table. There were helium balloons, baskets of flowers and several boxes of chocolates. Bob sat smiling in an ugly green vinyl covered chair. "Come on into the garden," he said. A large potted philodendron sat next to his head.

"Hello Jack," said a weak voice from the bed.

Martha sat in the hospital bed in a flimsy gown and white linens pulled up to her waist. Her hair was matted down on top and shaved on one side, where dark stitches and yellowish iodine intruded on her scalp. Her left eye was swollen closed; the eyelid marbled in black and blue. A cut had already scabbed on her lower lip.

"You gave us quite a scare, woman. How are you feeling today?" Jack asked.

"Well, I'm not ready to go out bowling tonight...but other than a throbbing headache and painful breathing—not bad."

"I called Susan Shaw last night. She was worried sick," Jack said.

"Susan dropped in for a short visit his morning," Bob said. "That lady is wound tight. She's worried how things will get done for the church bazaar. Now that's something she ought to know well—the bazaar part, I mean."

"Robert...be kind. You know her heart's in the right place." Martha said.

A loud bang on the door startled all three of them. "Are you in there, darling?" called a squeaky voice. A wisp of a woman in a wheelchair was being pushed on a collision course with the foot of the bed. An equally small man, whose head shook severely under a toupee, was pushing the wheelchair, which he seemed to rely on to keep his balance. The hairpiece screamed, "Cheap!" and from all appearances, looked as if, in a prior life, decades ago, it might have kept a beaver warm. At the last second Bob reached out—gently guiding the wheelchair around the edge of the bed.

"Hello, Aunt Francis," Martha said in a loud voice.

The little woman scowled at the two men as if they were encyclopedia salesmen, then turned to Martha with a sugary smile and squeaked, "Oh, you dear girl. Let me get you a doctor."

"He's been here already, Aunt Francis. Says I'll be fine."

The little lady had a dull red fox fur wrapped around her neck. From where he stood to the side of the woman, Jack could see two small ears sticking out of the fur like little teepees in a sea of matted animal hair. A lavender pincushion hat was cocked to one side of Aunt Francis' head. At least half a dozen paper poppies were propped up in the folds of the satin hat—each a lighter shade of red than the one next to it. VFW tags were attached to each flower.

"Hi Uncle Frank," Martha said smiling. The little man returned her pleasant smile. Martha nodded toward Jack. "This is a good friend of ours, Jack Flanagan and you remember my husband, Bob." When she cast the good eye on her husband and found a broad grin filling his face, Martha's good eyelid squeezed nearly shut and her lips turned down. The grin instantly evaporated from Bob's face.

"It's nice to see you again," Bob said.

Uncle Frank grunted an acknowledgment. He never took his eyes off Martha then said, "Well, we heard about the deer attacking you. Glad to see you're not dead." He patted the pincushion hat on his wife's head as he spoke, knocking it even more askew and continued, "For now, they're keeping us in that home back of here. Once our mansion is finished in Florida we're moving...stock, lock and wheelbarrow to where the sun don't shine!" His bushy eyebrows danced with each word.

Aunt Francis twisted her body to see her husband. "California, it's California...not Florida, you damn fool!" Jack could now see the glass eyes in her fox fur. One drooped from the socket on a yellowing piece of string. Uncle Frank sneered down at his mate then immediately softened his gaze when he saw that she could see his face.

"Yes honey," he agreed—displaying a survival technique he'd finely honed throughout countless battles. When the old woman turned her head toward Martha, the old man mimed the tongue-lashing he'd wished he had given her but not a word escaped his lips. He barked out the last of his silent utterance, snapping his head forward as if to bite his unsuspecting wife. The beaver pelt, which sat atop his head, slid over barren scalp and came to rest just above his eyebrows.

An attendant in a white coat craned his neck from outside the room to see if the visitors he had escorted there were behaving themselves. Bob nodded his way and gave the man an unconcerned look. Aunt Francis and Uncle Frank had been married for nearly sixty years. Their ways had become more eccentric in recent years. Martha now wished she had been better about visiting them in the nursing home, for their good hearts still shone through their peculiar behavior.

After a brief visit, Aunt Francis kissed Martha's hand and said, "You get well, Martha." Uncle Frank turned the wheelchair and began to hum the first few bars of *Seventy-Six Trombones* as he marched toward the door. Both held their heads high on the way out of the hospital room. Martha's good eye welled with tears. Aunt Francis had remembered her name.

The room was left in solemn silence. Thoughts of getting old and the fragility of life crossed each of their minds then Bob's stomach broke the silence with a hungry growl. Jack politely offered to stay with Martha so Bob could run out for a bite to eat.

"Nah, I'm really hooked on the fine hospital food they serve here. Wouldn't want to miss that pureed chicken," Bob laughed. "But I might take a short walk, if you don't mind keeping Martha company."

"Go ahead! I'm sure Martha will love talking about the art of motorcycle maintenance," Jack said.

Martha rolled her eyes and snapped, "Sit down here Jack Flanagan. I'm going to catch you up on what's been happening on *The Guiding Light*. You're not going to believe the scandal."

Jack plopped down in a chair next to the bed and feigned a bored yawn. "Hurry back, old buddy," he pleaded to Bob.

"I do need to paint the garage...but I'll be right back after that," Bob said with a devilish smile then tiptoed to the door, like a thief trying to make a clean get-away.

Martha moaned in apparent pain. She placed both palms on her temples and sniffled several times.

Bob stepped back toward the bed, watching her in concern. The pained look on Martha's face softened to an angelic little grin. "Don't be long, Sugarbear," she whispered through kissy lips then batted the eyelashes, on her one good eye, at him.

"Yes dear—I won't be long," he said.

"You never are!" Martha said and began to giggle.

As he turned to leave, Bob made a mental note to see Dr. Chompa about the dosage of morphine Martha was receiving. A privacy curtain was pulled completely around the bed on the other side of the semi-private room. As Bob passed by it, a weak voice from within snickered out, "She's bad." Bob silently agreed and walked into the hallway. He breathed in a lungful of air, permeated with the smell of Lysol and urine.

For as long as he could remember, Jack had never felt at ease within the confines of a hospital. There had been a couple times when an overnight stay there might have been advisable but he had always opted to "tough it out" with the assistance of friends, family and an occasional visit to the doctor's office. He now strained to carry on a conversation. The weather could only be stretched so far until it failed miserably to fill the gaps in small talk.

Martha fidgeted and finally blurted out, "Okay Jack, what's the dirt on this Fletcher woman? Are you serious about her?"

"She's a very good friend and I—I don't know. We write a lot and I do miss her but we haven't been together enough for me to really know anything for sure."

"Well, how are you going to figure all this out?" Martha asked.

"That's going to be difficult, with us being so far apart," Jack answered.

"Did you lose your driver's license?" she asked.

The puzzled look on Jack's face conjured up a single word thought in Martha's head: "Men…"

"Well, get your butt in gear, or that damn motorcycle in gear, and go out and see her! She's probably dying to get her hands on you."

A stupefied gaze on his face brought out more inquiry. "What's holding you back?"

"Well, my job and ahhh…"

"Have you ever heard of weekends? And Bob will be giving the work crew most of this week off, while he baby-sits me. Can you think of a better time? Bob can watch Darla. He'll love the company."

Cogs started turning and excuses seemed flimsy. Jack made up his mind he'd at least think about the possibility, but felt the ultimate decision should be made in the quiet of his own home. Plans for a trip like this could be complicated he thought and they were best made without distractions.

"I'll go!" he blurted out and slapped his knee to finalize the decision. "I better run it by Bob though…since he'll have two girls to watch after."

"I've never known Robert to have any qualms about girl watching. He's probably checking out that busty, blonde nurse as we speak," Martha said—her face etched in seriousness.

"Why…I've never known Bob to give another woman so much as a sideways glance," Jack said.

"Yeah, right!"

A more serious look overtook Jack's face. "You gave us quite a scare. I'm not sure if Bob mentioned it but…I was riding into town on the motorcycle—finally got her up and running—when I saw the ambulance. Damn, I was sick with worry when I realized it was you inside. Honestly, I was afraid to look. You and Bob have been like family and…" Jack's eyes began to water and he looked away.

"Sorry I caused such a stir. It was so strange. I wanted Bob to know I was all right but everything was moving in slow motion and it didn't even feel like I was part of it. It was like I was inside a bubble and things could filter in slowly but nothing could get out."

Jack patted her hand. A sudden pang of sadness swept over him. Twists and turns in his life had left him childless. The thought of a father sitting in a similar hospital room; next to a sick child; comforting his little one back to health, sent a stream of emptiness flowing through Jack's heart.

"Tell me more about Kate. I used to see her around town but never really got to know her," Martha said.

"Well, between Kate and that mutt of hers, they did get me to sober up. They both deserve medals for that. It's nice now waking up in the morning and actually remembering going to bed the night before. And I really feel at ease when I'm with her. There was never a time when I thought I'd need to go out of my way to impress her. I suppose only time will tell if we're completely compatible," Jack said.

"Jack! For God's sake, cut to the chase. Does she breathe hard when you kiss her? Do you tingle when you hold her? Is she still beautiful in the morning?" The twinkle in Martha's eye seemed to be dulled a bit, like she might have had several glasses of Mogan David.

"Listen old friend…Kate and I have only been together a few times. She's three hundred miles away and we do have some self-control, not to mention morals, unlike some…" The words trailed off in an innocent grin.

Martha stuck her index finger deep into her mouth and seemed to choke on something sicky-sweet. "Well, well—Father Flanagan in the flesh. It's always a pleasure to meet such a fine upstanding man of the cloth."

"I'll catch you up on this soap opera drama when I get back from Pough-keepsie. I'm sure you would make a fine counselor...for some sex fiend," Jack said and they both laughed.

"Sounds like you know what you're doing. Just make her happy, Jack. And make sure you're happy yourself." A weak smile on Martha's dried lips made her suddenly look very tired. Her good eye fluttered several times then she faded into sleep.

In the back of his mind, Jack began piecing together details of the little things that needed to be done before he could take this trip. Every since he first laid eyes on the Indian, Jack had been juggling the pros and cons of traveling across the state to see Kate. The void in his life was unmistakable but missing pieces were recently falling into place.

Footsteps interrupted his travel plans. Pastor Ingles nodded to Jack as he tip-toed into the room. "How is she?" he whispered. In one hand he held a lovely bouquet of wild flowers and in the other a Bible. His gawky features were soft-ened by the look of concern that filled his face.

"She's doing well...just fell asleep. I think the painkillers have got the best of her," Jack said.

The preacher laid the flowers down on the bedside table and stood at the end of the bed. He rested his hand on Martha's foot that hid under the bedcovers.

"Let's pray for her," the preacher said.

Jack bowed his head.

"Merciful Father, please shelter our dear friend in your hands. Give her doc-tors divine guidance from above. Make her whole again, so that we might all share her goodness and reap the rewards of her devotion to you. Amen."

Jack added his own "Amen" then raised his head.

"What are the doctors saying?" Pastor Ingles asked.

Jack shared all that he knew then pulled a second chair up next to the hospital bed. The two men sat by the bed, watching Martha sleep. "How's Bob doing?" the preacher asked.

On cue, the big man walked into the room. "Well, speaking of the devil," Jack said. "He's not really that bad," Jack added for the preacher's benefit.

Bob greeted Pastor Ingles then began to fill him in with more medical details. Jack waited patiently and when the conversation slowed said, "Think I'll get going now. I might be taking a little trip but we can talk about that later. Tell Martha I'll be praying for her."

"Where are you thinking of going?" Bob asked.

"I thought I might take a motorcycle trip out to Poughkeepsie," Jack answered.

Bob bridled his desire to tease his friend about the motive behind the trip and simply said, "Ohhhh." His face was filled with that look like he knew everything but, in un-Bob-like fashion, kept his mouth shut. "I guess you'll be needing someone to watch that mongrel?"

After giving Jack just enough time to feel uncomfortable, Bob said, "Don't worry—she'll be fine with me. I still have that old doghouse of Muggs out back. Darla can stay there in the daytime and have the run of the house at night. She'll love it!"

Jack knew she would. "Thanks," he said and walked from the room. "I'll give you a call tonight."

Kate was surprised to hear Jack's voice again that evening. He had called the night before to give her the news of Martha's accident and they had continued to talk for nearly an hour. Now she thought something was wrong by the way that he seemed to be thinking of each word before he spoke it. Her nerves tingled when he finally got out the question, "How'd you like some company? I have a few days off and Bob offered to watch Darla. If it's okay, I could ride up and be there by tomorrow afternoon."

"Tomorrow afternoon." The words rang in her ears as she looked around her apartment. It was in dire need of some aggressive cleaning. Kate was in the middle of doing inventory at work and tomorrow would be her busiest day of the month.

"Yeah, tomorrow will be great. I won't be off work until late in the afternoon though. We'll have to go out for dinner," she said.

"That will be fine. I'm going to ride the bike out," Jack said. The statement sounded very question-like.

An animated picture of her father's motorcycle with her clinging to a scruffy biker jettisoned through Kate's mind. She hadn't seen the bike in years and imagined one of those big choppers James Dean might have terrorized little old ladies with.

"I'll pick up a helmet on the way out," Jack added.

The mental movie continued in Kate's head. She was wearing a Buffalo Bills helmet, complete with chin strap, face mask and an oversized autograph of Cookie Gilchrist scrawled across the side. She shuddered.

"You be careful riding that thing. I don't want to be picking gravel out of your..." and she stopped, not wanting to sound mother-like or crass, "pockets,"

Kate added. "The Shady Rest Apartments, where I live, are on West Elm Street, just off Route 9 as you're coming into town. You can't miss them.

"I'm anxious to see you Kate. Is there a decent motel near your place?" Jack asked.

"Oh yes! The lovely Bates Motel is just down the street. Some nice showers, I understand," Kate joked.

"Sounds good," Jack said, totally missing any humor. "I'll take the scenic route and see you late in the afternoon. Bye."

"Be careful..." she said and before she could explain her joke about the Bates Motel, the phone clicked.

CHAPTER 18

▼

The Indian motorcycle engine purred as it started the long journey. Jack could still see Darla's sad eyes looking through the screen door. "She's pretty good at that sympathy act," Bob had said. "Looks like my mother-in-law at our wedding." Jack knew she'd be fine but missed her anyway. Dew glimmered on the wild phlox that bordered the rural roadway. In small hamlets friendly people waved as they stopped to watch the Indian pass. In Wellsville, Jack picked up Route 17, which would take him nearly all the way to Poughkeepsie. The road had a familiarity born not only from the numerous trips Jack had taken to Corning, Elmira and occasionally Binghamton but also from the subtle way the two-lane highway caressed the hilly landscape. The interstates and many secondary roadways were undoubtedly designed with a straightedge but Route 17 wove its way through emerald foothills and plush valleys like it had been stroked there with an artist's brush.

The Indian felt like a svelte black panther under Jack. Its growl was deep and almost imperceptible…but between each smooth stroke of the engine, inauspicious power lurked, ready to pounce at the slightest touch of the throttle. This highway seemed tailor-made for such an animal, allowing it to unwind on straight-aways and glide through banked curves in the road.

In a lush carpet of greens, Dyke Creek glimmered to the south. Over eons of flooding and meandering, it had created a rich flood plain, which now separated Elm Valley from Andover. On the outskirts of Corning, the Chemung River flowed gracefully. These radiant waterways were all perfect appetizers for the breathtaking Susquehanna. The regal river sported playful whitecaps then would widen and slow to a lazy crawl. Two men in hip waders stood thigh-deep in the water, casting red and white lures into a still pool that had pocketed itself on the bank of the river. Their bodies froze in anticipation of a trophy fish striking the lures that bubbled across the indigo water. Each man glanced up at the sound of the powerful engine, nodded, then focused his attention back on the river. A wall of evergreens shot heavenward on the south side of the road, commencing on a summit where the trees seemed to touch the clouds. Jack thought about Kate and imagined them riding together along this scenic highway.

With little effort, the concept of time and thoughts of the creations of man-kind were pushed from Jack's consciousness, leaving his memory a tabula rasa for recording the magnificent details nature was unfolding round every bend. The Indian hugged the gray asphalt and took control of the journey. Exhilaration pierced every pore in his skin as Jack glided down a tunnel of picture frames, each more beautiful than the previous, each taking him further into the picture. The rolling hills soon began squeezing closer and climbing higher as he rode into the picturesque Catskills.

The roadway cut unobtrusively through mile after mile of evergreen forests. Pines and spruce trees shrouded hundreds of mountain lakes. Their Indian names paid tribute to tribes that walked among them in a time before roads. An omni-present, majestic spirit still enveloped the mountain range. The Indian motorcy-cle slipped proudly yet insignificantly through the land of its namesake.

It was still late morning and the extra time Jack had allowed for this trip would be better spent here than wasting away several hours in Poughkeepsie, waiting for Kate to return from work. So shortly beyond Monticello, Jack turned from friendly Route 17 and let the wind guide him through the mountains. As he rode over the crest of a nameless summit, sunshine reflected off the surface of a tranquil lake. Several small sailboats played tag in the sparkling water. A crack in time might have revealed young braves racing across the lake in birch canoes. Attached to a fir tree, a small wooden sign announced Wanaksink Lake. The name stuck in Jack's mind because of the odd syllable "sink" and its poor associa-tion with any body of water. Neat little cottages surrounded by summer flowers stared across the still waters. This romantic setting could certainly beckon lovers to visit and to leave the rest of the world behind. Jack decided to ask Kate later that day if she knew anything about Wanaksink Lake.

Tiny mountain towns and rural roadways marked the haphazard sidetrack Jack was taking. The sun was nearly overhead giving no clues which direction his travels were taking him but early in the afternoon a road sign heralded Route 209—the road Jack had been looking for. He remembered it ran to Route 44, which would take him to her.

Now, his mind was on Kate. Nature's beauty would now have to take a back-seat to his daydreams of her. Just after crossing the Hudson River, Jack spotted a motorcycle dealer and pulled in to look for a helmet for Kate. A blue and red model was the closest he could come to anything feminine and it had the Buffalo Bills colors to boot. Jack placed the helmet in his saddlebag and was off to find West Elm Street.

The Shady Rest Apartments sounded so peaceful, yet Jack's chest pounded with anxiety as he parked the motorcycle. Jack began piecing together something witty to say to Kate as he walked toward the complex. When she opened the door he decided to greet her with, "It's been so long...I almost forgot how lovely you are." He repeated the line several times under his breath.

The walkway to the apartment was lined with large lilac bushes; their withered blossoms hid beneath heart-shaped leaves. Occasional park benches were nestled in small alcoves among the lilacs. Jack surveyed the entranceways to the apartments, each sporting a sign with a sequence of apartment numbers. There it was, directly in front of him. He wiped the sweat from his palms as he walked.

"Hello there, big boy. Looking for someone?"

The voice startled Jack and he quickly turned toward the source. There she sat, on a bench obscured by the lilac bushes and most definitely lovelier than he had remembered her. Kate's golden hair dropped over one shoulder and looked like sunshine flowing against her yellow and white sundress. The neckline of the dress dipped modestly but enough to show a little of her tanned breasts; a wisp of goosebumps covering them. Her lips broke into an impish grin as she watched Jack's eyes feast over every inch of her. A pair of sandals lay in front of the bench. Her legs were curled under herself and soft, peach-colored polish covered her toe-nails. Kate swung her legs to the ground and stood in front of him.

"Well...Hi," he stammered. His steel blue eyes were filled with the radiance of the woman he missed so much.

Kate reached out and took his hand between hers. "Is that all you have to say after all these months?" she teased.

"Well...No," he continued. "I ahhh...Wow! You look lovely." The word "lovely" was all he could remember from his hurriedly rehearsed greeting.

"How was the ride?" she asked.

"It was beautiful. There are a few places you have to see," he said.

"I've been traveling Route 17 for quite a few years now and it never ceases to amaze me just how beautiful this part of the state is. You'll have to come out again this fall, when the leaves have changed color," she said. For several seconds the distant look in Kate's eyes reflected the memory of leisurely drives amid rainbows of foliage.

"Let's go inside. You look hot and there's a pitcher of lemonade in the refrigerator with your name on it." She reached up and gently brushed a lock of hair off his forehead.

As the two strolled toward the apartment, Jack wrapped his arm around Kate's shoulder. She walked barefoot, the sandals swinging in her hand. Jack followed her into the cheery apartment. Kate closed the door behind them. Neither spoke a word. The quiet that bathed them was interrupted only by the sound of Kate's sandals hitting the floor. Jack slipped off his leather riding jacket and tossed it over an arm of the couch. Kate faced him then extended her hand. Jack took it between his own hands and pulled gently. She stepped close, her breasts brushing against his blue denim shirt. The faint aroma of Old Spice mixed with the earthy scent of leather filled her head. Jack raised her hand slowly and pressed it to his lips. As he kissed the back of her hand, Jack could smell the lotion that softened her skin and an alluring musky perfume. He turned her hand and lightly caressed her palm with his lips. Kate could feel any control she had been able to muster begin to slip away. She pulled her hand free and nervously smoothed little wrinkles from the shoulders of his shirt; her eyes piercing his; searching for feelings that might be hidden within his soul.

Their minds raced in unbridled abandon. Neither put their thoughts into words. Kate finally broke the silence. "Oh, Jack," was all she whispered then threw her arms around his waist and buried her head against his chest. Jack pulled her close, worried he might hurt her with the long overdue hug. He felt her breasts raise slightly against his stomach with each breath she took. For a moment she was still then slowly raised her head. Her eyes were closed. Jack lowered his head, lifted Kate to her tiptoes and began kissing her, softly at first but with self control severely weakened by months without her. She parted her lips and teased him with her tongue. Their mouths locked in a prolonged passionate kiss. Jack could taste the subtle sweetness of strawberries from her lipstick, his tongue starved for more of her. Both gasped for air amid torrents of wet hungry kisses. Kate's fingers pulled to draw Jack closer; her nails sinking into the skin on his back. Their tongues intertwined in insatiable desire.

The sound ripped through the room, startling both of them. On the second ring the two pulled apart. Kate drew a deep breath and held it while the phone rang two more times. Her shoulders dropped as she walked to the end table where the telephone sat next to a basket of yellow silk flowers. She cleared her voice and raised the receiver to her ear. "Hello?"

Kate looked sadly at Jack. Her eyes rolled in disappointment and her wet lips broke into a weak smile. "Hi Honey…yes he's here."

Kate's cheeks were pink. Jack touched his chin to find the half-day-old stubble a bit rough. He looked down at his jeans to see them dusty and spotted with the remnants of bugs that had been in his way earlier that day. *I could use a shower.*

"That's okay. We can have lunch tomorrow instead. I'll call you in the morning," Kate said into the phone. "Love you," and she hung up. A second later Kate took the phone receiver from the cradle and laid it on the end table.

"That was my daughter, Sarah," Kate said. "We had planned on dinner this evening but her husband, Adam is stuck at the store with some company big-wig. Guess we'll have to eat alone tonight," she added with a devilish grin. "There's a nice Italian place just around the corner. How's that sound to you?"

Yeah, that sounds great. I'll need to get cleaned up," Jack said.

"You can do that here or back at your motel…whichever is easier," Kate said.

"I guess I better get checked in there. I can shower and shave there then be back here in a hour if that's good with you. Where is the motel?"

"Just turn right going out of the parking lot and it's down two blocks on the left. There's a large sign with a bear in some goofy pajamas out front of the place. It's not really the Bates Motel," she said with a smile.

"Shall we ride in style?" The serious look on his face gave way to a crooked grin.

"Sure! Did you find a helmet for me?"

"One any good Bills fan would die for!" Jack said proudly.

The thought of a bloodstained football helmet worn by some brutish Neanderthal crossed her mind but Kate trusted Jack…somewhat. "I can't wait," she said, outwardly enthusiastic, inwardly apprehensive. "See you in an hour," she said and kissed him on the cheek.

She watched him walk down the sidewalk, leather jacket slug over his shoulder and a small triangular patch of sweat on the back of his light blue shirt. There was a detectable bounce in his step that Kate had never noticed before.

They rode the motorcycle to a little Italian restaurant that evening and sat at a cozy table in an intimate corner. The gold flecks in her eyes sparkled as she stared over the flame that flickered atop a red candle—one that had burned for countless other couples. Dried streams of wax wove their way down the side of the rounded wine bottle that held the candle. Sad violin music played in the background, harmonizing with the sounds of silverware clicking against plates and the voices of other diners talking softly. Scents of fresh bread, garlic and oregano intermingled. The aromas and the sight of Kate stirred hunger within Jack. "I'm so glad we're together again," he said. The candle flickered as the words whisked over it. "I'm sorry your daughter and son-in-law couldn't be with us tonight," he lied.

"You'll get to meet them at lunch tomorrow," Kate said. "It's too bad work sometimes interferes with family things." Jack nodded in agreement.

"Speaking of family…Darla gave me a big wet kiss before I left and asked me to pass it on to you. And she gave me that big sad-eyed look just as I was leaving." Jack paused, thinking of the canine friend who had become so much of his life. "She's quite a dog."

"I miss her," Kate said. Her eyes glimmered with the wetness of a tropical jungle pool illuminated by Tiki lights. "I'll try to get out to visit her, and of course you, sometime this fall."

A waiter cleared his throat to catch Jack's attention then handed him a wine list. For a moment Jack froze in speechless indecision. He hadn't touched a drop of alcohol for over half a year, but this night was special. Kate thought that Jack might have struggled with his drinking even though there was much he had never shared with her. His personal demons had remained personal. Jack swallowed and pointed to an eight-dollar bottle under the red wine column on the list. He promised himself this one bottle of wine on this special night would be the limit of his indulgence.

For the next five minutes they talked about family, friends, town gossip and how Martha was doing. But way back in a dark corner of his mind, Jack worried. He rationalized how innocent a couple glasses of wine would be, compared with the massive amounts of whiskey he would consume on bad nights. Back then he had called them good nights, but they surely led to bad mornings.

Another waiter cleared his throat. He was a dark-haired man in a short black jacket and held a bottle of cabernet sauvignon for Jack to see, then handed him the cork. Jack took the cork and glanced across the table. He turned his head slightly but enough to shield his face from the waiter then raised an eyebrow in puzzlement. Kate slowly lifted her hand, as if to deal with an itch that had found its way just under her nose. She held her index finger there for several seconds and stared silently at Jack. He smiled and raised the cork to his nose. "Very nice," he said to the waiter who then filled their glasses with the dark red wine and set the half-full bottle on their table. They both snickered as the waiter walked away.

The first taste of the wine felt bitter on his tongue. Jack held the ruby nectar in his mouth until the bite had subsided then swallowed. Comforting warmth followed the wine down his throat and an intoxicating memory came back to him— how good he felt after a few drinks. He quickly raised the glass to his lips again and as Jack took in a mouthful of the wine, he could see Kate over the rim of the glass. With the glass still between his lips, Jack lowered his head and allowed much of the wine to subtly flow back into the glass. He smiled at Kate and set the glass back on the table.

On Kate's recommendation, Jack ordered veal saltimbocca. When the waiter placed the steaming dish on the table, the aromas of many of the ingredients blended pleasingly up Jack's nose but the predominate smell was that of garlic— rich, strong, pungent garlic. Jack took the first taste of the veal and stopped in the middle of a chew. He closed his eyes and savored the flavors that floated around his mouth.

"Do you like it?" Kate asked. Jack nodded and had to summon conscious effort to keep from attacking the dish.

"Very good...Very good!" he said with a smile.

It was someplace between twilight and complete darkness when the two left the restaurant. There were few cars in the parking lot where the lonely motorcycle sat under a dim streetlight. Jack wiped the light dew from the pillion seat, straddled the bike, and held out his hand for Kate.

"You're quite the gentleman," Kate said. She took Jack's hand then lifted her leg over the little saddle that had been attached to the back fender. The helmet was not something you'd see at a fashion show, but not as bad as expected. Kate snapped the chin strap into place, wiggled to find a comfortable spot on the seat, although no such place existed, and rested her hands on Jack's waist.

With one kick the Indian started. A cool breeze swept over the two as they pulled from the parking lot. She snuggled closer to Jack, wrapping her arms around his chest. His body felt warm pressing against her and Kate thought of that day when she had found him in the woods, nearly frozen. She had done her best to thaw him out. Now it was his turn to give off some heat and return the favor. The wind in her face brought tears to Kate's eyes. She squeezed them shut and pressed her head against his back.

Minutes later Kate felt the motorcycle slow to a stop. As Jack turned off the engine, an envelope of quiet surrounded them. Hand-in-hand the two walked to the apartment in silence. Inside, Kate turned the switch on a small hurricane lamp until only the lower globe was lit. Pale light illuminated only a small part of the room in the soft yellows and pinks of the delicate pattern that adorned the lamp. Kate's rosy cheeks smoothed to a creamy peach in the dull light. Jack stepped toward her; his steel blue eyes locked on her face.

She looked up at him, placing her hands on his slim hips. For a minute her fingertips caressed him through the light cotton shirt he wore then Kate slid her hands under the shirt and rested them just above his belt. Her thumbs started tracing small circles against his skin. With every pass the circles widened. Jack tingled as the path Kate drew on his warm skin dipped under his belt. Her liquidy eyes reflected his passion.

Jack touched her cheek with one hand then inched his fingertips sensually to her ear. His hands were calloused and Jack could barely feel the light contact his fingers made with Kate's ear but her gentle gasps assured him that she surely felt his touch. His other hand stroked her bare shoulder; the soft locks of her hair brushing against the back of his hand. When his little finger slipped under the strap of her brassiere, a breath caught in her throat. The rough skin on his hand sent an erotic chill cascading through her, making the soft, tiny hairs on her arms stand on end. Jack eased his other fingers under the strap; their eyes still locked, but now invaded with wanton desire. Kate raised her chest slightly to meet his touch. The roundness of her full breast quivered under his hand. Jack lowered his other hand and pinched the top button on Kate's dress. He stopped for a moment until Kate nodded her head then he popped the button open. Her tanned breasts bulged under a lacy white bra. Milky white skin was harbored between them.

Kate momentarily turned her head from him and toward the couch behind her. She squeezed her fist around his belt and tugged gently. Several short steps backward and she was at the edge of the couch; her hands still clutching Jack's belt. A loving smile spoke to him as Kate released her grip and sat down on the couch. She took his hands in hers and pulled Jack toward her. Her legs spread, beckoning him to kneel between them.

Jack dropped to his knees; his heart pounding out of control. Kate pulled her hands from him then slowly unbuttoned two more buttons on the top of her dress. She leaned back on the couch and closed her eyes. As she arched her back slightly the cotton dress dropped back, exposing the cups of her bra, which barely held back voluptuous breasts. He leaned toward her, bracing his hands on the back of the couch. Kate turned her head slightly. A pearl earring brushed against her graceful neck. Jack lowered his head, parted his lips and slowly began to kiss a circular path around the earring. His tongue hesitated as his lips pressed against her soft skin. Then he tasted the sweetness and spice of her as he stroked the tip of his tongue behind her ear. Her breasts heaved to meet his chest and she gasped in a breath of air filled with the smell of him. The taste of red wine lingered on her tongue as she kissed his neck, gently at first then ever more consumed by hunger. Kate's fingertips pulled at his back and Jack gave up trying to hold himself above her. Their bodies plunged into one another, moving in a perfect harmony—arousing senses that had been dormant for more time than either wished to remember. Kate thrust her hips upward then cried out in ecstasy when she felt Jack meeting her. "Oh God!" she sobbed. Or perhaps they were his words echoing in her ears. Waves of pleasure flowed over her in a relentless onslaught of erotic thoughts and feelings. Kate grasped Jack's shirt, squeezing her fist over the top button. Any control she had possessed minutes before was quickly waning. Between gasps, a faint whisper escaped her lips. "Yes…yes…" and a loud knock punctuated her plea.

They both froze at that moment, each thinking their own imagination had played a paranoid trick on them. But the second knock erased any doubt and instantly squelched their desire. Jack jumped to his feet in panic. He stared wide-eyed at Kate for clues of what to do next. The word "damn" that she mouthed gave little guidance.

"Mom, are you all right?" a woman's voice called out. And a more desperate knock hit the door.

"Yes, Honey. I'll be right there," Kate called back.

Kate frantically jumped to her feet. In the time it took Jack to tuck in his shirt and run his hand through his hair, Kate had buttoned her blouse, straightened her clothing, fluffed her hair and as she opened the door with one hand, smoothed the makeup on her face with the other. Just as the door began to open, Jack hurriedly reached for the switch on the hurricane lamp. The light brightened considerably at each position he snapped the switch into.

"Come in…come in." Kate's greeting stopped abruptly as the room suddenly fell into total darkness.

She heard one apologetic word float across the room. "Whoops."

Jack fumbled with the lamp switch and finally released it when the lamp was at its brightest. He turned toward the door and greeted the visitor with an awkward smile—the kind that seemed to hurt his face.

"I was really worried, Mom. Your phone has been busy for hours," said the young woman in the doorway.

"This is Jack Flanagan," Kate said. A faint sneer invaded her cordial smile as she pointed to him.

He stepped forward with the grace of a mannequin and extended his hand to the petite woman who had just kissed Kate on the cheek. She smiled politely but hesitated to raise her hand. Her light blue eyes surveyed Jack from head to toe and finally (seeing no immediate threat) shook his hand.

"This is my daughter, Sarah," Kate said.

Sarah gazed about the room, her eyes stopping on the sight of a telephone receiver that lay next to the hurricane lamp. "Sorry to interrupt but I was worried about you, Mom. But I see you're in good hands."

The young woman continued to look about the room as if she might spot a candlestick, a lead pipe, or a noose at any moment. With a crooked grin, Jack stared at Kate but the return smile he was looking for did not materialize. Instead, Kate wrapped her arm around her daughter's shoulder and said, "Would you like a cup of coffee, sweetheart?"

Jack's eyes dropped in dejection then widened in horror at the sight of the buttons on Kate's dress being misaligned. He cleared his throat but failed to get her attention. Just as he was about to tap Kate on the shoulder, Sarah turned toward him. "No thanks, Mom. I can't stay. I'm sure you and Jack have lots to catch up on." She emphasized the word "catch" and made it sound dirtier than it should have.

The room was thick with tension. After several minutes of small talk, Sarah's Napoleonic posture softened and by the time she was ready to leave, mother and daughter were actually laughing.

"It was nice to meet you," Sarah said to Jack. "You be good to my mother." Her smile was sincere but showed a trace of concern.

"It was my pleasure. I'm looking forward to having lunch with you tomorrow," Jack said.

Sarah hugged her mother, said "goodbye", and was gone.

Kate looked emotionless at Jack for several seconds. He touched the top button on his shirt and stared at her dress. "What?" she asked then glanced down at her own buttons. Kate slapped her hand over her open mouth and a muffled, "Damn!" slipped through her fingers. Her eyes widened as thoughts raced across her mind. In desperation, Kate tried to recall if Sarah had given any indication that she had noticed the telltale buttons. Then, gripped with the realization there was absolutely nothing she could do, Kate burst into laughter—tension releasing, belly shaking, laughter.

Jack placed his hand on Kate's shoulder as she bent over, laughing away concern. He shook his head and in a low, scolding voice said but one searing word— "Hussy."

Her sides shook even more and Kate gasped for breath. When she finally stood upright, Jack could see rivers of tears flowing down her face. Her mascara looked like black watercolor applied by a nearsighted schoolgirl. Jack chuckled at first then, seeing the absurdity of worrying, lost control. He pulled Kate into his arms and felt chuckles work their way up to, what a Laugh-O-Meter scale might call, "unrestrained guffawing". She heaved in his arms then held her breath and in her softest, sexiest voice, whispered, "Pervert," in his ear. The two laughed in supportive embrace as time slipped by and the world outside surrendered its meaning. Words lost their necessity. Kate and Jack stood together—cleansed of guilt and concern. They had stepped beyond the "worrying what other's think" stage of their relationship.

His bed at the Long View Motel squeaked as Jack tossed and turned much of the night away. Outside, a neon sign buzzed and cast colorful shadows across the room. The smell of bleach and thoughts of Kate's laughter were the last thing Jack remembered before falling asleep. He held one pillow close to his chest and dreamed of making love to a woman who he hoped was also thinking of him.

The Hitching Post was nothing fancy but the food there had an indescribable quality that kept the regulars coming back for more. Sarah and her husband, Adam, were sitting at a table tucked between a small bar and an electronic bowling machine. Sarah waved and Adam stood when Jack and Kate stepped into the dimly lit room. The bartender smiled at Kate as he buffed a shotglass with his snow-white apron. He nodded toward the table where Kate had already spotted her daughter. Few patrons—busy themselves with baskets of fried shrimp, triple-decker cheeseburgers and mugs of beer—noticed Kate and Jack zigzagging their way to the table in the back.

Adam kissed Kate on the cheek and extended his hand to Jack. "Have you been here long?" Kate asked. The whiskey sour in front of Sarah was nearly gone.

"No, we just got here," Sarah said.

Kate politely introduced the men. As Adam shook Jack's hand, he attempted to grip it firmly but his stubby fingers could barely reach beyond the callused palm. Out the corner of his eye, Jack could see the shiny bottles behind the bar. Several seemed to call out his name, but he ignored them, then pulled back a chair from the table, and waited for Kate to sit. He noticed bottles of catsup, mustard, Tobasco sauce and one with simply an "XXX" proclaiming its potency. Adam looked to be the mustard type. Jack was sure he wouldn't see this milky-skinned man touching the triple-X sauce.

"How was the Long View Motel?" Sarah asked.

"It was fine. Not exactly the Waldorf Astoria but the sheets were clean," Jack said.

"I understand you're in the construction business," Adam said. "What do you do during the winter time?"

Jack debated the merits of being honest—deciding that the fact that he typically drank away most winters was not exactly something that would endear him to Sarah and Adam. "I usually do fine carpentry work...you know, picture frames, jewelry boxes, walking sticks. And some occasional dog-sitting," Jack said and smiled at Kate.

"Oh right. How is Darla?" Sarah asked.

Jack told the story of Darla's run in with the racoon, followed by several other less exciting tales. He described the little things the dog would often do—like resting her head on the arm of a chair until she got his attention, or that contented sigh she always let out just before falling asleep, or the way she would look sadly out a window if he was outside and she wasn't. While Kate listened, she could see every image of the dog. She missed Darla but knew Jack cared for her just as much as she did. In silent admiration Kate watched Jack and knew she would miss him just as much as she missed Darla...or more!

Sarah had two more whiskey sours and Adam lined up four empty beer bottles in front of the now empty basket of shrimp he had attacked. Kate nursed a Sloe Gin Fizz and picked at the pile of fried clams in front of her. Jack drank several glasses of ginger ale, wondering if Sarah and Adam were guessing why. He pushed his chair back a bit from the table and stretched his long legs under it. Their conversation grew happier and louder. Jack began to feel relaxed and told several innocent jokes. (They were not ones he'd heard at work!) The bartender continued to shine his shot glasses and watched the four strangers laugh away most of the afternoon.

In the parking lot, Adam slapped Jack on the back, as if they were old friends. Sarah stood on her tiptoes to plant a polite kiss on his cheek and Kate wrapped her arm around him. She smiled proudly up at him, sensing "the kids" approval. Jack thought the lunch had gone reasonably well, but was glad he would soon get some time alone with Kate. Sarah and Adam followed behind in their Ford Fairlane, as Jack and Kate pulled slowly onto the highway, aboard the motorcycle. Even with the car windows up, the sound of the Indian could be heard after it disappeared beyond a bend in the road.

Kate walked into her apartment and had just set her purse down on the kitchen table when she felt his arms slip around her waist. "They're real nice," he whispered in her ear. "And so is their mom." He squeezed her from behind and softly kissed her ear. The moan he heard was quite different than he had expected. It seemed filled more with pain than with passion.

Kate wiggled from his grasp then held her hands against her stomach. "Owww," she cried and then winced. She quickly brought her hand up to her mouth as her cheeks puffed out. Two words explained her agony as she ran toward the bathroom: "The clams!"

Jack paced around the apartment as distressed sounds filtered from under the bathroom door. The emphatic "No!" he'd heard when he asked if there was "anything I can do", removed any doubt that Kate just wanted to be left alone. On a shelf under the coffee table Jack found a stack of old *Life* magazines. Colorful pictures of Clark Gable, Marilyn Monroe, the Beatles and JFK adorned the covers. Sitting on the edge of the couch, Jack absentmindedly picked up a magazine with Richard Burton and Elizabeth Taylor dressed in glitzy Egyptian-ware splashed on the cover. The muffled sounds of retching, emanating from the bathroom, worried him. But when Jack called out, "can I help?" a curt, phlegmy voice snapped back, "I'm all right!" He thumbed through the magazine, looking at the pictures, too worried to read. A couple of small, perforated baseball cards with images of Mickey Mantle and Roger Maris—the old M&M boys—hid between glossy pages advertising Sunbeam Frypans and Post Cereal. Jack carefully removed each card and slid them into his shirt pocket. He was sure Kate wouldn't mind, but intended to ask her later.

A picture in the magazine reminded Jack of Martha. He wondered how she was doing and decided to call home to find out. "Mind if I use your phone to call Bob?" Jack called through the closed bathroom door. "I'll leave you some money for the charge."

"Just go ahead. Don't worry about the charge." Kate's words were short and it was obvious she was not in the mood to talk.

Bob answered the phone and told Jack the good news that Martha was home. "Doing fine…as demanding as ever," he said. As for Darla, just as Jack suspected, she was being spoiled.

"I'm going back to work tomorrow, but don't worry about it. Take off as long as you want," Bob said. "You usually just slow us down anyway," he kidded. Jack knew that working with even one man short, made for some very long days. There was no way he could extend his stay in Poughkeepsie.

Just as Jack said, "Goodbye," Kate stepped from the bathroom. Her face gleamed with sweat and red splotches covered her cheeks. The sparkle that usually filled her eyes had been washed out and they now looked very tired.

"You got an extra stomach pump out in those saddle bags? I sure could use one now." The words appeared to hurt, as Kate tried to make light of the obvious pain she was in.

"Can I get you something…maybe some Pepto-Bismol?" Jack asked, as Kate eased herself into a well-worn chair. He stepped behind her and gently massaged her shoulders. Even through her cotton blouse, Jack could feel her skin was clammy with perspiration. Now was not the right time for him to mention the coincidence that the clams she had eaten at the Casa Nova might have brought on this condition.

"Yeah, maybe Pepto would help. There's some in the cupboard next to the refrigerator," Kate said. "Jack, I'm sorry you have to play nursemaid. My timing sort of stinks."

Jack quickly retrieved the pink-stuff from the cupboard and a tablespoon from a drawer next to the sink. Had her visitor not been there, Kate might have drunk the medicine directly from the bottle, but she knew the *Vanderbilt Book of Etiquette* would frown on such a departure from the social graces. So instead, with hands shaking, Kate poured three drippy spoonfuls of the wonder drug and slurped them down. A drop of the pink liquid rolled down her chin as she checked the bottle for the proper dosage.

Thoughts of time slipping away crossed Jack's mind. He had planned on leaving the next day, sometime early in the afternoon, and right now it didn't appear that the evening would be filled with romance. The burden of responsibility awaiting him back home battled with his desire to spend more time with Kate. He knew deep inside that he would be saying "Goodbye" to Kate the next day. There would be other times to say the things that needed to be said and to let feelings take them where they may.

Without saying a word, he walked to the sink, found a clean dishcloth hanging next to it and ran cold water over the cloth. After wringing out the excess water, Jack stroked Kate's sweaty face with the cool rag. She closed her eyes and raised her head. A weak smile told her appreciation. "Thank you, Jack," she whispered.

He continued to caress her forehead and the skin near her hairline with a tenderness that slipped well beyond concern for her health. With the cloth rolled tightly around his index finger, Jack stroked her lips. At that moment he knew he wanted to care for her a very long time. "Kate I...I," he said slowly. His brain stumbled, trying to find just the right words. "I hope you're feeling better."

"Yes, I feel I'm in very competent hands, Doctor. Do you need to examine me any further?" she asked playfully. Kate still looked sickly but her mood had certainly improved. Dr. Flanagan's bedside manner had worked its magic. Kate took his hand and held a kiss softly against it. "Jack, I haven't felt this way in a very long time. And I don't mean with the upset stomach. What I do mean is...I really like being with you." She stopped, not groping for words, but allowing time for what she had said to sink in. "I wish we lived closer but, with my job and the lease on this apartment...I guess that's not possible."

"I really like being with you." Those were the last words Jack comprehended. The loving sincerity that Kate had used when uttering that phrase gripped Jack with its naked honesty. She was exposing feelings that were not masked in humor or opaque light-heartedness. Without the aid of whiskey or a joke, Jack knew he needed to say something. His feelings were several rungs higher on the clarity ladder than his vocabulary. Somewhere, there was just the right thing to say, but that phrase hid well in the recesses of uncertainty.

Jack touched her cheek with his fingertips. "Kate...I'll treasure this time I've spent with you." The words echoed in his mind and, for a moment, he had to reassure himself that he had spoken them. The words continued to flow. "There are times, especially at night, when all I think of is you. When it's quiet in the house—sometimes when I'm just about to fall asleep, I can hear you whisper. And I hear you say how much you miss me. Then I'll hear Darla breathing and know there's part of you in her. When I hold my hand against her, and she sighs, that part of you floats into the room. And I'll drift into a dream—not sure if I'm asleep or captured by the thought of you."

He sat down on the edge of the couch and smiled at her. The feelings that had escaped him seemed to carry some of Jack's strength away with them. A familiar sensation swept over him, and, for a moment, the source of it escaped him. Jack almost laughed when he realized the total contentment that now consumed him was exactly how he felt many years ago. It was when he truly loved his ex-wife and after they would make love, Jack would lie in bed, basking in a state of relaxed euphoria.

"What's the matter?" Kate asked. "You look like the cat that just ate the canary."

"Oh, I was just daydreaming," Jack said. The emotional coincidences he was now feeling would be too difficult to explain, so he just left it at that.

"I thought you were the stoic type...that never lost control of his heart? You're getting soft in your old age," she kidded.

"No—I've always been a romantic at heart, but just don't like to wear it on my shirtsleeve. And it's not often that the right person comes along and sparks the Don Juan I keep well hidden." Jack grinned, a bit embarrassed by his own boldness, hoping Kate didn't think he was being boastful.

"Jack...I'm not the steady rock that I might appear to be. There are issues that I've never dealt with well. And there's a reason I'm not living in Friendship right now," she said.

He looked at her questioningly and Kate continued: "There are some ghosts— oh, not real apparitions but they haunt me just the same—and sometimes I'm afraid to even go back there to visit." She swallowed and stared into his eyes with a seriousness he'd never seen in her. "You know I was married but I haven't told you any of the details. I think it's important you hear them."

Jack leaned back on the couch and she began: "His name was Michael and we were very much in love. Both of my parents adored him. I know it's odd, but my father treated Michael more as a son than he treated me as a daughter. When we married in 1939, Michael had just enlisted in the Navy. I became pregnant with Sarah while he was on leave. At the time I was envious that he had just received orders that he would be stationed in Hawaii. That's somewhere I had always dreamed of going. He was assigned duty on the USS Oklahoma and once he was there, we corresponded two or three times each week. I still have all the letters and postcards he sent. Every now and then I'll read every one of them and have a good cry."

"You don't need to do this," Jack said. But deep inside he knew she did.

"We hadn't heard a thing until the morning of December 8, 1941. Someone called Dad on the phone and I can still remember the look on his face. He was like a wild animal when he ran to our radio. I don't remember him saying a single word. When I heard we had been attacked, it still didn't strike me why he was so upset. We all thought our country would be in the war sooner or later. Then I heard someone on the radio mention Hawaii. And at that moment I knew he was dead."

Jack could see tears welling up in Kate's eyes. He wanted to plead with her to stop but knew she couldn't. These were words that had to be spoken and heard if their own relationship was ever to flourish.

"We listened to President Roosevelt and that phrase, 'a date which will live in infamy', pierced my heart like a dagger. News that the Oklahoma had taken direct hits and rolled over in the water only made me more sure that Michael was gone. It was nearly a week before someone from the Navy called. Dad answered the phone and after a few seconds, held it out for me. He looked like a painting at that moment—not a single emotion that I could see. To this day, I'm not sure just what was said on the phone before he handed it to me. I guess it's not important but at the time I wanted to know. The only thing I remember that voice on the other end saying was, 'We regret to inform you...' and it sounded like the voice was crying. I dropped the phone and as I started to fall, Dad caught me in his arms. That's the last time he ever really held me. I wanted to think he had saved Sarah's life, but I guess that was my own way of conjuring up some positive memory of Dad. Mom was weeping and when Dad spoke her name, she ran into the kitchen. It was so strange—she started baking pumpkin pies. I'm sure that was just her way of escaping. From that day on, any time she'd bake a pumpkin pie, I'd catch her crying."

Kate's eyes were dry now. The story had probably been acted out in her mind thousands of times and the ending never changed. When she told Jack about the bad scene with her father at the funeral, her words snapped out, like a drill sergeant barking orders at new recruits. A notion with no foundation chewed in the back of Jack's mind: There was more to this story than even Kate knew. He was sure of it, but didn't know why. It was odd, but Jack actually felt sorry for Kate's father. He must have been plagued by some horrible demons.

Kate stared into nowhere and continued. "When Sarah was born, I submersed myself in everything she did. Sometimes, when she was just a baby and I was feeling lonely, I'd wake her in the middle of the night then rock her back to sleep. We were still living with Mom and Dad. Sarah and I were really trapped there. Any jobs I'd find were always menial—not paying enough for us to get a place of our own. Those days were good for Sarah…I suppose. Not having a daddy can be really tough on a little girl. Mom was great with her and even Dad seemed to enjoy bouncing her on his knee—telling stories about brave knights and days of old. Once in awhile, I'd catch him looking at me but as soon as our eyes met, he'd look away. Even when he seemed so happy with his granddaughter—I never forgave him for holding me back at Michael's funeral, and for that look he gave me there."

Jack wanted desperately to take Kate into his arms—to sweep her away to another place, another time, where the hurt that she felt would disappear. Her eyes were full of steadfast resolve. He knew any effort to sidetrack her would be in vain.

"When he was out of the house, Mom and I would have some good, heart-to-heart conversations. As Sarah grew, the three of us were almost like a family. Mom loved rocking her and telling stories of my childhood. Sarah would cuddle up, sucking her thumb and listen for hours about the mischief I'd get into. The story she liked the best was the time I got into Dad's fishing tackle box and stole a bobber. We had a foxhound at the time. His name was Sam. I swear that dog's howl would wake the dead. One day I was playing with that bobber when Sam came snooping around. Without thinking of the consequences, I hooked that bobber onto old Sam's tail. Well…all hell broke loose. That hound started chasing his tail, trying to catch the bobber. He was howling up a storm, knocking over furniture—just about destroying our living room. I ran and hid in my room until the commotion stopped. Then I claimed total ignorance when Dad questioned me about how this could have happened. He never punished me and it was years before I confessed to the crime. Dad started laughing and admitted that it was all he could do to keep a straight face when he thought of the sight of his hound dog chasing that bobber."

A little-girl-like grin crept across Kate's face. It soon melted away to seriousness and she continued:

"My father wasn't usually mean…he just always seemed detached, like there was another life being played out in the back of his mind. He worked hard, running the farm and the way I picture him to this day is with a tired, sad look on his face. After he had a stroke, things around the farm seemed to take on less urgency. There were things that just didn't get done and finally he had to take on some local help to run the farm. It was in that last part of his life that Dad finally began to look like he was at peace with himself. But he never talked about it. Maybe the stroke washed away some of his anger. There would be times I would see the glow of his pipe burning in the dark. He'd sit alone in his easy chair when the rest of the house was sleeping. Sometimes I'd think about going downstairs just to talk to him—but that's all I would do—just think about it. I never did forgive him for his shortcomings as a father."

"How do people get to that point, Jack?" As the question tumbled about Jack's brain, he wasn't sure if Kate was talking about just her father or if she was including herself.

"I don't know Kate. I'm sure your dad must have had some regrets, even if he never shared them with you." There were feelings churning inside Jack that he wanted to share with her, but now was not the right time for them. "There will always be questions in this world that don't have answers," he said.

"When Dad had his final stroke, it paralyzed him. I can still see his eyes—he was afraid of something. Sarah was a teenager then and was really good with him. She'd feed him and carry on one-sided conversations that seemed to calm her grandfather. Whenever I'd walk into his room, the peacefulness would be shattered. His eyes would start twitching and I'd think he wanted to say something to me. Or maybe I just irritated him…I don't know. Oh, Jack, his wake was at the same funeral home as Michael's. We sat in the same stupid folding chairs—on display—right up there in the same damn places we'd sat for Michael's funeral. Except it was Sarah next to me, instead of Daddy. And she was the one to break down this time. I tried to calm her but she was almost out of control. At one point I had to hold her back from the casket."

Kate's face was shiny with tears and sweat—her eyes puffy and red. But as Jack looked through the hurt, he'd never seen anything more beautiful. He wanted to tell Kate he loved her…but she might think he was doing it out of sympathy, so he simply said, "I'm glad you told me, Kate."

"Now it's your turn, Jack," she said looking him straight in the eyes. "Are there things you haven't been telling me? Sometimes I get the sense you want to say more but for some reason you stop. Maybe I'm wrong or maybe it's none of my business, but we've come to a point in our friendship where I want to share things with you…and some of the things are very personal. I never want you to worry about being able to say something to me."

Jack sat silent for a moment. The vileness of his alcoholism was something that he kept under verbal lock and key since meeting Kate. Shame had shackled him. The words, "I have a problem, Kate," did not come easy.

"There have been times, and not so long ago, when you would have been sickened to see me. I drink a lot Kate, and I drink to forget…and when I've drunk enough to forget my troubles, I also forget how to act with any sense of decency." He swallowed then continued:

"A few years ago any time I got into the booze I'd feel good and could be the life of a party, but I didn't know when to stop. People would tell me things I'd done the night before and I'd just laugh, pretending I knew what they were talking about…but I didn't.

It got really bad. The first night we met I was just getting started. You caught me at a "good time". At that point in my life I was constantly feeling sorry for myself. Damn, I'd rather drink than do anything else!

The night that Darla stayed outside was worse than I ever told you. I was blasted and after letting her outside I passed out. She could have frozen to death…and that scared the shit out of me. That night left its mark! Since then the sip of wine I had with you last night was the first drink I've touched. So whether you knew it or not…you and Darla have helped get me sober."

"Oh, Jack…I had no idea it was that bad," she said then tenderly kissed him on the cheek.

"If it weren't for you two, who knows where I'd be today. She's great company for me, Kate. But God, she's scared me a few times—chasing raccoons, getting lost and that episode at the farmhouse."

Kate's eyes questioned Jack.

"Something happened at the farmhouse when we were staying there. I don't mean to scare you but it was almost like she had another spirit inside. I thought at first she was walking in her sleep but it was something way beyond that. The poor dog was like a zombie. I'm sure she didn't know what was going on around her and when she retched, nothing came up…just the smell of peppermint. I don't know what the hell got into her, but she's okay now."

"Jack, why didn't you tell me this?" Kate asked.

"Well, I was worried it would scare you and…"

"Has there been more?"

"There were a few things around the farmhouse that worried me. Some strange marks on the bathroom mirror, fog around the foot of your bed and ticking I heard one night. I guess everything could be explained but it still bothered me. It was like something was trying to reach me. Did you ever see weird things happening around there?" Jack asked.

Kate seemed disturbed, thinking back into unpleasant times. "There were a few odd things that happened around the house after Dad died. But I always thought it was something that Mom had done, then forgot she did it…like marks in the dust in her sewing room or furniture getting moved or the clock in the hallway often stopping then starting again. I sort of pushed that stuff out of my mind and eventually it went away."

Her stomach churned again and Kate grabbed at her stomach.

"Are you okay?" Jack asked.

"Yes, just more tired than anything else. I'd like to talk more, but I'm really whipped."

Before he left, Jack ran the cloth under cold water in the sink and helped Kate to the bedroom. "You get a good night's rest and I'll see you in the morning." He caressed her forehead with the cool cloth and stared with concern into her eyes. "Is there anything you need before I go?" he asked.

"No…I don't think so. Sorry I messed up our plans." Her weak smile told him that she had wanted more that evening, too.

"You didn't," he replied.

The curtains at the Long View didn't quite meet in the middle—allowing early morning sunshine to stream in. Jack had already been to the motel lobby and poured a cup of fresh coffee. A column of sunlight that peeked between the curtains overexposed the steam that curled above his coffee cup. The morning newspaper sat folded on the edge of the bed next to Jack. He planned to read it cover to cover, giving Kate some time to do her morning things. Then he'd give her a call to see how she was feeling and to make plans for their final day together. Jack watched the steam roll off the coffee cup and picked up the newspaper.

By midmorning Jack had read the sports page, local news, then a review of a new movie—Doctor Zhivago. He wished that they had just one more night together to see the romantic movie, but he knew Bob would be back at work and his crew overworked in Jack's absence. "Another time," he thought, then called Kate.

They spent the hours before noon doing little things around the apartment. After watching a mindless game show on the television, they played a game of Scrabble. Both of them avoided mentioning the topic that filled each of their minds—Jack's trip back home.

"Hey, there's a nice little park just down the street. Let's go for a walk," Kate suggested.

Ten minutes later the two strolled into the wooded park. Majestic spruce trees lined a meandering footpath. The path was covered with brown spruce needles, which muffled their footfalls—making the walk seem as if it was over a padded quilt. The spruce trees gave way to a grove of hardwoods—their leaves forming a canopy that softened the summer sun. In the middle of the park several wooden benches surrounded a small pond. Except for the swans crowding the pond, the park was empty. An ancient sycamore extended two massive limbs around one of the benches. Jack held Kate's hand as they walked to the picturesque spot—a place where they would say "good bye" and keep secure in their memories. Two swans swam in graceful converging circles near the edge of the pond. Finally the two beautiful birds turned from the shore and swam side-by-side toward a private cove on the far side of the pond.

"They look happy," Kate said. She watched the swans until they were gone from sight then turned to Jack. "These days with you have been very special, Jack."

"They have for me, too. Sometimes I forget there's another world outside of my own little town. It was time for me to break away…at least for a short time and you've given me something to look forward to," he said.

"You mean you're coming back—especially after the time I showed you last night?" she asked with a grin.

"Well…it's not often I get to play doctor with such a pretty patient. I reckon I can make a few more house calls." He raised her hand to check her pulse then pulled it slowly to his lips. Kate closed her eyes as Jack spread soft kisses across her palm. "Yes, I'll be back," he whispered.

They spent their last hour together on the cozy park bench—talking very little but sharing a great deal. The swans remained hidden in their romantic hideaway.

As the Indian motorcycle carried him away, Kate stood in the corner of the parking lot, tears filling her eyes. Jack thought of turning the bike around but decided against it. Instead, he waved as he turned onto the main highway and vowed to return. For much of the ride home Jack rehashed the events that had made the last three days the fulfillment of a dream. The only mishap on the return trip occurred as he rounded a bend in the road heading into Elmira. A gust of wind blew the two baseball cards from Jack's pocket and as they dropped, each of them was sucked into the spokes of the motorcycle and shredded.

As soon as he arrived back home, Jack switched his motorcycle for his truck and drove to Bob and Martha's place. Darla acted like a little pup when Jack stepped into the kitchen. She yipped and washed his face with her tongue when her long lost friend bent to one knee to greet her. Then she rolled over, waiting for a few scratches on the stomach and tried to lick Jack's hand, as he obliged her. "Did you miss me, old girl?" Jack asked.

"Well, that's a fine way to treat a friend," said a voice from across the kitchen. Martha sat at the table, smiling at Jack, who had not seen her when Bob and Darla greeted him at the door.

"It's nice to see my *old* friend is back where she belongs. How are you feeling?" Jack asked as he stepped up to her and placed a kiss on her forehead.

"Oh, Nurse Bob has done a fine job waiting hand and foot on me. I'm feeling 100% better than when you last saw me. Just an occasional headache every now and then, but nothing a couple aspirin won't cure." Martha looked weak but her eyes had regained much of the sparkle the accident had stolen from her.

"And how's Queen Darla been? You guys didn't spoil her, did you?" Jack asked.

"In between bed pans and enemas, I found time to toss her an occasional bone," Bob said. Martha shook her head at the implication that she needed any assistance with her personal hygiene. "She's been the perfect house guest," Bob added.

"How was your trip?" Martha asked, her eyes wide in gossip-craving curiosity.

Jack and Bob both pulled up chairs to the kitchen table. Over coffee and cinnamon rolls the three talked about the innocent details of Jack's visit to Poughkeepsie. There were several things Jack would never share and soon the conversation turned to Darla and the news around Friendship.

When the news began to wear thin, Jack yawned and said, "If I'm going to whip that work crew back into shape, I better get some sleep. Where are we working tomorrow?"

"We're roughing a new place up on the West Notch Road…across from the Scott place. See you bright and early," Bob said.

"See you then. And thanks again for watching Darla," Jack said. The dog wagged her tail at the sound of her name and followed Jack out the door. In the front seat of the truck, Jack gave Darla a big hug then drove silently home. When his head hit the pillow that night, the thought of how nice it was to be in his own bed followed Jack into a deep, much-needed sleep.

CHAPTER 19

▼

Late August brought with it a searing heat wave. Nights gave little solace, with temperatures never dropping out of the 80s and the high 80s at that. Jack ran several window fans around the clock. When he returned from work each day, he would find Darla lying in front of a small fan—one that did little more than circulate the air in the kitchen. One evening after work, Jack walked in his sock feet toward her and, as he knelt to pet the dog, he noticed that the floor seemed cooler there. The spot she always seemed to pick must have been directly over a cold water pipe, which ran across the basement ceiling. It made the floor a couple of degrees cooler in that spot.

"Well, aren't you the smart one," he told the lethargic dog. Darla wagged her tail once in response to the compliment then dropped her head back to the floor. During those oppressive weeks she ate very little and panted constantly. She began to shed her coat at an alarming rate. The fan swept the fur that she dropped to the far side of the kitchen where it collected in gobs large enough to be mistaken for a stuffed animal. Few local businesses had air-conditioning and none of those allowed dogs.

On a stifling Sunday morning, Jack was in church service, dressed in an open-collared, short sleeved blue shirt and light colored slacks. Fans were flapping and several worshippers hurried from the church during prayers, not wishing to find themselves unconscious on a church pew. Mrs. Ingles sat in her usual spot in the front row and several times Jack noticed her head start to bob. Pastor Ingles shortened his sermon that day—very conscious of the discomfort his congregation was feeling. As Jack left the church, he glanced down at his light blue shirt. For the most part it was now dark blue—saturated with perspiration. The only part of the shirt that was still light blue was under his arms—a most peculiar place to find dryness amid the river of sweat that had flowed from him. He had recently tried Mitchum Deodorant and apparently it worked. As Jack stepped into the church parking lot, he decided to do something about the heat—at least for that day.

Darla was always up for a ride in the truck, but when she hopped up into the passenger's seat and felt the blast of heat, her ears drooped and her head hung low. Once they were on the open highway her mood changed quickly. She stretched to get her head and neck out the window. With eyes squinting, the dog checked out every bug, bird and bush that flew by. The breeze cooled her but sent fur flying inside the truck. "You're going to look like a Mexican Hairless before we get there," Jack said. But Darla's attention was elsewhere. Her flapping cheeks were pushed back by the wind into a fiendish smile. Darla was happy!

Jack stopped at a small diner called Red & Trudy's on the outskirts of Portville. The place had the best malted shakes in the county. Jack bought a large chocolate one. He drove into northern Pennsylvania, fighting to get the thick shake up the straw. When he had nearly finished, Jack tipped the waxed paper cup and let Darla have a taste. A bit of chocolate ice cream lodged on the top of her nose, but Darla spotted it and made short work of the last remnant of the tasty milkshake. She looked up at Jack then back at the empty container. With sad brown eyes and a slight whimper, Darla played the guilt routine, the likes of which would have been the envy of a Jewish grandmother. Jack laughed out loud and reached over to scratch under her ear. The dejected dog soon forgot about being slighted and turned her attention to the world beyond the truck window.

Half an hour later Jack pulled under a large, hand-painted sign that announced, "The World Famous Ice Mines". It led into a small, unpaved parking lot where several dozen cars and trucks had parked. Jack snapped a leash onto Darla's collar and grabbed a folding chair from the back of the truck then headed toward the only opening in the rope fence that surrounded the parking lot. There, a man in a dingy top hat sat on a barstool behind a podium collecting entrance fees. "Addmision $3" had been painted on a piece of plywood that leaned against the podium.

"No dogs allowed," said the admission man.

Jack winced…then looking the man square in the eyes said, "She's a seeing-eye dog."

The poor soul looked totally confused and as he juggled pieces of an objection, Jack pulled a five-dollar bill from his wallet and said, "Keep the change."

The man slowly tugged at his ear lobe—most likely to pull-start the high-finance section of his brain—then squinted at Jack through one accusatory eye. He started to pull two tickets from a large roll then abruptly shifted his fingers and ripped off one ticket. A smile full of teeth and chewing tobacco indicated he had just realized a fast one had been pulled over someone...and he was sure it wasn't himself. A nod of the top hat pointed Jack and Darla toward two large doors, which were set in the side of a steep hill. Another figure stood in front of the doors, also adorned with a top hat. As Jack and Darla got closer, it was obvious that this was a woman, but she bore a scary resemblance to the admission man. (Probably his sister or his wife—or perhaps both.) She took the solitary ticket then looked back at the admission man. He nodded his approval and she pulled one squeaky door open. A rush of cool air hit all three. Jack and Darla stepped cautiously into the dimly lit cave.

It took several seconds for his eyes to adjust to the darkness, but when they did, Jack could see a large chamber opening at the end of the short passageway in front of them. As they stepped into the chamber, the air became instantly cooler. A handrail, made of wrought iron pipe, encircled the chamber. It left a six-foot walkway between the outer walls of the cave and a pit that lay beyond the barrier. As Jack walked up to the handrail he could see the pit gleaming from spot lights that illuminated its walls. The walls were actually sheets of ice that sparkled in a partial rainbow of whites, silvers, blues, purples and greens. Jack leaned over the handrail and peered down. A floor of rippling ice, at least twenty feet below, reflected a carpet of coins that covered it. The tinkling sound of metal echoed in the chamber. Jack looked up to see a man standing directly across from him, holding a small boy in his arms. The child had apparently thrown a coin into the pit for good luck and now was giggling—pleased that he had been allowed to partake in this sacred rite of adulthood. Thousands of quarters, dimes, nickels and pennies covered every square inch of ice on the bottom of the pit. There were even a few silver dollars scattered about.

The thick layers of ice brought back memories repressed for years—of a happy honeymoon taken to Niagara Falls in the wintertime. These Ice Mines were like a miniature version of the frozen falls but unlike the great Niagara, they remained caked with ice year-round. Jack shivered for the first time in months, as the coolness of the cave met his sweaty T-shirt—a welcome reprieve from the heat that had drained his energy.

The walkway around the chamber was filled with other weary travelers, all looking for the same thing—a place to get cool. Several children teased for coins to throw into the icy pit, knowing their wishes would come true only at a price. A withered elderly couple leaned over the pipe railing and fanned cool air into their faces with opened hands.

Twenty feet to his right, Jack spotted a cubbyhole in the cave wall. He led Darla to the spot and opened the folding chair he had been carrying. The indentation was deep enough for Jack to sit comfortably and not cause a traffic jam with people who wished to pass by. Darla plopped down next to the chair on the chilly stone floor. For the next 45 minutes the two sat in the soothing coolness until a frigid memory gripped the fright core of Jack's brain—that night last winter when he had fallen asleep in the woods.

Jack and Darla walked back into the sweltering reality outside the doors of the *World Famous Ice Mine*. The ride back to Friendship was certainly hot and sticky, but any time it approached unbearable, the recollection of the ice blew an imaginary cool breeze through the truck's open windows. As they pulled into the driveway, Jack saw a small pool of moisture on the truck's seat, in front of Darla's paws. Her tongue hung low. Drool and foam covered her entire muzzle. A photograph of the dog, viewed at another time, might have portrayed her as mad, but anyone standing in the oppressive heat for more than a few seconds would have instantly known her problem. Poor Darla was just too damn hot!

"Let's get you inside and cooled down," Jack said.

Darla followed her master at a snail's pace. In the kitchen Jack grabbed a dishtowel and rolled up several ice cubes inside of it.

"Here, girl. This should cool you down." And he removed Darla's thick leather collar and tied the towel around her neck. Gray had invaded the fur on her face and her eyes drooped, exposing bloodshot pockets under them. Jack absentmindedly ran has fingers over the collar as he watched her. Darla was looking old and he worried about her.

Jack's fingertips ran over small indentations on the collar. He peered down at the imperfections. Small letters had been punched on the inside of the collar. There had only been a couple times since Darla had been with Jack that he'd removed her collar, but this was the first time he'd noticed the letters. If not for feeling them, Jack was sure he would never have known they were there. He stepped to the kitchen window and held the collar at an angle with the incoming sunlight. Small shadows revealed the letters, which Jack read aloud: "Under the moon."

It appeared the letters had been punched long ago and had nearly worn off the old collar. Although the letters were neatly aligned, there were minute spacing variations, which led Jack to believe that a human, rather than a machine, had sent the message. Where had they come from? Darla licked the hand that held the collar—an act of gratitude from, perhaps the only one who knew the answer to that question. And in the back of Jack's mind the three words tumbled, desperately trying to find a match with words he'd heard before—"Under the moon."

Late that night Jack tossed and turned under a sheet moist with his sweat. He listened to Darla's labored panting. Through an open window he could hear the sound of leaves beginning to rustle. Distant thunder rolled over the parched valley, teasing nocturnal listeners with the prospect of relief from the stifling heat. The oppression of the hot August night was cut with a cool breeze that lifted the bed sheet and tickled Jack's sweaty neck. He threw back the sheet and sprawled out spread-eagle across the bed, allowing the coolness to sweep over him. Darla's panting soon changed to a contented snore. Jack reached down to stroke her neck. As his fingertips ran over her soft fur, they touched the leather collar. The three words "under the moon," drifted like clouds across his mind—carrying Jack into his first sound sleep in several torrid weeks.

CHAPTER 20

▼

Autumn in Western New York typically would bring colorful foliage. But even the most eloquent linguists would have found themselves tongue-tied, attempting to describe the breathtaking spectacle that filled the forests that year. A glorious rainbow of brick red, bright yellow and warm orange painted the rolling hillsides in a splendor that begged residents and visitors alike to hike along some woodland path or bubbling stream.

In early October, a high front stalled over the Northeast. Day after day the sky was drenched in a cobalt blue, so bright that it hurt to look at it directly. Evenings tingled in early fall crispness. The sweet aroma of burning leaves would often drift through an open window, carrying memories back to the autumn nights of childhood.

Several times Jack would find Darla curled up, sunning herself in a pile of leaves he'd raked during a warm afternoon. She started retrieving half-ripe apples that had fallen from an old Macintosh tree behind the garage. The spirit of a young pup showed again in her eyes.

Even the newspaper began printing various pieces noting the exceptional beauty of this autumn to remember. One Saturday afternoon, Jack was trying out a hickory rocking chair he had purchased that morning from an Amish carpenter who lived on the outskirts of town. The bent hickory sticks fit perfectly with his back and the rocker squeaked in seesaw cadence against his front porch. Jack's eyes became heavy as he read the editorial page of the Olean Times Herald. His head nodded several times as he began a poem entitled, *"Allegany Green"*. The words seemed to flow with an easy rhythm, which Jack enjoyed even in his sleepiness. He sat up straight and began again—mouthing the words as he read.

Have you ever seen?
Allegany green.
Its hillsides defined
By emerald pine.

Dark shadowed hemlock,
Deep forests of spruce,
Sometimes a balsam
Mid tamarack root.

Small painted cabins
On hillsides so lush
Green heathered meadows
In full verdant thrust.

And so can you say?
That you've ever seen,
Autumn's jade canvas,
Allegany green.

Dare you to behold!
Allegany gold.
Yellow poplar leaves
Dance soft with a breeze.

Sunbursts of maples,
The oaks' tawny creams,
Burnt ochre ash leaves
In willow-kissed streams.

An amber sunrise
Brings warm to its morn
Gold rays through the mist
A new day's new dawn.

Dare I to ask you?
To truly behold
Autumn's full glory,
Allegany gold.

Have you yet to tread?
Allegany red.
Woodlands all dappled
In scarlet maple.

Maple like rubies,
Maple so crimson,
And Maple maroons,
Maple vermilions.

Each autumn blossom
Renaming its name.
Sumac to russet,
Sunset to red flame.

My fond wish to you,
When all has been said,
Discover its warmth,
Allegany red.

Colors so many!
That's Allegany.
So let it be known
The colors it's shown.

Pumpkins in orange
Beneath azure skies.
Copper creek bottoms,
White clouds floating by.

Sun silvered cascades,
Tan reeds in the dale,
Red coals in the fire,
A deer's flagging tail.

So when someone asks
What colors you've seen,
Start then to tell of
Allegany green.

The author, William G. Bernbeck, had obviously visited Allegany State Park and it was also obvious he had fallen in love with that special place. Jack had been in the park many times and as he read the poem the second time, each line painted an image he had seen before. When he read the line, "An amber sunrise", Jack thought of the way Kate's hair had looked that day on the park bench. The day they had watched the swans swimming together now seemed like a lifetime ago. Jack felt strangely alone until Darla bounced onto the porch and dropped an apple in his lap.

"Thanks, old girl. I suppose you'll be wanting a pie now." He smiled and thought how happy her gray face looked. "Let's go for a walk," Jack suggested. Darla pranced at the sound of those words she had grown to love.

Dry leaves swished underfoot as Jack and Darla walked the familiar path into the park. Jack unsnapped the lead from Darla's collar and let her run among the majestic oaks and graceful maples. Her nose worked overtime, exploring the abundance of scents that filled the air. The dog began to zigzag in excitement at the base of one of the twin cannons. She moved leaves with her paws to get closer to the intriguing smell. Jack stepped closer to examine just what it was that had Darla so excited. He knelt down and flicked several leaves aside, exposing the moist earth underneath, which held the evidence. In the gray mud dozens of imprints resembling something made by a baby's hand told Jack the story behind Darla's excitement. "Raccoon tracks," he said to himself. "You leave them alone!" he commanded Darla. Jack knew well that the dog would love to be hot on the trail of one of those wily varmints. "I don't want you chasing one of them into the next county. Now settle down."

Darla dropped her ears and looked up at Jack. "You're no fun," her body said. He picked up a stick and waved it in front of her face. Darla's disappointment evaporated, as she stared—totally focused on the stick. Jack heaved it far from the cannons, hoping to distract her from the obsession with the smells of the wild. The dog dashed in the same direction his arm had pointed and whipped her head from side to side, watching for the stick to land. The scent of the raccoons was tucked away safely in the back of her mind.

Day after day the sights, sounds and smells of this magnificent season stirred a longing to share them with someone. Jack clipped the autumn poem from the local newspaper and sent it to Kate. Poughkeepsie was not to be outdone and had put on an equally splendid foliage display. Kate struggled to describe what she was seeing there, in a four-page letter she sent the day before the poem arrived.

CHAPTER 21

▼

Winter made an abrupt entrance into Western New York. A mid-November storm dumped over a foot of snow on the area, which would remain until late spring. Kate had made plans to spend Thanksgiving with Jack, but on the Tuesday before the holiday those plans changed. Heavy snowfall was forecast for the next four or five days and, according to Kate, the car was making a grinding noise. The dangerous road conditions were enough to postpone her visit and the possibility of a breakdown was the final nail in the cancellation coffin. They both hoped for a break in the weather and maybe…just maybe they could then be together at Christmas.

On Thanksgiving Day Jack spent the morning carefully preparing the motorcycle for winter storage in his garage. As he pulled the protective tarp over her, an empty feeling flooded through his veins. He ran his hand over the tarp until he felt the pillion seat he had installed for Kate to ride. Jack smiled at the memory of her arms wrapped around him as they rode through the streets of Poughkeepsie on those warm summer days.

That afternoon Jack had Thanksgiving dinner at Bob and Martha's. The threesome ate and laughed and ate and watched a football game then ate some more. Darla had also received a dinner invitation. She, too, feasted on scraps of turkey, several scoops of mashed potatoes and butternut squash. For dessert she had the crusts from three pieces of pumpkin pie. Her manners slipped as she curled up for a long nap after dinner. By the end of the football game all three of her dinner mates had joined her and none of them knew the final score of the football game.

Over a snack of turkey sandwiches on homemade bread, Bob mentioned that it looked like their construction jobs would have to go on hold for the next few months. Jack was not a bit surprised and had actually counted on the winter break to get caught up with projects he had planned around his house.

"You flying south for the winter with the other snowbirds?" Martha teased. "I hear there are some great retirement villages near Miami."

"Nah, I guess I'll rough out the winter up here. I got a few orders for some small furniture and several picture frames that I can get started on now," Jack said.

"How's Kate doing?" Bob asked.

Martha shot a dagger filled glance his way. She knew Jack missed Kate and just the mention of her name might get him feeling lonely.

"I just got a letter from her yesterday. She's having dinner with her daughter and son-in-law today. Probably will get back here for a visit over Christmas," Jack replied.

By the time the sandwiches had hit bottom, all three were yawning and ready for a more serious nap. "Darla, wake up!" Jack called. "You're going to have to drive home. I'm too tired."

December brought with it more snow and gloomy skies. The sun's trip south and a perpetual bank of thick gray clouds were stealing several minutes of sunshine each day.

Jack would often completely miss the light of day as he busied himself with small carpentry projects. The basement, where he had set up his table saw, lathe and drill press, had no windows. On one occasion, after laboring over a disagreeable hutch for hours, he had climbed the cellar stairs and walked into total darkness. From that day on, Jack always turned on a small table lamp in the hallway before he descended into his workshop. He built a maple coffee table for the Davidsons and a beautiful cherry bookcase for the Madisons, which finished up the projects he had promised families about town.

For the next couples days Jack spent much of his time with organizational jobs around the house. He filled plastic bags with the accumulation of years, from closets throughout the house. With the closets in order, he turned his attack to the kitchen cupboards. Standing atop a footstool, he spotted a bottle, which had tipped over behind a set of mixing bowls stacked inside one another. As his hand gripped the neck of the bottle, a tingle swept through him. His old friend, Jack Daniels hadn't been around to visit for quite some time. There were only a couple shots left—certainly not enough to do any damage. He sat down at the kitchen table with bottle in hand and stared at the black and gray label.

Depression was not something Jack would talk about openly. In fact he viewed it disdainfully as a sign of weakness. The pinpricks of boredom, loneliness and self-doubt worked together, forming an emotional battering-ram that smashed against the doors of his inner-peace. The amber whiskey inside the bottle looked warm and inviting. Jack twisted the cap off and took a deep breath—filling his lungs with the sweet aroma of his long-lost friend. He closed his eyes, remembering the strong oaky flavor that burned so well going down. Jack could feel the inside of his mouth watering in anticipation.

The tapping of Darla's nails caught his attention as she walked to the table then sat on the floor next to him. Her eyes were curious and inexplicably cast with concern.

"Don't worry old girl. There's only a little bit here. Just enough to take the edge off." Jack listened to his words ring hollow across the kitchen. "I really need this. Don't you know how lonely it gets being here day after day after day—all by myself. Oh…you're such a good friend but I need someone to talk to. I know you don't understand but just this little bit won't hurt."

Jack raised the bottle to his lips. His tongue touched the inside of the neck of the bottle. The familiar flavor talked seductively to him. Jack tipped the bottle back slowly and watched the golden nectar roll toward his mouth.

The piercing ring of the telephone echoed off the kitchen walls—breaking the mood of that moment. With care, he lowered the bottle to the table and begrudgingly walked to the phone.

"Hello," Jack said and was ready to snap out, "What the hell do you want!" but thought better and waited for the caller to reply.

"Hello, Jack. This is Pastor Ingles. The reason I'm calling is that we're expanding the vestibule at church and need to remove two pews. I know you do some woodworking and thought you might like them. I'm not sure but I think they're oak. If you want to take them out for us, they're yours."

"Well, that's a kind offer. I'd love them. What do I owe you?" Jack asked.

"Oh, there's no charge. I just hated to let some good lumber go to waste. You could do me one favor though. I need an usher at church this Sunday. If you don't have any plans…"

"I'd be glad to, Pastor. And I'll pick up the pews first thing in the morning…if that's convenient," Jack said.

"That will be fine. The church is unlocked of course, so just help yourself. How's everything with you?"

"Everything's fine here! Couldn't be better," Jack lied.

"Great…well, I'll see you Sunday."

"Thanks for thinking of me, Pastor," Jack said.

Jack stood numb, staring across the quiet kitchen. The whiskey bottle sat in solitude atop the table—an aura of innocence surrounded it. A minute later the Tennessee whiskey found itself plummeting down the dank drain of the kitchen sink. He watched as the last drop clung to the lip of the bottle before falling into obscurity. "Church pews," he thought. There was something about them—an unmerited significance—that picked at Jack's brain. "That dream," he whispered.

Parts of the dream had already faded from his memory but the vile act of smashing the pews still lingered there. *What the hell prompted such aggression?* Then he remembered that he had built something with the wood from the pews…something for Kate. *A house—that was it—a house!* Vague pieces of the dream fell back into place until Jack finally forced his thoughts elsewhere.

Like a lifeline thrown to a sinking swimmer, the phone call had rescued him. *There must be someone watching over me,* was the only explanation Jack could attach to such luck. He brushed the coincidence aside and went on as if nothing had happened.

As he thumbed through a woodworking magazine that evening, Jack noticed plans on how to build a jewelry box and also some blueprints for several houses. He hurried to a cupboard, grabbed a tablet of yellow writing paper and a pencil then began sketching plans for Kate's Christmas gift—a miniature house with each room doubling as hideaway for jewelry. For the better part of an hour he drew, changed his mind, erased and redrew. By midnight his plans were complete and his eyes were weary. Darla had already retired to her favorite spot, under the bed, when Jack plopped down on it.

It turned out the pews were maple. When the finish was removed, Jack found the wood was too light for his taste and decided to stain it cherry, but there was lots to do before that. He shaped the lid of the jewelry box like the roof of a house and hinged it to one side. With a fine chisel, Jack even cut tiny lines in the roof, which gave the appearance of shingles. Under the roof he built a level that looked like the attic of a house. Miniature trunks were glued to the base to give a more authentic look. Jack covered the floor of this attic with a thin layer of blue velvet. The upper level was built separate from the outside walls and could be removed to expose rooms underneath. Each room contained a piece of miniature furniture but still had plenty of space for more of Kate's jewelry. A toilet had been a tasteful omission.

Within the week, Jack was putting the finishing touches on the gift. He glued shutters next to the windows he had carefully painted, and fastened a chimney on top of the roof to act as a knob for opening the jewelry box.

"What do you think?" Jack asked Darla, holding up the finished product for her assessment. She sniffed the handy work and once she determined it couldn't be eaten, walked away. "Thanks, for the encouragement."

CHAPTER 22

▼

The radio station in Wellsville had been playing Christmas carols each evening since the beginning of December. Jack lifted his head from the pages of Reader's Digest and listened to the silky voice of Nat King Cole. The dreamy lyrics "Chestnuts roasting by an open fire", swept over the room. Darla was lying against Jack's feet, keeping them warm. She suddenly stirred from her sleep and perked her ears. Her nose worked the air for subtle signs. Several seconds later there was a light rapping at the front door.

Jack dropped the magazine along with his reading glasses on the coffee table, stretched out his stiffening back muscles and walked toward the door. Darla literally pranced beside him. "What's got you so worked up?" he asked her.

He flicked on the porch light and could see footprints in the light snow leading up to the door but no one outside. Apparently the visitor had stepped to the side, not wanting to be seen. Jack pulled the heavy door open.

There she stood to the side of the door in a blue ski jacket and matching ski cap. Her cheeks were rosy and when she said, "Hello, Jack," he could see her words float through the stillness of the cold night air. His heart leaped at the words and at the sight of the woman he had been thinking about so much lately.

He gave her a quick hug and said, "Come in...come in." Jack brushed the snow from her shoulders and slid his arm around her waist—guiding her into the hallway. Kate stamped her feet then unzipped the ski jacket.

"Surprised?" she asked.

"Oh God, Kate. I can't tell you how much," and he eased his hands inside the jacket and pulled her close to him.

She buried her face in his warm flannel shirt and squeezed him tightly. Jack dropped his head and kissed the top of her head. Kate's hair was cool and the faint fragrance of pine lingered about it. Finally she looked up at him.

Memories of the first night he'd seen her at the *Black Horse Inn* filled his head. Here, in his arms, was an answer to so many prayers. Kate's blue eyes invited more.

At first he tried to kiss some warmth into her cold cheeks then totally surrendered to his desire for her. His lips met hers. A moan escaped Kate's mouth and she pulled at Jack's back, trying to get closer to him. One of her cold hands worked under Jack's shirt and he flinched at the frigid touch. Kate pulled back and grinned. Then both of them felt something pushing on their hips.

In a rare breech of etiquette, Darla jumped up against them—wanting badly to be part of the joyful reunion. She nuzzled Kate's hand for some affection. It was obvious the dog still remembered the friend who had been gone so long. Kate ran her fingers through the thick fur on Darla's neck. "Yes, I missed you too, Darla," Kate said, lowering her head for a sloppy kiss.

"I think I've got a little competition here," Jack said. He stared at Kate, not knowing what was different about her but sensing a change. As she pulled the ski jacket off, it clicked. "Wow, you've lost a lot of weight. You look great!" he said.

"Almost twenty pounds and it wasn't easy. I bought one of those stationary bikes and I swear the Marquis de Sade designed the damned seat!"

"Has Playboy called you yet...for a calendar pose?" Jack kidded.

As Jack gawked at her, Kate smiled demurely. After so many months of working to get her weight down, and now to be showered with compliments—especially by the one she was doing it for—made all the pain worth it.

"You want some coffee or hot chocolate?"

"No, I think I'll just put my feet up and relax for awhile. It's been a long day," she said.

"God, I still can't believe you're here, Kate. I wasn't sure if you were even coming. And I thought it wouldn't be until next week at the earliest."

"You better sit down, Jack. Have I got some news for you?"

Jack sat down at one end of the couch and Kate walked to the other end and sat down. She swung her legs around and rested her feet on Jack's lap. Her toes wiggled under gray wool socks. As Jack began firmly massaging her tired feet, Kate closed her eyes in ecstasy.

"There was a break in the weather this week and with the winter like it's been, I thought I better get home while I still could. Yesterday, I put in my last day at work. Sarah and Adam actually have someone with a college degree to replace me. And the other waitresses at the diner can fill in for me. Business has been slow there anyway." Kate opened her eyes in time to see Jack's jaw drop.

"You quit?" he said in high-pitched disbelief.

"Well, I wasn't fired and I talked to the kids several months ago about looking for another job. They were both fine with it." Sarah hesitated, giving Jack time to absorb only the tip of this news iceberg. "And…"

"Go on! Don't keep me in suspense," Jack pleaded.

"Tomorrow morning I have an interview at Friendship Dairy for a bookkeeping job. One of the big wigs there, was a close friend of my dad's. He indicated the interview was only a formality and that I could start work there the first of the year."

Kate had been anxious about Jack's reaction to her move. It wasn't as if she was moving in, but now—with both of them living in the same town—things would be different.

"I miss this place," she said then sat quietly, waiting for a reaction from him.

His hands stopped massaging her feet and he reached to her. Kate took his hands and Jack pulled her toward him. She squirmed into his arms, laid her head against his chest, curled her feet up and then looked at the man she had secretly fallen in love with. His eyes were moist and she knew instantly how he felt. The tension that had been building all day, melted in his warm embrace. His crooked smile answered the question she had been asking herself every minute of the long car ride home. Kate Fletcher had made the right move.

They talked about Darla, the weather and the remodeling job. It would have been so easy to simply fall asleep in his arms. Her day had begun very early and her body spoke to her in soft, provocative words, "This feels so comfortable. Just relax, close your eyes and leave the world behind…sleep, sleep…" but rationality interrupted. It was clear that the short drive to her farmhouse would become much more difficult if she stayed even another five minutes.

Before Kate said a word, Jack knew she needed to leave. Feeling her resting against him had raised a tide of emotion within his heart but he also knew there would be a next time—an evening that would be just right.

At the doorway they kissed again and as she looked up into his eyes Kate said, "You're invited over tomorrow evening for dinner. If you bring a nice dessert, I'll take care of the rest."

"You sure I can't do something more than the dessert? I do know how to boil water."

"No…just bring Darla and we can make a party of it. I promise to be a little livelier. Today has been…"

Jack interrupted, "I know, you must be bushed. Get a good nights sleep and tomorrow at the interview, wear that mohair sweater I first saw you in that night at the Black Horse."

"I didn't think you noticed that sweater. And hopefully it's too big now," Kate said.

"I noticed," he said smiling and kissed her once more on the cheek.

Darla yipped to make her presence known. Kate immediately kneeled and hugged the dog, pressing her head against Darla's, who promptly returned a wet kiss.

"Yes, I missed you too, girl," Kate said then walked down the snowy front steps. "See you both tomorrow," she called from the car then drove away.

Jack and Darla both stood on the front porch, watching her car's red taillights until they had gone from sight. He didn't feel the light snow as it melted under his sock covered feet.

A postcard worthy Christmas scene spread over the town the next morning. Fresh fallen snow covered evergreens, sunshine glistened off snowdrifts like diamonds on a bed of cotton, and a cardinal whistled a morning song from the bough of a blue spruce in Jack's backyard. A few rabbit tracks crisscrossed the otherwise virgin snow. And all Jack thought about as he stared out his kitchen window was seeing Kate again that evening. Minutes passed like hours for the entire day. Jack had planned to pick up dessert at the little bakery in town but decided baking chocolate chip cookies might help pass the time. The first batch he pulled from the oven appeared a bit overdone—perhaps edible but not presentable. He noticed the streaks of flour zigzagging across his shirt and prayed that Bob wouldn't pop in and catch him in such an unmanly act. The second batch looked perfect but a small sample puckered Jack's mouth and left a slightly bitter, salty aftertaste. Checking the recipe he found it called for one tsp. of salt, vanilla extract and baking soda. He had leveled the tablespoon when measuring the ingredients, so that couldn't have been the problem. "Good enough," he said, but none too convincingly. A Tupperware container would at least present them well.

Jack whistled several romantic Christmas carols as he drove to Kate's that evening. Darla sat straight up in the passenger seat, sensing his excitement. She touched her nose to the frosty windshield several times, leaving dark, wet poke-a-dots. Pausing on the back steps at the Fletcher's farmhouse, Jack thought of the many changes in his life that had taken place since standing in that very spot a year ago. A gust of winter wind tingled on his cheeks where Old Spice had been splashed a short time before. Darla wagged her tail, excited to be home.

Kate opened the door and let her guests into the brightly-lit kitchen. Her hair was pulled back—French braids holding it tight against her head. Her cheeks glowed under just a touch of subtle makeup. The weight she had lost gave a graceful angularity to her face. "Merry Christmas," she said and stood on her tiptoes to give Jack a warm kiss. The taste of cinnamon was left on his lips.

"And Merry Christmas to you, too." Kate said, as she knelt to greet Darla. The dog closed her eyes and purred as her old friend found just the right spot to scratch behind her ear.

"I'm so sorry, Jack. I searched high and low in this house but couldn't find the Mohair sweater. Guess this old thing will have to do." Kate stood up before him in a snow-white cashmere sweater held together at the neckline with mother-of-pearl buttons. It fit her new shape to perfection and as Jack gawked speechlessly, Kate turned her head—embarrassed by the excessive attention.

"You look incredible," he finally stammered.

Jack set the container of cookies on the kitchen table and took Kate's hands into his own. He kissed one then the other. Looking into her eyes he whispered, "I've dreamed of having you back here…now it looks as if my dream has come true." A sizzle on the stove interrupted and Kate hurried to move the pot that was boiling over to the side of the burner.

She stepped back to Jack and slid her arms around his waist. Her eyes told him all he needed to know and as Jack lowered his head to kiss her, the grandfather clock in the hallway began to chime. As soon as the clock had rung out six times, Kate said, "The cow jumped under the moon."

Jack stepped back, stunned by the words. His face contorted in confusion. "What did you say?" he asked.

"The cow jumped under the moon. It's what my father always said when the clock rang six o'clock. There's a dial on the face of the clock with a picture of the cow jumping over the moon, like in the nursery rhyme. At six o'clock the dial is actually up side down, so the cow is under the moon. Dad never failed to announce the cow was under the moon at that time. It was just some silly little quirk he had."

"Kate, you've got to see something," Jack said.

He knelt down beside Darla and removed her collar. "Look at this," he said to Kate, stepping under the bright ceiling light.

At first she saw nothing but when Jack tipped the collar, Kate could see the very slight indentations. She squirted then recoiled as the words pierced her eyes. "What's this all about? Did you put those words there?"

Jack tried to summon a calm voice and replied, "No, I found them there this summer and forgot to mention it to you. I didn't think they were important. But this is so strange. I bet your father put them there. Or maybe your mother."

"Oh, I'd guess Dad put them there…but why would he do that?" Kate asked, not expecting an answer.

It was at that moment that something clicked in Jack's brain. He had heard a clock ticking during one of the nights he had stayed in the farmhouse. It was something he had dismissed as a dream, but deep inside he never really believed that. His mind wandered back to that week. The slashes on the steamy mirror—they were like the hour markers you'd see on the face of a clock. And the way Darla had frozen like a statue in front of it—something peculiar was going on and all hands pointed to the old grandfather clock.

"Do you remember me talking about the odd things that happened when I was staying here at the house? I guess I could have explained any one of them but this seems to tie in with them," Jack said, staring down at the collar he held in his hand.

She didn't need to answer. Jack knew it was something Kate could not forget. Both of their heads turned slowly toward the hallway. Darla's claws clicked against the linoleum as she walked from the kitchen. Between the sounds made by her claws, mechanical ticks snapped in a rhythmic cadence. Jack and Kate followed Darla into the hallway. It took several seconds for their eyes to adjust to the dim light there but, as their vision cleared, the outline of the dog staring up at the grandfather clock crystallized.

"There's something there," Jack whispered. Out the corner of his eye he could see Kate nodding in agreement.

Kate snapped on the hallway light. She could see Darla's eyes were locked on the face of the clock. "Let's see what this is all about," she said. Over the years she had dusted the clock, raised its weights and adjusted the time but not once had she seen anything unusual. Now her fingertips scoured the frame of the clock, searching for something, yet clueless to what it could be. Jack reached over her shoulder and opened the small door that shielded the face of the clock. The picture on the dial was inverted—making the up-side-down face, which had been painted on the moon, look like it was frowning rather than smiling. And the cow was on its back, udders pointing up at the full moon.

Jack gently touched the dial, the hands of the clock, the beveled glass on both sides of the housing and the wooden floor at the base of the housing. The floor plate moved, almost imperceptibly, but it did move. As Jack looked closer, he could see the wooden plate had not been attached to the side of the frame. It was odd that the builder of such a fine piece of furniture would fail to secure this piece. Jack thought that perhaps the plate had been left unattached to allow for easier access to the hardware of the clock.

"Let's take a look at this," he said, pointing at the plate. "Do you have a pocketknife or something I could pry this up with?"

Kate hurried to a desk in the corner of the living room and pulled out a letter opener from the center drawer. Jack took the opener and eased it under the wooden plate. As he lifted it, Jack could see a second floor underneath. "It's a false floor," he said.

He raised the plate until it hit the base of the clock's dial then tipped it to the side and pulled it from the clock. The plate had been stained on the top to match the wood in the frame of the clock perfectly. Jack looked closely at both sides of the plate but found nothing. He then stretched to examine the real floor under the face of the clock. Kate's heart pounded as she saw him reach for something inside. Jack pulled out an envelope that had yellowed with age. The single word "Kate" was written on it. He handed it to Kate and she looked up at him—wanting Jack to tell her what to do.

"Open it," he said, shrugging his shoulders for lack of another choice.

Kate grasped the letter opener, took a deep breath, then sliced the top of the envelope open. Inside was a thick letter. Kate immediately recognized the handwriting. "It's from Dad," she choked.

She walked to the living room couch, sat down on its arm and held the letter under a light on the end table. Jack sat down beside her as Kate began to read aloud:

Kate,

As you're reading this letter, it's most likely that I'm no longer of this world. It was several months ago when I first found out about my cancer and the doctors were not very encouraging. What I share with you comes from my heart, which has ached for many years with the burden of things I've never been able to tell you. You see, your mother and I have disagreed about things that needed to be said. So I have decided that the hands of the Lord will determine the fate of this letter. I'm hiding it, and if it's you, my dear wife, who is reading these words, please understand I'm just taking one of our most important decisions out of our hands. God can decide what our precious Kate will learn of her past. And if it is you, my dear wife, looking down at this letter, let me say one last time, how deeply I love you.

However, if it is you Kate, before you read these words, you may wish to simply destroy this letter and carry on with your life. Just know that although it might have seemed like a shallow love I held for you, it was really much more. You should stop reading now and give yourself some time to think about whether you really want to know more about your past. If you're happy and old ghosts never haunt you, then you should burn this letter now.

Kate looked to the ceiling, her eyes filling with tears. "Oh, you bastard...you know I can't stop. It's way too late for an apology," and she looked back down at the letter and continued.

If your eyes are touching these words, then you have obviously made up your mind to hear what I have to say. I most want to say "I love you" but I'm sure those words will ring hollow in your ears. So let me just tell you a little about yourself that you might not know.

Your mom had a very difficult time when she delivered you. You were born in the late morning and she was in labor the entire night before. The doctor came into the waiting room and told me I was the proud father of a healthy baby girl. But the look on his face told me something was wrong. He said there was a second baby that your mom hadn't delivered yet and there were some complications. As I'm writing these words now, the thought of how much your mother suffered has my eyes filled with tears.

After such a long night and painful delivery, your mom could barely stay conscious. I've always thought the doctors waited too long but when they finally decided to do a Cesarean, it was too late. Your twin brother was stillborn. We named him Michael and if you go to the cemetery, the small stone marker behind your grandparent's with the letters M. F. is his grave.

That day something died in me, too. I never took much stock in what the doctors called depression. Truthfully, I always thought it was just some excuse for weak-willed slackers to be moody. But now I know firsthand that it's very real and can be devastating. For all those years I tried to deal with it myself and looking back, I see I didn't do a very good job of it. I'm not making excuses for the way I acted, but feel I owe you, at the very least, an explanation.

I have many regrets now that I've lived my life near to its end. Surely the one that has left the deepest scar is the illogical blame I held for you being the cause of Michael's death. It was never a fully conscious thing, my darling daughter, but just a dark little notion that hid deep inside my head and cropped up every once in awhile. It made me wonder if he would be alive if it weren't for you. I didn't want to think those black thoughts and I always tried to push them out of my head. Sometimes, when I'd see you playing with your dolls, I'd imagine a son going hunting with me. And I hated myself for thinking that way.

There. I've said it as best I could. This damn secret has eaten away my soul. I have lived with so much shame that these last days of my life are coming as a relief. It was my fault that you lived your life without much of a real dad. The little emotion that I did have after the tragedy was spent feeling sorry for myself and once I started ignoring you, it kind of snowballed and we fell even farther apart.

You're probably cursing me at this moment, realizing I was too much of a coward to admit things had gone wrong and didn't have the courage to change them. Your mom always pretended to understand when we'd talk quietly in the dark. She cried enough for both of us and I couldn't find even one tear. There were times she'd tell me to just pretend nothing had happened and start a new life in the morning—to go into your room, give you a big hug, and tell you how much I really loved you. But I'd always drag my feet and end up doing nothing. It's too late for us now, but if God has helped put this letter in your hands, maybe it can make some of the anger you must have for me go away.

When you met your Michael and brought him home to meet us, it made things better. I truly thought God had stepped in and given me back at least a substitute for my lost son. And when you introduced him as "Michael", it was as if a sign was being sent to us. From the very start I liked him. It was as if you had stepped in and made things whole but I couldn't even thank you for it. I was so proud at your wedding. You put some sunshine back into my life and I began thinking how happy we were going to be.

The day Michael left for the Navy broke my spirit. I worried I'd lose another son. My spirit crumbled when the bad news about Pearl Harbor came. For weeks afterwards, I could barely remember my name. It was like my mind had shut down. I swear that nothing at Michael's funeral ever made its way into my head. Your mother talked with me about it later but I couldn't remember a thing. My actions must have caused you such agony. Now there is nothing in this world that hurts me more than the knowledge of the enormous pain I have cast on my beloved daughter.

About all I can do these last few days is lie in bed and think about mistakes I have made. It has taken me many days to finish this letter but they have been days that have finally restored some of the feelings I lived without for untold years. Your sweet mother was always by my side and without her I may well have ended my life long ago. I'm thankful she passed on some of her strong will to you. Hopefully it will help you to cope with some of the great disappointments life has to deal.

As for me. my body is too tired to go on struggling, but I have found new life to my spirit. It feels so good now to cry. Many tears have punctuated this letter. From a better place I'm sending my unspoken love. At this moment. a most perfect dream has unfolded in my mind. A little girl sits on my knee. giggling at a funny story. And I hug her and tell her. "I love you. Kate."

Dad

Kate sat frozen in a time and reality unknown to her only minutes before. Her cheeks were tracked with tears and several had fallen onto the letter, which Kate held in her lap. Jack rested his hand on her shoulder. His fingertips caressed the white cashmere, trying to think of soothing words to say but none came. Kate's shoulders drooped and her head hung low as she pieced together the enormous burden of enlightenment. The truth had been dealt with the swiftness of a drug being mainlined and it paralyzed Kate in an emotional overdose.

Through teary eyes she looked at Jack. "I guess I should be relieved but…but, damn it. I can't think straight," she said. "I've hated him for so long. Now I can't figure out how I'm supposed to feel." The answer she searched for in Jack's eyes was not there.

Darla laid her head down on Kate's knee and looked up—her sad brown eyes bleeding sympathy. Kate ran her fingers through the soft fur on Darla's neck and gazed blankly at the dog. Kate took a deep breath interrupted by several sniffles.

"Oh, my God! The roast!!" Kate gasped and ran toward the kitchen. Jack hurried behind her. As he stepped into the kitchen, she was grabbing a towel and pulling the oven door open. Kate squinted as the greasy heat hit her eyes. She pulled out a pan, which held a smoking brown chunk of meat. "I'd say it's done," she said over her shoulder. And Kate started to laugh. She set the roast atop the stove, turned to Jack and threw her arms around him. With her head against his chest she reassured him, "I'm okay."

Jack carved the very well done meat while Kate whipped a bowl of mashed potatoes and tossed a green salad. She lit two thick red candles cradled in plastic holly wreaths. A minute later the two were smiling across the flickering flames, not really tasting their food. They ate in peaceful silence.

The secret letter sparked thoughts in the back of their minds, but for that evening it would remain outside their conversation. Jack sensed that Kate needed more private time to digest what she had learned and although passion churned inside of him, the goodnight kiss at the doorway was polite.

"She can stay here tonight," Kate said, nodding at Darla.

The suggestion caught Jack off guard. He hadn't given much thought to where Darla would stay now that Kate was back. The dog was ready to follow him out the door and Jack's command to "stay" caught her off guard as well. Darla looked from Jack to Kate and back again.

"Looks like you've made a life-long friend…but I bet I've got something here that might soften her up a bit." Kate walked to the refrigerator and pulled out a large piece of the roast beef. Darla sniffed the air once then hurried across the kitchen—not embarrassed the slightest to take the delicious bribe.

"Why you two-timing little chow hound," Jack chuckled. "I guess I know where I stand."

Kate walked back to Jack and gave him another kiss. "We'll get together tomorrow night, if your social calendar is open," she said.

Jack held her hand for a moment then was gone. Darla licked Kate's fingertips, where the taste of the roast beef still remained. The dog followed her old friend into the living room and curled up at the foot of the recliner where Kate had sat down. It was the same chair where Ed Fletcher had spent countless evenings, his head buried in a newspaper or eyes glued on some mindless television show. Kate unfolded the letter he had written so long ago. As she read the painful words again, her thoughts lingered on each sentence—piecing together her mental images of the past with each fragment of the stunning revelation. The tears that had flowed like a great river the first time she read the letter, now filled her eyes like serene pools. She still had questions, but Kate also had answers, which filled in many voids of her life's puzzle.

On the other side of town Jack tossed in bed, worrying about the woman he had fallen in love with and missing the contented sighs he heard every night just before falling asleep.

CHAPTER 23

▼

Even in small-town America, the days before Christmas were often hectic, with last minute shopping and dozens of those little details to attend to that would make the holiday perfect. Kate and Jack did almost everything together over those days. And as the big day approached, Jack saw a woman not frazzled, but one that found joy and the happiness of the season in just about everything.

On the day before Christmas Kate, Jack and Darla hiked into the forest behind the Fletcher farm. They spent nearly an hour picking out a beautiful fir tree. Jack crawled under its thick branches and had just touched his bow saw to its trunk.

"Wait," Kate yelled. "I think I like this one better."

Jack stood and brushed the snow from his coat and surveyed Kate's change-of-mind. He cocked his head to the side and was about to say, "it looks a little crooked". The words hung in his mouth when he saw Kate staring at the tree he had crawled under. There, snuggled deep within the boughs, was a bird's nest. Jack knew immediately that her thoughts were of a homeless bird.

"Yeah...I think you're right. This one's beautiful!" he agreed.

Darla checked out a variety of new scents in the woodland while Jack cut the perfect Christmas tree. Kate watched a chickadee perched upon a nearby tree. She wondered if the nest in the fir tree was the little bird's home.

Jack bound the tree with bailing twine and it slid easily from the forest on the blanket of snow. Kate threw several snowballs for Darla to hunt down but the dog lost interest, or perhaps energy, in the game she never seemed to win. Back in the barn Jack trimmed branches from the trunk of the tree to ready it for the tree stand.

The tree looked a lot bigger in the living room than it had in the woods. When Jack cut the twine that secured the tree, its branches dropped nearly the entire width of the living room. "Guess I've got some pruning to do," he said and they both began to laugh. While he pruned the oversized branches, Kate disappeared into the kitchen.

Soon the farmhouse was full of the aroma of the season as hot apple cider steamed on the stove, a pumpkin pie baked in the oven and popcorn, for decorating the tree, snapped inside a covered frying pan.

When Kate walked back into the living room, the fir tree stood erect near the front windows. The fresh smell of evergreen permeated the room. In her father's recliner Jack had stretched out and was snoring in two-part harmony with Darla.

"You better get up. It's time to get ready for the Christmas service," Kate said, gently shaking Jack's arm.

"Oh…I'm not asleep. Just resting my eyes. What time is it?" he asked.

"Time for you to get into your Christmas finest. I have a little something for you before you get dressed," she said. Then Kate reached behind the couch and pulled out a brightly wrapped package with a shiny blue bow.

Jack tried to open the package without tearing the paper. His mother had always used Christmas wrapping paper for decades before discarding it and the habit had worn off on her son. Finally Jack made his way into the package and found a silk tie, adorned with a subtle pattern of green pine boughs, red holly berries and dark brown pinecones.

"I got it at the Big & Tall Men's Store in Olean," Kate said. "I think it will be long enough." She didn't mention the fact that his only other tie would struggle to get within two buttons of his belt.

"Wow, thank you! I'll wear it tonight."

Although Kate and Jack left early for the church, it was filled to near capacity when they arrived. An usher by the front door handed each of them a small white candle. As the two surveyed the sanctuary for a place to sit, a hand popped up from a pew near the back of the church. Jack spotted Bob and Martha with enough room beside them for two more people to squeeze in. Kate sat next to Martha and by the time the service began they seemed like old friends.

Pastor Ingles stepped onto the pulpit, cleared his throat and greeted the congregation: "Good evening friends. Please take a moment and extend your hand to your neighbor and wish them a Merry Christmas." A joyous buzz filled the sanctuary. When the pastor cleared his throat again the throng of worshippers quieted. He continued: "This is a season of giving. So let us give praise for the greatest gift of all…the Lord Jesus Christ. As he lay in that manger in Bethlehem, so many years ago, the angels sang out a joyous song to honor the Savior of mankind. Let him hear us now in joyful adulation as we sing hymn number 201...*Angels We Have Heard on High*". The pastor's wife sat at a piano in front of the church and gave a rousing introduction to the song, her fingers slapping at the keys and her feet pounding the pedals. Jack slipped his hand over Kate's as she held the hymnal. "Singing sweetly through the night," she sang and he wanted to kiss her.

That night the spirit of Christmas truly visited the little church. It manifested itself in uplifted hearts and renewed commitments. When the lights dimmed near the end of the service, lit candles were passed through the aisles. One-by-one the congregation used the candles to light the ones they had received before the service. Soon the room was lit by a multitude of tiny lights. The beautiful words of *Silent Night* echoed about the church, filling it with excitement, and peace, and love. The candlelight was not bright enough to illuminate the pages of the hymnals but every single soul in that church sang out as if they had personally penned the flowing lyrics. Teary eyes and smiles filled their faces as the worshippers filed out into the peaceful, silent night.

Back at the farmhouse Jack turned on the lights on the Christmas tree then lit kindling underneath a stack of applewood in the fireplace. Kate poured eggnog and placed a dozen shrimp atop a red bowl filled with ice. Darla paced about the kitchen and whined to go outside. "You hurry up. There's a big party going on here tonight that you won't want to miss," Kate said. She held the shrimp bowl high with one hand and opened the door for Darla. The dog barked several times on her way out the door. "I wonder what's got her all worked up?" Kate asked herself.

The past week had been eventful, to put it mildly. Little-by-little the contents of the letter maneuvered their way into the realm of acceptance. Kate struggled under the weight of the revelation, which she had yet to classify as "welcome", but the disdain she had held for her father had softened. When the time was right, she would share the monumental news with her daughter. And Christmas Eve was not the right time to talk with Jack about it either, but soon they would sit down and have a heart-to-heart. Tonight would be a special night—nothing too heavy—just a time to eat, to enjoy Jack's company and perhaps a time for romance.

CHAPTER 24

▼

Ron Lyman had worked for the Friendship Dairy for twenty-six years. He and his wife Barbara had two teenage daughters, Colleen and Sue. Six days a week he drove a milk truck—one with a large, stainless steel tank to haul milk from local farms to the dairy. Ron had grown up in Friendship. He knew the people and the roads well.

The day before Christmas he was making his last pick-up at the Hamilton farm. It was nearly dark and the farm's driveway was too narrow for the tanker truck to turn around. So Ron backed the truck down the driveway. A gust of wind blew up snow and Ron failed to notice a slight bend in the driveway. He buried the back set of tires in a ditch near the road. Three hours and one tow truck later he pulled onto the open highway. His family would be impatient, wanting him home with them on Christmas Eve. He may have touched the accelerator down just a bit more than usual, but he was a careful driver. There was no sense taking chances.

The little town was quiet as he drove through deserted streets. Snow hadn't fallen in several days and the roads were bare. On the outskirts of town, strings of Christmas lights drooped over many spruce trees and porches. A Christmas carol played softly on the radio. Ron couldn't remember the singer that made the promise, "I'll be home for Christmas", but he sang along, an octave lower than whoever it was.

Ed Fletcher's place was just ahead. Ron wondered if old Ed had ever finished that Indian motorcycle he'd been working on before he died. The Fletcher farmhouse had lights on. "I wonder who's got that place all lit up?" he asked himself. As he drove in front of the house, Ron craned his neck to look through the front windows. Out the corner of his eye he saw something move. His head snapped forward just in time to see a raccoon dart in front of the truck. It was far enough away that the truck would just miss the lucky night bandit. An instant later, Ron saw something larger bound into the road. As he locked the brakes on the tanker truck it become clear that "the something" was a dog. Rubber screamed against the blacktop just before that awful "thump". Then all was quiet.

CHAPTER 25

▼

In the time it would take for a snowflake to melt in the crackling fire, the meaning behind the dreadful sound registered in Kate's mind. She screamed and as Jack rushed into the kitchen, the vision of her there—hands over her mouth, eyes popping in terror—was seared into his brain. Kate dropped her hands and cried out, "The dog!" Her finger shook as she pointed toward the door.

At first Jack failed to understand. He didn't know that Kate had let Darla outside. She choked as tears and emotions flooded from her. As Jack ran from the house, Kate dropped to her knees and sobbed.

Smoke and the smell of burning rubber filled the air in front of the farmhouse. A man was kneeling at the side of the road. Faint Christmas music drifted from the open door of the cab. Jack slowed to a quiet walk as he approached the man. "Is she dead?" he half whispered, half choked.

"Yes, I think she is," the man said, not raising his head. "I couldn't help it. She ran into the side of the truck."

The man dropped his hand to the dog's nose and held it still. He looked up at Jack and said, "I think she's still breathing."

Jack turned and ran back to the farmhouse. He took a deep breath as he pulled the kitchen door open. "She's still alive. Call Doc Morrison and tell him we're on our way," he told Kate. The calmness in his voice was soothing to Kate but deep inside Jack struggled to mask his true feeling.

Jack grabbed a quilt from the back of the couch and ran from the house again. By the time he had wrapped Darla's limp body in the quilt and lifted her in his arms, Kate had the pickup truck running in the driveway. She ran around to the passenger's side door and held it open as Jack gently placed the bleeding dog in the middle of the seat.

Doc Morrison's place was just across town—not more than five minutes away. The vet had been enjoying Christmas Eve with his family but told Kate to come right over. The office would be open.

In the darkness, Kate stroked Darla's neck until she felt something wet. She cringed at the thought, then rested her hand on the dog's side. Kate turned her head and stared blankly out the window.

At the vet's office Jack carried the dog inside and carefully placed her on an examining table that the vet pointed at. Darla looked very small, curled there on the cold stainless steel slab. She had not moved a muscle. The vet's face looked grave as he held a stethoscope to the dog's heart. His hands delicately touched one of the Darla's legs, which was caked with blood. He examined the dog thoroughly.

In a kind face, filled with sadness he shook his head. "I don't think she's going to make it. The leg is broken so badly that it can't be saved and I don't think she'll regain consciousness. There's not much you can do. I'll stay out here with her, but I think unless something changes, we better put her down."

Jack looked into Kate's eyes. They were filled with tears—mascara running down her cheeks.

"I think you're right," she whispered and took Jack's hand. "What do you think?" she asked him.

He swallowed and nodded his head.

Kate started, "Can you…"

"I'll take care of everything. We'll talk tomorrow," said the doctor in a comforting voice. "What's your phone number?"

Kate told the doctor the number at the farmhouse then ran her hand across the matted fur on the still dog's neck. As she turned from Darla, Jack put his arm over Kate's shoulder and the two of them walked silently from the office.

They sat for a moment in the truck. "Oh, Jack…why did this happen?" Kate asked in sobs. And she waited for the answer she knew would never come. In the darkness she could see Jack's head shaking.

"Let's stay at your house tonight. I don't think I can stay there…where *it* happened. At least not tonight," Kate said, sniffling between every other word.

"That's a good idea," Jack agreed. "Do you need to get anything from your place?"

"No…I'll rough it tonight," she said. Kate rested her head on Jack's shoulder as they drove to his house. "She was a wonderful dog."

Tears streamed down Jack's face and words would have been choked with grief, so he sat silent. For Kate's sake he would try to be strong.

There was something about the house that was stark and lifeless. Nothing seemed important at that moment as Jack and Kate sat on the couch in his living room. *Miracle on 34th Street* played on the television, not so much for entertainment, but to soften the painful silence. In unison they yawned—physically drained and emotionally exhausted.

"I'll sleep on the couch and you can have my bed," Jack suggested.

"I'm tired Jack…but I need you to hold me. God, I miss her so much," Kate said. She wiped tears from her eyes and stood up. "Come on."

Kate took Jack's hand and walked quietly up the stairs to his bedroom. She lay down on the bed facing a wall. Jack stepped around the bed then cuddled up close to her. He wrapped his arm around her shoulder and pulled her close. His lips tenderly touched her ear in a sympathetic kiss. And she fell asleep in his arms. Jack did not move for nearly an hour but sleep failed to come. He could only think of the way Darla would stare into his eyes, chin resting on his knee; the way her nails would click as she walked across the kitchen floor; the way she would sigh just before falling asleep beside his bed…and Jack thought of the sadness Kate would have to endure. Sleep finally came, a reprieve from the troubles that would return in the morning.

"Merry Christmas, Jack," were the first words he heard. Sunshine lit the bedroom and Kate sat on the edge of the bed, a cup of coffee in hand. Her eyes were swollen, her hair was disheveled, her clothes were the same as she'd worn to bed and she looked more beautiful than he had ever seen her.

"Good morning and Merry Christmas to you," he managed. She handed him the coffee. A big gulp brushed a few cobwebs away but he still struggled with reality. The first clear thought that he had was that Darla was gone. A dog that had become such a large part of his life had been taken away in a cruel twist of fate.

"I guess we should get some breakfast. Then…" and he hesitated to add that they would need to stop by Doc Morrison's office to pick up the dog's body for burial.

"I know what we have to do Jack. It won't be easy but it has to be done. We can't leave her there," Kate said. "I'll go with you."

"You don't have to Kate. I can handle everything."

"No, I want to do this. If I avoid it, things will only get worse," she said.

Jack glanced at the alarm clock on the dresser. It was already 10:00 am. He tried fruitlessly to brush out a few of the wrinkles from the clothes he had slept in. After toast, scrambled eggs and much more coffee, the two climbed into the truck and drove slowly to the vet's office. They could see a light on.

For a moment Kate felt like driving away from the office, away from the town and forgetting this had ever happened. Knowing that was not an option, she forced herself to pull the handle on the truck door, get out and take those agonizing steps to the office. Jack walked behind her. He held the door open for Kate then followed her. Doc Morrison was nowhere in sight but the door leading into the working part of the office was slightly ajar. Muffled words came from inside the room.

"Hello, Doc," Jack called out.

"Come in," a voice called back.

As they walked into the room, the vet was kneeling next to a cushion in the corner. He turned to look at them and a measured smile crept across his face. "I've been trying to call you all morning," he said.

"We couldn't stay at the farmhouse," Kate started to explain.

At the sound of her voice a head stretched out and peeked around Doc Morrison. Kate threw her hand over her mouth and blinked to make sure what she was seeing was real. "Oh, Darla," she cried out and ran toward the dog.

"Be careful. She's very weak," the vet warned.

Kate slid on her knees to the cushion where the dog was resting. Darla kissed her hand as Kate touched her fingertips to the side of the dog's face. Tears, which had flowed in grief the night before, now turned to tears of joy.

"What happened to her?" Jack asked in amazement.

"Well, as best I can tell…she ran into the truck, maybe one of the wheels. If the truck had hit her head on she wouldn't be with us now. There's a large cut across the back of her head and she sustained head trauma, severe enough to keep her unconscious for nearly an hour after you left last night. When she woke up the dog was much more coherent than I might have imagined. It doesn't seem like she has any internal injuries except for the leg. Now that's the good news."

"The good news?" Kate choked.

"The truck must have run over her leg. Maybe she slid into the tire and her head hit on the inside of the rim. That would make sense with this type of injury. I'm afraid I can't save her leg. And that's one of the reasons I was anxious to talk with you folks this morning. I don't know how to put this delicately…but some owners might feel it was more humane to put the dog to sleep rather than have it deal with getting around on three legs. I wanted to see how you felt about this," the vet said.

"Oh, God no. We want her back. There's not any question," Kate said and Jack nodded in agreement.

"I can operate here, but she'll have to stay with me for a few days. And it will be a while before she's steady on the one front leg. You can call me tonight to find out how things went."

Jack dropped to one knee and stroked Darla's neck. "You gave us quite a scare, old girl," he said. The dog lowered her head to the cushion and whimpered.

"She's had a long night. Probably has a bad headache and I'm sure the leg must be paining her a great deal. She was fussing a bit, so I gave her a painkiller just before you came. Right now, sleep will do her good and speaking of that…I could use about forty winks." Doc Morrison looked as if he might fall asleep while he was talking.

"We'll call tonight," Jack said. He stood then helped Kate to her feet. "Thank you, doctor. You don't know how much she means to us." He held his hand on the doctor's shoulder, wishing there were words to convey his appreciation.

Outside the office, Kate folded her hands, closed her eyes and simply said, "Thank you, God."

That evening Kate and Jack celebrated Christmas together at the farmhouse. Before dinner they called Ron Lyman, the truck driver, to tell him that Darla was going to be all right. Ron also thanked God.

After dinner, Jack started a fire in the fireplace. Kate brought coconut spice cake and coffee to the living room. They ate the dessert and sipped coffee by firelight. When Jack got up to throw another log on the fire, he stepped to the hall closet and pulled out a brightly wrapped present.

"What is it? A house," Kate asked as Jack set the oversized gift in her lap.

She ripped the paper from the package, rolled it into a ball and tossed it into the fire. "We won't be using that next year," she said, then grinned at Jack.

"What *is* this?" The roof of the house-shaped jewelry box that Jack had made was all that she could see. When she finally freed it from the box, Kate's eyes scoured the miniature house. "It's beautiful," was all she said.

"Here," Jack said, lifting the roof on the little house.

Kate gasped at the sight of the miniature furniture adorning the inside of the house. She ran her fingers over the velvet and felt like she wanted to cry. "Jack, this is incredible. Did you?" and he nodded in embarrassment. "I think it's the nicest gift I've every received." She kissed him on the cheek and said, "Thank you, sweetheart."

Kate reached under the couch and retrieved another Christmas present. "This is for you. Merry Christmas."

Jack started to ease his way into the package then smiled. With one yank, he ripped all the paper from the package, crumpled it and tossed it into the fire.

Inside was a hand-knit sweater. Four shades of blue were woven within the delicate crew neck pattern. He held it up to his shoulders. It looked like it would fit perfectly.

"I love it, Kate. Thank you. And I love you," he said.

She fell into his arms. "Oh Jack, I adore you. You've made this Christmas so special."

As the fire flickered away each of them knew their worlds had become inseparable. And Darla, in her own way, had been a bond for their relationship.

Jack sat on the couch and Kate stood in front of him. She glanced at the framed wedding picture of her parents that now stood on the end table. Kate turned it face down, ran her fingers through Jack's hair then bent to kiss his forehead. His strong hands caressed her hips and a fingertip slipped under her silk blouse. She stepped back then slowly unbuttoned the blouse. Jack pulled her toward him. His lips brushed against her soft skin and would stop every few inches, teasing her with a tender kiss—each provoking a little gasp of ecstasy. Kate cradled his head in her arms. Her breasts pressed against the side of his face, his whiskers rubbing a warm path over the silky skin that they touched. All Jack could hear was the beating of her heart and a tiny voice in his head whispering, "She's the one."

They moved as one, gracefully to the floor in front of the fire. Kate unbuttoned his denim shirt then whisked her fingernails over his muscular chest. She touched spots that sent shivers through him. Soon her fingers dropped to an erotic path across the lower part of his stomach. She teased him until Jack could stand no more.

He rolled his body over hers. Kate's breath caught in the middle of a passionate moan. Powerful arms held his upper body far enough from her to see the flames of the fire reflected in her eyes. "Oh God, Kate," he whispered as his slim hips rocked down toward her.

Kate's fingers pressed into Jack's back as she pulled him closer. She dragged them across the small of his back. Her head turned and Kate squeezed her eyes shut as a wave of ecstasy swept through her body.

Jack pulled from her, then struggled to stand. His body seemed lost in the pleasures of the moment. He extended his hand. She looked questioningly then smiled. Kate took his hand and pulled herself up beside him. Arm-in-arm the two walked up the stairs. The old farmhouse was quiet, at least for the moment, as they closed the bedroom door behind them.

CHAPTER 26

▼

New Years Eve would be a low-key affair this year. They had received an invitation to join Bob and Martha for a small party, but Jack and Kate decided to stay home. The canine princess needed to be waited on hand and foot. (Perhaps paw, paw and paw would be more accurate.) And New Years Eve was a time to be with loved ones.

Darla was somewhat tentative at first but was soon hopping around the house with ease. A bandage still covered the stub of her leg. (Kate was glad of that.) Sometimes she'd forget there was only one front leg to support her but Darla always seemed to catch her balance by taking a quick sidestep. Jack still helped the dog outside with a lead, worried that she'd slip on icy steps or have trouble negotiating deep snow. In time his protectiveness would pass, but for now, he treated Darla as an only child.

As the New Year approached, Kate brought out three party hats. She took a picture of Jack and Darla sitting by the fireplace, wearing the shiny hats. Jack tried to look serious but a little grin betrayed him. Darla looked like she was smiling, probably thinking, "Cheese!" Kate would cherish that photo for the rest of her life.

As the clock on the television struck 12:00, Kate gave Darla a hug then threw her arms around Jack. Their midnight kiss, ushering in 1966 would be a tender, private affair. Just Jack, Kate, Darla and of course, Guy Lombardo and his Royal Canadians.

978-0-595-34619-6
0-595-34619-7